LIFE
BEFORE

LIFE BEFORE

MICHELE BACON

Sky Pony Press

New York

This is a work of fiction. Names, characters, places, and incidents are either the products of the author's imagination or used fictitiously.

Sky Pony Press books may be purchased in bulk at special discounts for sales promotion, corporate gifts, fund-raising, or educational purposes. Special editions can also be created to specifications. For details, contact the Special Sales Department, Sky Pony Press, 307 West 36th Street, 11th Floor, New York, NY 10018 or info@skyhorsepublishing.com.

Sky Pony® is a registered trademark of Skyhorse Publishing, Inc.®, a Delaware corporation.

Visit our website at www.skyponypress.com.

10 9 8 7 6 5 4 3 2 1

Library of Congress Cataloging-in-Publication Data is available on file.

Cover design by Sarah Brody.

Print ISBN: 978-1-63450-639-7
Ebook ISBN: 978-1-63450-640-3

Printed in the United States of America

for Charles, my S. H.

PREFACE

The epic road trip of my dreams features two bags of junk food, one awesome girl, and ample music. No murders.

This . . . this is all wrong. Four hours and a hundred miles ago, I escaped my police escort and left everything—Gretchen, my friends, my summer hijinks—behind.

Headed east on this stinking, stuffy Greyhound bus, I am alone. I *hope* I'm alone. If Gary's on my tail, I'm done.

Right now, I need to disappear. In shorts and a navy T-shirt, with my ball cap pulled casually over my face, I look like any other guy.

Any other guy, analyzing every single car on the road to ensure I haven't been followed. Any other guy with two IDs—one genuine, one fake—running scared from a murderer.

That sounds more ominous than it is. No serial killer is stalking the cow towns of northeastern Ohio. There's just one guy—one murderer—and he only wants me.

He killed once, and now he's stalking me, waiting me out, watching my every move. I have no choice. I have to skip town.

One

(Three Weeks Prior)

"Are you naked under there, Xander?"

Jill is the world's most annoying alarm clock. Every morning, she calls my phone ten times over the course of four minutes. She bangs on my front door for a few more before things escalate to a critical state of Get Xander To School. This heightened state of emergency involves her ripping off my covers.

After two solid years of early mornings, I'm just about done.

Jill's patience is thin. "I asked whether you're sleeping naked again."

"Nope." I haven't slept naked since my unfortunate exposure last September. Cringing, I await the inevitable.

Jill whips off my sheet. "Boxer briefs. Figures. You have three minutes. I'll find breakfast."

Jill is a great friend—my best friend, truly—but I strongly suspect sadist tendencies.

On my way to the john, I wish for the millionth time for a normal family. Mom finally gets by with just one job, but apparently a nine-to-five is too much to ask for. I get

1

it—Mom needs all the help she can get, and encouraging Jill to prod me to school probably seemed practical to her. But giving Jill a key to our house and authorizing her to kick me out of bed? That's unforgivable.

Exactly three minutes after the rude awakening, I stumble out of the house in clothes that smell fine. For the last time, I run across the lawn between our houses and slide into Jill's vintage brown Beetle.

The free ride is not without sacrifice: the front seat's faux white leather has been baking in full sun for an hour. Perching on the seat edge to spare my skin isn't remotely comfortable, but it's better than the crusty pink faux fur Jill used on the back seat. We call the car Neapolitan, but it's only cool in winter.

I shouldn't complain. When I turned sixteen, I got a used ten-speed, so a blistering car seat is still a pretty good deal.

Jill tosses an off-brand diet granola bar in my lap. "Sorry. I couldn't find anything good in your kitchen."

My mom still shops like we're totally broke.

Jill peels out between a Dodge SUV and an ancient blue Oldsmobile. "You missed a great lecture last night. Evolution of the human brain? The discussion lasted past my curfew."

And yet, still, she was at my house at the crack of dawn.

Jill sings along with the radio and asks, "You awake yet?"

"Yes, thanks to you."

"Super. I've been thinking. We should go somewhere for Infinite Summer."

She says this as if Infinite Summer is a celebrated tradition and not a moniker of her own invention. Jill sincerely believes this summer—the one between high school and college—will bring the best months of our lives: no AP homework, no college obligations yet, and no responsibility (unless you count my part-time job at the batting cages, which I don't).

Personally, I think the best time of my life will start in August, when I trade my current, messy life for my real life, at college.

I *would* like one big adventure under my belt before then. Well, I want a dozen, but one would be great. For all my dreaming of a cross-country tour, I've never actually left Ohio (unless you count numerous trips over the Pennsylvania border for chicken wings, which I don't).

Infinite Summer or not, a road trip sounds awesome. Somewhere sunny with a beach and no parental guidance would be perfect.

Jill has other plans. "Before I go off to swim camp—I still can't believe I got in as a counselor, can you?"

"No." I have a sneaking suspicion they hired counselors with experience sneaking out or sneaking contraband in, but I can't tell *her* that. "Focus, Jill. Where are we going before your swim camp?"

"Oh! I think we should all take a camping trip—a real one, with tents and backpacks and stuff—all together for one last hurrah . . . in the Adirondacks!"

No.

Jill is the champion of The Big Plan. Last July, she bent a lot of rules to scope out a funky Cincinnati dance club. We had plenty of cash and made the trek without raising parental suspicions. Everything was great, except Jill hadn't anticipated the enormous sign that read 18 AND OVER ONLY. (Their emphasis.) Jill and two of our friends got in on fake IDs. Tucker and I were left outside for two whole hours before the threesome emerged from the club soaking with sweat and stinking of stale marijuana.

To Jill's credit, she did buy me a fake ID after that. Since I'm Alexander, she chose the name Graham Bell as a joke. Except the guy who made the fake misspelled it. Graham Bel is nineteen, and he's been helping me see obscure bands in tiny venues all over northeastern Ohio for nearly a year. I don't feel guilty using it, either, because a club's entry age is an arbitrary rule, not an actual law. When I turn eighteen in August, I'll pitch it.

Jill's fake uses her full name—Jillian Bernard—and makes her twenty-one so she can drink in public.

But I digress.

At seventeen, or eighteen, or twenty-one, roughing it in the Adirondacks does not appeal. I prefer a real bed and a roof. Not to mention my somewhat irrational yet totally genuine fear of being dismembered by bears. I absolutely will not be camping in the Adirondacks.

"You're remembering that grizzly bear annihilating a housecat at Cleveland Zoo, aren't you?" Jill says. "There are no grizzlies in upstate New York, you know. This would be fun! You, me, Tucker. A few others, including Gretchen."

She has me there.

"Gretchen." She stretches it to three syllables: *Guh-ret-chen*.

Gretchen Taylor could scale anything the Adirondacks have to offer. She's lean and strong and somehow, even in Ohio's darkest January days, she's tan. Not in a leather type of way, but in a healthy kissed-by-the-sun kind of way that suggests she belongs outdoors. Since the day she showed up in Laurel Woods—wearing an I ♥ NY T-shirt on April 8 in the seventh grade—I have wanted to date her. She's brilliant. And funny. And hot.

Gretchen is everything. Amazing. Her stories about exploring Europe and New York City excite me at every turn. And even though she's practically a junior chef, she loves cheap Dairy Queen treats as much as I do. And she reads a book a week for fun.

I guess I can risk my life camping if it means a long weekend with Gretchen. I'm a fast runner, and I'll pack light.

I'll even let her share my tent if she also is scared of bears.

To Jill, I say, "I guess I would rough it for you."

"For me." Jill's sarcasm is part of her charm. Her many charms, actually. She taught me how to braid hair, gave me a list of phrases never to say to girls, and occasionally forces me to watch a tearjerker—all of which helps with girls I actually want to date. Or it will someday.

"Is that Gary?" Jill waggles a finger toward the school visitors' parking lot, where a bright blue Mustang shines in the morning sun. Red fringe, which may or may not be a nipple tassel, hangs from the antenna. As we round the corner, we can read the plate: HACK U.

I can't handle all the saliva flooding into my mouth. Gary—I can't stomach the thought of calling him Dad— is my father. Or he used to be. I guess he still is, but we don't exactly have a normal relationship. He used to beat on my mom, but then they separated, and now they're divorced. Ever since Mom forfeited child support—to our own financial detriment, it should be known—he has left us in peace.

My whole past—the horrible family life, Gary's dual personalities, the abuse—starts churning around in my brain. Gary does not have a single reason to be at my school.

He lives way on the other side of town, maybe twenty minutes away, and I haven't seen him in ages. Mostly, I try to forget he exists.

In this parking lot right this second, he actually doesn't exist, so we're okay. Jill and I hustle into the school to avoid a confrontation.

Tucker hops down from his radiator perch when he sees us. "Morning Jilly."

"Hey, Tucker. Everything ready for the party?"

"Not hardly."

"We'll be ready, I promise." Jill disappears into a sea of backpacks and bare legs.

Teachers come down hard on anyone wearing shorts above the knee. To make a point, the girls have—blessedly—rebelled in their shortest miniskirts. Some arbitrary rules are okay in my book.

Tucker and I wend through nuzzling couples on our way to my locker. I half expect to see Gary around the corner, but he's not in here, either.

"Jill tell you about camping?" Tucker says.

"She did."

"I told her black people don't camp."

Shuffling books between my locker and messenger bag, I have to ask. "How'd that work out for you?"

"She didn't buy it. Worse, Mom heard me say it, and she smacked me upside the head. She even promised Jilly she'd pack my bags and kick my ass out the door on the appointed date."

"She would, too," I say.

Tucker heads to first period, shouting over his shoulder, "See you for lunch."

I turn toward the science wing and run smack into Gretchen.

"Morning, Xander!" The hair she used to wear in braids now cascades over her shoulders in waves.

I try to force my heart back down my throat but, as with the rest of my body, it refuses to obey orders in the presence of this one particular person. My attempt at a nonchalant smile feels giddy.

Gretchen doesn't notice, or is kind enough to overlook it. "It's ridiculous that we're here today at all. We could have turned in our books during exams. It's like blow-off day for seniors. They're just trying to imprison us as long as humanly possible."

Mouth open, I nod instead of speaking. I imagine her words in a comic's dialogue bubble, and I want to hold the bubble—her voice—in my hands. How do those words feel in that instant, coming up from her lungs, dancing over her tongue, and darting out through her lips?

"Tongue tied, Xander?" My own name slips between those pink lips. "Something Tucker said, no doubt. Or I have a yogurt mustache?" She brushes her fingers over her lips.

This is going horribly wrong. "No, your mouth is perfect. It's—you're fine."

"Are you genuinely ill?" Everything goes in slow motion as Gretchen reaches toward my forehead. She gauges my temperature, first with the back of her hand, then the pads of her fingers.

I pull back before she detects the nervous sweat oozing from my pores. "I'm fine, Gretchen, I swear. I have a lot on my mind this morning, what with the speech and all."

It's a lawyer's answer: true, if not relevant. Our school has two speakers at graduation: the valedictorian and the kid voted by his peers to address the class. The latter would be me.

I sort of know how it happened. My soccer captain thought it would be hilarious to start a social media campaign to get me behind the podium. And it was funny, but then people started taking it seriously. Jill convinced the rest of the swim team to get on board, then the emo kids from her art class. Tucker's trumpet section and the rest of the marching band got behind it. My fellow physics Olympians. Everyone else who sat for AP exams.

I have too many interests. And friends. Friends who are eager to watch me make an ass of myself in front of the whole town.

So Saturday night—in two days—I have to speak in front of hundreds or thousands of people in an enormous music hall. Public speaking? Not one of my interests. But also nowhere near front of mind when Gretchen is in front of me.

"We're all behind you, so relax," Gretchen says. "No one is going to remember any of this, anyway. It's just high school graduation."

Easy for her to say. She still has at least two college graduations ahead of her, but high school graduation is a really big deal for some people—the ones whose parents didn't finish high school, or the ones who are banking on that diploma to open a few doors.

For me, graduating was never a question. My mom didn't go to college, so you bet your ass her kid will. When Tulane awarded me three scholarships, she threw me a party. Well, a small one: she, Jill, Tucker, and I got Royal Treats at Dairy Queen. After I wolfed down my banana split, I ate all but the bottom layer of a Peanut Buster Parfait. That was a party.

"Hey, I was thinking of heading to Pizza Works for lunch today. You interested?" Gretchen's voice sounds pinched.

I definitely am, except my wallet is pretty much empty. And Jill will never forgive me if I cancel our last high school lunch for some girl . . . even for *the* girl.

"I already have plans, thanks." Besides, I want a date, not a casual lunch. I am so tired of being every girl's Great Friend Xander Fife.

"But you're definitely going to Tucker's party tonight, right?"

"Yep."

"I promised my mom we'd get a jump on college classes," Gretchen says. "So I'm bringing my calc book."

"You're joking."

"Of course I'm joking. You can't drink and derive."

I want to freeze time right here, the two of us grinning at each other. I love that Gretchen always has a pun on the tip of her tongue. She looks at me, expecting something, but I don't know what.

Brushing past me, she shouts over the warning bell, "See you in German!" I turn to watch her walk away. Who wears jeans when it's ninety-three degrees out-side? Gretchen does, but they hug her butt, so I'm okay with that.

I swear she had more than pizza on her mind just now but that doesn't make sense. She and Jameson have been dating nearly two years. They're the most irresistibly perfect couple. But . . . it almost felt like she was asking me out.

Only Jill can make sense of this.

My mother will kill me if I go over my monthly text limit again. Instead, I go old school, dashing toward the lit wing, where I scrawl a note to Jill: *Urgent Question: Status of Gretchen's relationship with Jameson?*

I find her deep in discussion, sandwiched between Grant Blakely and her locker. On paper, Grant could be my twin: taller than average, skinny build, scraggly brown hair, brown eyes. The similarities end there, though. Jill says Grant is mainstream cute to my quirky cute.

I think that means you have to be weird to find me attractive.

Maybe that's my problem.

Two

Between periods, Jill presses a crumpled wad of paper into my hand, triggering a brief twinge of sentimentality.

The last note we will ever pass in the hallowed halls of Laurel Woods High reads: *No idea about Jameson. She hasn't been talking about him at all lately. Other stuff to talk about or an issue with Jameson, not sure which. Sorry. P.S. Could have told you all of this via text AN HOUR AGO if you got on my phone plan.*

Jill and Gretchen co-edit the yearbook, so they spend endless hours together, especially now with end-of-year deadlines. Either Gretchen is completely immersed in the task at hand, or she is now a free agent.

I spend all of third period in Assistant Principal Graber's office. While he edits my pity speech, I start making plans. Free-agent Gretchen is a whole different ball game. She'll have more time for Infinite Summer, for sure.

Graber says, "Remember what we said about diplomacy."

"Yeah."

Gretchen doesn't work. I only work twenty hours a week, and that's nothing. I could work two ten-hour days and spend five twenty-four-hour days with Gretchen.

Every week.

Graber crosses out another sentence. "Tact is getting your point across without stabbing people with it."

"Right."

There's just that little issue of whether Gretchen is unattached. And that much larger problem of convincing her to attach herself to me.

Graber says, "Have you heard a word I've said?"

"Yes. Of course. Diplomacy. Tact."

Focus.

Graber recites a paragraph with his suggested changes. I nod. Focused.

I know exactly what I want to say in the stupid speech, but I'm having trouble saying it without offending the valedictorian or the administration. Turns out it's hard to inspire *everyone* without offending the people who will live their whole lives here, or the people who wanted to leave but didn't get into college, or the people who hope to leave and never return.

What I want is for everyone to stick together this summer, before life pulls us in opposite directions. I love these people. We share a history.

Well, mostly. We share social and academic histories, for sure. But my fellow seniors know only the happiest version of my life. I've kept some things secret, like how I actually broke my clavicle in the second grade. Or why my mother used to wear turtlenecks in summer and never had any friends until after the divorce.

Jill knows, of course, but she's Jill. A best friend loves you no matter how awful your life is. Instead of expecting everyone else to overlook my family's abuse, I'd rather they not know the truth. And when I go to college in August, I can leave all that truth behind.

THREE

After the final bell, the senior lot teems with overeager near-graduates crammed into cars of every vintage.

In the wild wind, Jill's blond hair clings desperately to her scalp. "Come on, Xander! Do I need to light a fire under your skinny white ass?"

I pick up the pace. Jill's ass is just as white and even skinnier than mine, but this is no time for fighting.

"Tucker called shotgun already, so you're in the back."

Damn. Neapolitan is a sorry excuse for a car. Any car with a back seat needs four doors, unless the passengers have four legs or are under four feet tall. Tucker is two whole inches shorter than I am, so he legally belongs in the back seat.

"Where is he?"

"Kissing the girlfriend good-bye, I imagine." Jill lays on the horn and screams, "Tucker!"

We have left Tucker in the parking lot on more than one occasion. If he isn't in our car in two minutes, Jill will leave. And I can ride shotgun. Perfect.

"Hey, guys!" Gretchen is right next to me.

I don't know what to say to the girl who may have asked me out this morning.

14

"Happy last day of school," she says. "See you at Tucker's."

Jill and Gretchen kiss each other on the cheek. Is that a thing now? I'd take a kiss on the cheek.

Gretchen turns to me, but no kiss. "Xander, I saw your dad in the front office this morning?" Pulling her hair out of her face, she tries for a ponytail like we're not hanging onto her every word.

Jill and I have one of those private conversations that involve eyebrows and foreheads. Maybe Gary is cyberstalking me again and knows about last week's senior prank. Who knows? Neither Jill nor I can imagine what Gary wants now.

Gretchen isn't privy to our silent conversation. "Why does he need two extra tickets for graduation? I mean, I get that divorced parents don't necessarily share, but why would he need two tickets? Did he remarry?"

"Dunno." I had no idea he would be at graduation! And, frankly, no matter how big the music hall is, his attendance doesn't jive with my mom's Order of Protection against him.

Gretchen doesn't know about the Gary situation, so I have to play it cool. Everyone knows my parents are divorced, but Gretchen believes that I broke my arm falling off my bike in sixth grade. And that the two-inch scar on my forehead is the result of playing too near our brick fireplace when I was four.

Gretchen has probably heard rumors of how Gary treated my mom, because the Laurel Woods rumor mill never forgets its juiciest topics. But everything else is between me and Mom and Jill. Tucker knows not to ask, and no one else has ever been interested.

15

Amazing Gretchen changes the subject, "How was Graber today? Is your speech ready?"

"It's done. He threatened to yank me off the stage if I try any hijinks. Like I would."

I totally would, if I could address the crowd after receiving my diploma. As it stands, my speech is before diplomas, so I must deliver exactly what Graber has approved.

Gretchen says. "Great. Con-*grad*-ulations. See you at Tucker's then?"

"Yeah."

Gretchen spies Tucker first. "Here he comes. See you guys later."

Jill and I say farewell in unison as Gretchen heads to her car. When she's out of earshot, Jill whispers, "What the hell? Maybe Gary is trying to impress a client? The *Vindicator* and the *Trib* ran stories about your triumphant election to the graduation podium. Maybe that's it. Is he working these days?"

"No idea. Maybe?"

Gary is a self-taught computer programmer, so sometimes he has a job and sometimes he doesn't. I never know. He's the quintessential two-faced person. Jovial, good-natured guy-next-door Gary is good fun at neighborhood barbecues—playing freeze tag with the kids and working the grill like a pro—and he's happy to help people build a new shed, or move furniture around, or whatever. But lurking beneath that guy is the Gary who kicked me down a flight of stairs when I ate the last frozen egg roll. The evening of the neighborhood barbecue.

I never know which version I'll get. That first guy is awesome. I could hang out with him. But the second guy is always just under the surface, ready to pounce if I put one toe out of line or otherwise piss him off. And then he apologizes like five days later. *Sorry you broke your arm . . . save the last egg roll for me next time, okay buddy?*

Living with Gary was a terrifying emotional roller coaster. He's a phantom to me now, and as long as he keeps his distance, I'm happy. In a crowd of thousands of people, I still won't feel safe from him.

My stomach turns over as Tucker joins us. His skinny (black) ass is barely in the seat when Jill puts the car in gear.

"Seatbelt, Tucker!" Jill yells. Turns out, when your dad is the chief of police, you refuse to drive unless everyone is buckled up.

I do, too. Or I would, if I had a car.

Tucker buckles and we're off. I get another twinge: the days of our little threesome are numbered. This is our last drive home together. In August, Tucker will move south to Ohio State and I'll move much farther south to New Orleans. Jill starts at Oberlin the first week of September. This is the beginning of the end of our joyriding.

I want to memorize this feeling, hang on to *right now* as long as possible.

My real life starts when I get to Tulane, but I can hardly fathom life without Jill. College hijinks probably won't include jumping from a second-story window on a dare. I probably won't sneak off for pizza at midnight or attempt to discern the melting point of everything in the kitchen. Will there even *be* hijinks without Jill?

We stop at her house for our bags. I toss my gear in the trunk and run a few laps around our neighborhood.

Running usually calms my nerves, but today the Gary-related nausea persists.

I had convinced myself all that Gary stuff was over, but I was wrong. Panic and nausea build in my stomach as our secrets consume my mind. I need to tell Mom that Gary will be at graduation so she can be on full alert Saturday night.

Tomorrow. I'll tell her tomorrow. For now, I need her to think everything is fine because I want to go to that party.

When we finally head to Tucker's house, I'm 80 percent sure I'm going to vomit. Jill's driving doesn't help.

———

Tuck lives on the hill, which means his house is twice the size of mine and his yard goes on forever.

Tuck's mom keeps us on our toes for three hours—shifting food around, cleaning up the bathrooms, mowing the lawn. It's our party, so we have to work for it.

She bought the beer, so I can't complain.

Gretchen arrives at seven, followed closely by Tucker's girlfriend, Ashley.

Ashley grins at Tucker. "The Booremba twins are coming. I told them I don't think there will be enough beer."

Tucker says, "I'll check the larder."

Tuck's larder, or what I would call a pantry if we ever had that much extra food, is in his basement. His mother stockpiles groceries; if World War III broke out at this instant, the five of us could survive in Tuck's house and repopulate the world.

I'm sure that's what Ashley is thinking when she volunteers to help Tucker audit the alcohol.

Jill rolls her eyes and redirects. "So, Gretch, did you decide to join my book club?"

I declined a week ago because it's a terrible idea. Gretchen and Jill are straight-up contemporary fiction, and I am almost exclusively a nonfiction guy. I devour biographies, science, and travelogues in single sittings, but every time I read a novel, I think *now you're just making up shit*.

Genres aside, Gretchen is on my side here. "Book clubs are for old people, Jill."

"We'll still share what we're reading," I say. "But because it's brilliant and insightful instead of a forced dissection of some long-dead author's motives."

Gretchen says, "And we won't be limited to books. Last weekend: the merits of reality versus scripted television. And I opened Xander's eyes to abstract impressionist art."

True. And while I still think it's complete bullshit, I'm a better person for understanding. I think.

Jill says, "Just as long as you keep reading, Xander. I don't want your brain to atrophy over the summer."

"I feel like you're my mom today."

"Yeah, and I have been utterly terrified since we saw Gary's car this morning, too."

I can't believe Jill is bringing this up in front of Gretchen, who believes my family is sort of normal. If I had my way, Jill wouldn't know about the Gary stuff either, but she witnessed his abuse firsthand.

Jill's second little brother was born during the hottest summer ever. While her parents were at the hospital, Jill and I unrolled our sleeping bags on my parents' bedroom floor because only their room had A/C. My father thought we had fallen asleep, but when he tried to get some action, Mom refused. When she refused again, their mattress moved slightly and she yelped.

Six years later, I can still hear Mom's yelp in my head.

I was mortified, both because it was happening and because Jill was there. In the pitch black, Jill grabbed my hand and held tight until my parents' bed started creaking in rhythm. I put my hands over Jill's ears and she covered mine as we laid there, holding onto each other for dear life.

We haven't talked about that particular night for years, though it repeats in my mind when I'm stuck in a cringe-loop, and now Jill is bringing it up *in front of Gretchen*. If Gretchen *was* asking me on a sort-of lunch date, this definitely is not the time to reveal family secrets.

Gretchen focuses instead on our friends in the basement. "Should I go get Tucker and Ashley, you think?"

"You wouldn't want to walk in on anything indecent," Jill says. "Give them another few minutes."

I guarantee nothing indecent is going on down there. And even if it is, Gretchen has seen it all anyway; she has been dating Jameson for two years.

Jameson!

I'm totally casual. "Is Jameson back from OU yet?"

"OU gets out in mid-May." Gretchen excuses herself to track down Tucker, leaving Jill and me in the kitchen.

Jill says, "Straight out of left field, Xander."

"What?"

"We're talking about the make out artists in the basement, and you blurt out some random question about Jameson. We all know where your mind went between topics."

"Yeah, well look where your mind went. Talking about my idiot father right in front of Gretchen."

"Sorry."

"Yeah, thanks. And come on, Jill: Infinite Summer! I have to know about Jameson. If Gretchen is genuinely free this summer, imagine what a summer it could be!"

Spectacular. It would be spectacular. Summer brings lots of co-ed pick-up soccer, which puts Gretchen's legs on the same field as mine. Our legs could get tangled up together, possibly. When she's on her game, Gretchen is utterly unlike herself. She is super focused and super aggressive. And that competitiveness is super-sexy.

If Jameson is out of the picture, some of that super-sexy could move to my couch.

Jill doubts it. "Xander, if you could untie your tongue and find the balls to make a move, something great could happen. Otherwise, Gretchen will just be the twelfth in your long line of first dates."

"She would be number thirteen. And I already know we fit. Familiarity and intelligence put her lightyears ahead of the last three."

"Ahead of the vapid daisies, yeah, Xander. But you're the same guy: timid and shy. Grow a set and go after the girl you really want."

Someone rips through the neighborhood and parks less than two feet from Neapolitan. Jill freaks out until Grant Blakely steps out of the car. Grant Blakely is one of those guys who plays sports year round: football in fall, basketball in winter, soccer in spring. And in summer, for good measure, he competes in the Youngstown Swim League. Girls

21

swoon over him like he's a movie star; that's probably why we always call him by his full name.

Five other guys tumble out behind him like it's a clown car.

Tuck's mom makes us drag some huge logs out of the woods and arrange them around what will be a campfire. We won't be breaking any of her lawn chairs tonight.

———

Our party grows remarkably quiet when Pizza Works delivers. My first slice of sausage and onion doesn't sit well in my stomach, so I hang back while everyone else devours the pies.

I can't get Gary out of my head.

If I could fast-forward through the next three days, this Gary episode will be over, and so will the speech. No more nausea, and hello summer!

Smooth sailing. No seasickness.

It's still choppy waters in my stomach at this juncture. I probably can't even touch the beer. Nausea plus alcohol is a surefire recipe for barfing in front of—or all over—everyone I know.

Free beer isn't worth a reputation I can't possibly live down in the next ten weeks. Damn.

My stomach and brain are on overload. Can Gary even come to graduation? Maybe he got special dispensation from Mom's Order of Protection for my really special life event.

Or what's supposed to be special. Instead, I'm nine years old again, scheming about getting out of his way. I used to swear that if my parents' fighting got any worse, or if I took one more beating, or if Mom wound up in the ER one more time, I would skip town. Jill and I called it the Youngstown Escape Plan, and any time my parents did something annoying, one of us would say, "YEP."

Jill helped me plot the whole scheme—hell, she practically plotted it singlehandedly—and promised I could hole up at her grandparents' house in Youngstown, a mere seventeen miles away. (When you're nine, you don't think big.) I had just wanted some peace. I hated both of my parents, and I hated my life, and I hated all our family secrets. Having a plan made me feel better—nevermind that Jill's grandmother would have called Jill's house the second I showed up on her doorstep.

I never told another soul about that exit strategy. And now I desperately need a new one for graduation. Bonus points if it gets me out of the whole public-speaking thing.

I am in serious danger of barfing, even without the pizza and beer. Maybe I could go the other way: chug several beers and my mind will float away, taking my nausea with it.

Too risky. Damn. Double damn.

Four

Maybe because the world is quieter, or maybe because the truth is easier in dim light, or maybe because the visual landscape shrinks—whatever the reason, intimate things are more apt to happen after dark.

Several couples—mostly the newly dating—have retreated to tents at the far end of the lawn. The socially awkward people are fumbling through conversations and board games in the garage, but most people are hanging out in the yard again.

Jill and I settle around the campfire with a group of her friends and my soccer buddies. The logs are perfect benches for those of us who aren't drunk. Everyone around my campfire has a red plastic cup. Mine is half-full of Cola. Not Coke. Not Pepsi. Turns out, if you're feeding a hundred teenagers, you go generic.

Someone plays guitar nearby, because someone is always playing a guitar. Play a measure, stop. Play a measure, stop. I think the musician is going for Modest Mouse. The harder he tries, the harder I cringe.

No one else notices the party melting all around us. People are slurring their speech or losing their thoughts in the allure of open flame. Being the only sober one in a huge group of drunk people is . . . sobering. I can't alter the slippery slope; I can only watch as everyone else slides down it.

Unfortunately, Jill has slid right down with everyone else. "In two months, you will disappear for good. I know you will, Xander. You will never come back from New Orleans or your new best friends, Mr. Mardi Gras and Little Miss Beignets. Tucker will go to Ohio State and find ten thousand new friends. I'm just not ready for it to end."

Managing Jill is my job. God knows she's done far more for me—letting me stay at her house during the really bad times with my parents and sharing her mom's amazing breakfasts every Saturday—but it's still a drag. While Grant Blakely plots his midnight soccer scheme and Tuck pitches a tent of one kind or another with Ashley, I slide from the log to the grass and put my arm around Jill.

"You get to stretch out the end as long as you like," I promise. "And then you also will make ten thousand new friends, at Oberlin."

Jill's heavy head falls onto my shoulder.

We're all silent for a while, the drunk ones mesmerized by the fire and I by their vacant stares. I have known these people all my life, and soon our paths will diverge into the world.

"Take a walk, Xander?"

Gretchen is standing right behind me. The firelight catches her hair and she is literally luminous. She should have posed for senior portraits right here.

"Xander?" Gretchen often has to address me twice, apparently. "Will you walk with me?"

Grant Blakely kindly—blessedly—puts his arm around Jill. "Go ahead, Xander. I got this."

Is our whole class aware of my affection for Gretchen? Does it really matter? Grant is totally responsible. Jill is in good hands. I realize I'm making Gretchen wait again.

"Yes, sorry. A walk, yes." In my attempt to seem blasé, I catch my toe on the huge log and fall into several stargazers.

A million apologies later, I walk into the void of night with Gretchen.

"It took me forever to find you in the dark," she says as we abandon the drunken civilization of our senior class.

Gretchen and I talk all the time. Every day, almost. But we've never talked in the dark. Alone. When her inhibitions might be stifled by a few beers. What would Gretchen say if completely uninhibited? What would she do?

She guides me through a small opening in the trees at the edge of the lawn and reaches for my hand. "I found a path."

I am completely calm. *Completely. Calm.*

Within minutes, we are lightyears away from everyone else. And, somehow, I've left my nausea with them. It's just us out here.

She leads me deeper into the mini-forest. "Did you bring a tent tonight?"

"Sleeping bag."

"Me, too. I don't think anyone is actually going to sleep, though, do you?"

"Probably not." Just as well. I've felt crawly about my sleeping bag since the fateful night with Jill in my parents' bedroom. Gary would be thrilled to know his actions have so crippled me. Maybe that's why he's coming to graduation: to inflict a little more psychological damage.

Freaking Gary! Even when he's not around, he gets inside my head. Alone in the dark with Gretchen, I can't even pay attention.

I've lost the thread of our conversation. Gretchen is talking about hiking. Something about her family? She's wearing shorts, and her bare legs show a little blue in the moonlight. This is just how she looks in my dreams, but with a looser T-shirt.

The dream ends abruptly when I walk right into those blue legs.

"Sorry."

"No, it was me." Her voice is sweet. "I thought we should stop. This is a better face-to-face kind of thing."

I can't quite reconstruct her recent words in my head. Hiking? Taxi lights? Flip-flops?

I give up. "What's a better face-to-face thing?"

She can't really look at me. "This is awkward."

Well, now it is. In this grove of walnut trees, we're not walking and not talking and not knowing what to do.

I don't mind much. I mean, the drunks are so far away that I can't really hear them. And the scenery is excellent: I could stare at Gretchen for the rest of my life and be happy.

It's not quite as easy to stare at someone for the rest of your life when she is staring back, though. I study Gretchen's flip-flops.

Finally, after an awkward eternity, she says, "I'm sorry. I just. I don't know where to start. I had this whole speech planned out, and I . . . I broke up with Jameson."

"I'm sorry." All I can come up with is that complete and utter lie? I guess it's the truth if I look at the relationship from Jameson's perspective. I'm sorry for him, truly.

"*I'm* not sorry. I just—argh!" Gretchen walks in circles, shaking out her hands like a crazy person. Or someone who is trying to deny she is in serious physical pain.

Neither alternative is good.

"This is supposed to be poetic." She holds a young tree's trunk and spins around it a few times. "Okay. Okay."

This is completely unlike my articulate friend Gretchen.

"Have you been drinking?"

"No. No, Xander, I have not been drinking. I have not been doing anything." She shouts skyward: "Anything! For almost three months!"

Her wildness makes my arm hair stand on end in the most electric way.

"Okay," she says. "Okay. Do you remember that day in February when we were discussing *In the Lake of the Woods*? I hated it. Half the class was trying to defend it, some people were defending me. And you said, 'Gretchen, it's not the answers authors give, but the questions they raise that make them interesting.' And then you rattled off a bunch of other books that leave readers with more questions than answers. Remember?"

Not really. But I recognize it as a thought in my head, so it's plausible. Also, I want this craziness to continue, so I nod.

"It struck me that I've been with Jameson for years, and he's sweet, don't get me wrong, but you look at the world differently. You counter my ideas and make me think. You challenge me and you get my bad math jokes, and—I don't know. We fit. I'm trying to say we fit."

I can't say anything to that.

"Xander, we have been friends for years. I think you're the peanut butter to my jelly. The Pierre to my Marie Curie? I don't know, maybe we're twin primes? Point is, I know you want to date me."

Cringe.

"No, it's mutual. I'm telling you I'm interested. Really interested. I broke up with Jameson in March, and the rule is you have a mourning period of 10 percent of the length of your relationship—or two weeks, whichever is longer— so I'm done mourning now. I know your taxi light is on. I know you think I'm your anglerfish life partner."

I have no idea what half of that shit means, but I know this is my moment. I step forward and kiss her square on the mouth.

Our lips are pressed together and I'm not sure what to do next. I pull back to find her wide-eyed and grinning, so I lean in for more, this time with my arms around her back. Gosh, she is warm. And electric. Touching her is magical. I want our heat to melt us together so we are one hot mass of flesh and pleasure.

I want to slip my hand up her shirt, to feel the heat of her back with my palm. And then maybe slip it up the front of her shirt.

I'm going to screw this up. I have dreamed about making out with Gretchen for years. And in my copious hours of television watching, I've seen ample kissing and on-screen sex. But I have never done any actual kissing.

When Gretchen opens her mouth, I close mine and wait my turn. She closes her mouth and I open for my turn, and she opens hers again so I clam up.

Gretchen pulls back, panicked. "Are you not into this?"

Wracking my brain for the right thing to say, I come up empty. Some guys get excited about virgins, but I have never—not once—heard a girl say she wanted to make out with an inexperienced guy. It's something I should have learned before graduation. Hell, I should have learned it before high school!

I blurt it out. "I sort of need a little tutoring in the lip department."

"Are you being cute?" Gretchen squints in the most adorable way.

I wish I were being cute. "Gretchen, I want more than anything in the world to be kissing you instead of having this discussion. But, here's the truth: I have spent most of my life mastering the English language, so I am a prolific raconteur, but I have spent almost no time practicing the whole kissing thing."

Those squinty eyes again. The moonlight isn't illuminating her freckles properly, but I know they're folding in on one another as she studies me.

I feel naked, and not in a sexy way.

Gretchen wraps her arms around my neck in a very sexy way and pulls my face close to hers. Her whisper is somewhat patronizing. "Okay. Lesson one: keep your eyes closed."

Eyes closed.

"Lesson two: don't think, just feel. Okay?" Gretchen pulls me closer and her lips warm mine.

Are my lips warm, too? And soft like hers? My blood rushes southward as I try desperately to focus, then to un-focus and feel instead of thinking.

I'm doing it wrong again.

Gretchen parts her lips slightly, and I follow suit, tipping my head toward the left.

We are kissing.

I stop thinking and feel. Everything.

Delirious happiness.

A few minutes later, I cup her head in my hands and slowly draw my fingers through that long hair, which is no longer taboo.

"That feels really nice," Gretchen says.

"I love it," I say before our mouths are busy again.

———

Hours later, we stumble from the mini-forest into the yard, which looks like a narcoleptic convention. People are passed out in open tents, upright in chairs, and smack in the middle of the lawn. Alone, Tucker clutches his phone, fast asleep by the snuffed-out campfire.

The sun threatens to pierce the horizon, but I am nowhere near tired.

Gretchen fishes around in her pocket and offers me her Chapstick. "Need lip balm? It's Labello, not a girly flavor."

"I've never heard of Labello."

I lick my lips before accepting her Labello, which is clear and flavorless and utterly smooth. If our health teacher is right, and kissing someone means kissing every other person she's ever kissed, using this lip balm must be like kissing Gretchen again. "It's German," Gretchen says. "You can keep it if you want. My mom buys it by the carton when she's abroad." She takes my hand like it's the most natural thing in the world. "Gosh, I'm not even tired."

The royal blue plastic cylinder fits in that tiny extra jeans pocket where nothing else ever fits. "I'm hungry, actually. Do you think Mrs. Tucker made breakfast?"

"Let's hope."

It's remarkably quiet as we head toward the house. I drag my feet a little, because everything will change when we reenter civilization.

"So, Sunday, then?" I just want to hear her say it again.

"Sunday. Noon." Gretchen scopes out the landscape before one last kiss. It's a bit chaste for my taste, but we'll have more on Sunday. Actually, there may be more than kissing on Sunday. After years of pining, I have a date with Gretchen Taylor. And it was her idea!

A swift breeze brings the scent of stale vomit (and not-so-stale vomit) and the stench revives my nausea in full force. With Gary back on my mind, happy thoughts about our mini-forest start to dissipate. Quickly.

Sunday can't come fast enough.

Who the hell am I kidding? I'll probably sleep all day before tonight's dinner with mom. Graduation takes up all of tomorrow: rehearsal in the morning, ceremony at night. I'll wake up on Sunday for Gretchen Day. It's practically here, really. I just have to get through the next forty-eight hours, and life will finally begin.

FIVE

Two hours later, I leave a note for Mom on the kitchen table: *Gary's coming to graduation. Maybe find your Order of Protection? See you for dinner. X, X.*

In the shower, I can't stop thinking about Gretchen.

Despite all my dreams of peppermint or strawberries or sweet cherries, Gretchen didn't taste like anything. Or maybe we both just tasted like pizza. Pizza Works may forever remind me of Gretchen in those trees in that time and space.

Hot water runs over my navel. Just three hours ago, I was pressed up against Gretchen, our shirts brushed aside, so the warm flesh of our bellies touched. It was weird to be in a cooling forest hanging onto the only other ninety-eight-degree thing. She's so warm. How warm are those other parts of her? Those few parts I am not yet but soon will be acquainted with? I can only imagine.

Her legs are so smooth. Those tiny dimples at the small of her back . . . I could have run my hands over them for hours.

I guess I did. And oh, the kissing.

The kissing is amazing. We know each other's best stories and have lived each other's worst days (mostly), so the kissing is like playing catch-up, physically. Before tonight, I didn't know about the weight of her hair—so heavy!—or the heat of her lips or the muscles in her back.

Catching up is awesome.

I don't know what we were before today, but kissing Gretchen and running my hands through her hair—and, let's be honest, over her hips and around her back—for seven straight hours means we are now something very significant.

After a quick towel-off, I pass out in my bed.

———

Mom brushes my hair from my forehead. "Xander. It's five o'clock. We should go soon."

Mom is a thousand times gentler than Jill. *This* is how wake ups are meant to be.

"Thanks."

When she's gone, I find exactly one appropriate outfit. Chinos and a button-down shirt are okay for a celebratory pre-graduation dinner, right? They're from my Tulane interview. Mom couldn't swing a campus tour, so Tulane hooked me up with a recent graduate who lives in Pittsburgh. He told me everything I needed to know about my home for the next four years.

That interview was important, so these chinos are from the mall, not Goodwill. They're already a little short, but it's only dinner with Mom.

I find her swishing around the kitchen in her green dress.

"You're swishing."

"I'm sashaying, Xander," she says. "It's the dress."

It's always the dress. "Right."

"You're lucky I'm not singing 'I Feel Pretty' while I sashay."

I've heard plenty of that, too. "I'm ready to go."

Unflappable, she picks up her purse and sashays downstairs to the garage.

Minutes later, when she's focused on the road, I tread lightly. "Hey, uh, think I could use the car Sunday afternoon?"

"Absolutely . . . not." She thinks she's funny.

"It's kind of important. No, strike that, it's the most important thing I have ever done. And I promise I will remember to pick you up from work this time."

Mom puts on her serious face. "Xander, are you going to pay me for gas this time? And where are you going to go that doesn't involve money? Last I checked, you weren't working."

"That's your fault, not mine." I would work year-round for cash and freedom, but Mom only lets me work in summer.

"You know, as a freshman, you were happy to help around the house for a little bit of cash."

It was a very little bit of cash, when she was working two jobs. These days, her new warehouse salary is supposed to be all we need.

"But we have more money now, you said."

"We do, but you're not earning it anymore. I am constantly cleaning up your dishes. Your room is a sty, and until that changes, no allowance."

"Fine." I tune to the one radio station new enough that I'm interested, but not so new that Mom hates it. Window down, I'm mouthing lyrics when we pull into the police station.

Mom cuts the engine. "I couldn't find my protection order, so one of Dale's guys is making me a copy. Back in a jif."

Dale Bernard is Jill's dad, and it still feels weird that our lives are so intertwined with the chief of police.

Whatever. In just over twenty-four hours, Laurel Woods High School will be a part of my past and Infinite Summer will take hold of us—a vast wonderland waiting to be discovered. Camping last night wasn't too bad. I can endure a couple nights of camping if it means more time in the dark with Gretchen. Sunday may be the first of many, many dates. Mom works so much that Gretchen and I can spend many, many hours alone in my house.

All of life awaits me on the other side of tomorrow. And no one has to know about life before this moment.

Mom tosses an enormous file folder in my lap. "The new guy, Nolton, copied my whole file, from the beginning. Everything they had."

I shouldn't look.

The very first thing is a color copy of my mother's eleven jawline stitches. Behind that photo are more—dozens more—of Mom's injuries after what the police call domestic disputes. Interview notes, official complaints, police reports. In my hands is the history of my parents' sordid and storied relationship. It turns my stomach, but I can't stop reading.

"You should have told them no thanks."

"The poor guy is like an overeager puppy. I couldn't refuse," Mom says. "It probably can't hurt to keep it on file."

I don't need a file. My very first memory is of Gary throwing a knife across the kitchen at my mother. I lived through their marriage, and I remember their fights in vivid detail. So really, what I need is less information.

Morbid curiosity compels me to thumb through it anyway.

————

At Olive Garden, once we've covered the usual topics, I try again. "So, about the car . . ."

"I said no." Mom tears off an inch of her breadstick and pops it into her mouth. She enjoys dinner out like normal kids enjoy Christmas morning. Mom is like a whole new person: sitting up straight, smiling, wearing normal summer clothes. She once confessed that she stayed with Gary because she thought we couldn't make it without him. We were broke for years after the divorce, but look at us now: we are actually eating out at a family restaurant like normal people. We're almost normal.

Halfway through my lasagna, Mom's curiosity gets the better of her. "What did you want the car for?"

"Nothing. Maybe I'll borrow Jill's."

Mom laughs. "She'll never let you."

"She would for this. I have a date."

"On a Sunday?"

"It's summer! Every day is Saturday until Tulane. We could go out every night. Well, not tonight because I'm here with you. And tomorrow is graduation. So, Sunday."

Mom shakes her head.

"What if I clean up my room?"

"No."

"And the kitchen?"

"No."

"And mow the yard?"

"Jesus. Who is this date with? An honest-to-god celebrity?"

I separate my lasagna layers with a fork. "Gretchen."

Her eyes are so wide that I can see white all the way around her irises. "Gretchen Taylor?"

Mom missed a lot of stuff when she was working two or three jobs, but the name Gretchen Taylor means something to her. "You never cease to amaze me, Xander. How did you manage that?"

"Forget it."

"Fine." It was two syllables and a double-dose of sarcasm. I wish I could ground her from the car for being sarcastic. Maybe Gretchen and I could go without a car. Spend the afternoon at my house while Mom is out. Maybe movies and a long chat on our L-shaped couch. Maybe—

"Alexander Fife?"

Next to us stands an eager, perky blond creature with tacky red nails, a tight suit, and (it must be said) enormous fake boobs.

I'm chewing a breadstick that is way too big for my mouth in the first place, so Mom half-stands in the booth to greet her. "Yes, this is Xander."

The woman gushes. "I have so been looking forward to meeting you!" She thrusts her right hand and a half-dozen bracelets toward me.

Half-chewed half-baked bread slides down my throat as I reach for her. She shakes my hand with enthusiasm.

"I have just been dying to meet you. I'm Renee, your dad's fiancée."

My quick breath sucks another bite of breadstick down my throat. *Stop eating, seriously.* I flex my diaphragm to expel the demon. No dice.

This is it. I am going to die right here in freaking Olive Garden before my life has even started.

Mom tries desperately to get out of her bench but Renee is frozen. These two women are watching me die.

No graduation.

No date with Gretchen.

No kissing.

No naked nights on the couch.

No Infinite Summer.

Finally—and before I have to Heimlich myself—the bread returns to my mouth and glorious air fills my lungs.

My eyes gush as I sip my water and draw some long, welcome breaths. "'Scuse me. Went down the wrong way."

Renee pats her bare chest and fans her face. "I almost lost you before we really knew each other."

Gary has enjoyed lots of women since the divorce. Since way before the divorce, if I'm being honest. Renee seems different from the get-go. She's about Gary's age, for one thing.

"I am so glad I recognized you." Renee's enthusiasm seems genuine. "I expected we would meet at graduation, but here you are!"

As the pieces fall into place, I reach for the bench to steady myself and my hand finds the police portfolio that was too important to leave in the car.

Two minutes ago, I almost died. And I am just pissed enough at Gary to raise a little hell. My smile broadens. "Renee, why don't you join us? This is my mother, Helen."

Renee startles at the mention of my mom, as if I'd be having Friday dinner with any other middle-aged woman.

Mom scoots toward the wall to make room.

Renee sits as far from Mom as she can, an inch of her thigh hanging over the booth's edge. "One of my clients invited me to dinner as thanks for finding her a house, and the second you walked in, I couldn't keep my eyes off you. I knew it was you. I just knew." Her penciled eyebrows bob as she nods.

She sure seems genuine. Maybe she has merely cultivated the sincerity required to succeed in real estate, but I almost like this person. Does she have any idea what's in store for her if she marries Gary?

I'm starting to fear for her. Keeping my eyes on Renee, I reach down and open that manila file folder.

"Renee, you seem like a really nice person. You deserve to be happy. In what I can only call a bizarre twist of circumstance, I happen to have with me some photos of my mom from a few years ago." I prop the stack of photos on my lap facing my abdomen and slap them on the table one at a time: bruises in varying degrees of healing on Mom's spine and legs, stitches that covered a puncture wound to her torso, finger-shaped bruises on her upper arms.

Mom raises her voice. "Xander, I think—"

"Mom. I think she deserves to know. Don't you wish you had known?" To Renee I say, "This is why Gary is prowling the singles scene."

Renee picks up a photo of Mom's back.

"Yeah, you can tell from that one that some bruises are old, huh? Some are weeks old. Some days, and some are fresh." I tip the photo back toward me and point to my mom's lower shoulder. "That one, right there? If you hit the wall or the floor just right on the shoulder blade too many times, eventually the body gives up trying to heal. She still has a shadow right there, but you only see it when she's walking around in her bra."

Mom's shoulders sag as she studies the plastic table tent advertising Olive Garden's summer desserts. She's folding in on herself emotionally and physically. Gary has defeated her again and he's not even here. This time I did it. I'm embarrassing her, but I can't stop.

Renee picks up the photo with Mom's stitches.

"Oh, that's a good one: the last straw, so to speak. At twelve, I had been living with this BS for years. I always, always expected beatings on one or both of us. But on this morning, after she'd lost consciousness for a few seconds, something changed."

Actually, everything changed. It wasn't her last beating from Gary, but it was the catalyst for their divorce. Mom and I ran to Jill's house in our pajamas. Jill's parents thought Mom was crazy for never saying anything before.

"Our neighbor was a cop—he's now the chief of police—and my mom's act was so good that even he didn't know how bad things really were in our house. We all stood there looking at my mom, and do you know what she said?"

Renee shakes her head very slightly.

I remember every single second of that afternoon: the seven doughnut varieties Jill's mom offered us, the argument about whether to file a police report, Jill's too-big pajama pants dragging on the checkered kitchen floor.

"She said, 'I never dreamed that he would kill me.' That's what she said, as though everything else—the cuts, the bruises, me wetting the bed until age ten, her three broken bones—hadn't signaled a big enough problem."

Mom is tearing up now, but I can't shut up because I'm on a roll. "So, Renee, let me tell you: you deserve to be happy." I pick up the photos one by one until only the stitches are left in Renee's jittery hand. "And you're not gonna get there with Gary."

Renee focuses on nothing in particular, her right hand massaging her pale throat. Finally, faintly, she says, "I deserve to be happy."

I catch Mom's eye and mouth the words, "I'm sorry." She keeps her hands in her lap when I reach across the table toward her.

Renee sniffles a bit, though she's not crying. A minute later, as if she's just processed everything, her eyes snap back to mine and she says it again: "I deserve to be happy." She scoots out of the booth and whispers, "Thank you, Xander. Helen."

We're silent for a long time. Eventually, I pick up my fork and work through my lukewarm lasagna. Mom doesn't eat another bite.

After our waiter delivers the dessert menus, Mom says, "That poor woman."

How many people have said the same thing about us?

Six

Graduation day. Finally!

Between catching up on sleep, dinner with mom, and Jill's very late Friday night date, she and I still haven't talked about what went down at Tucker's house. She doesn't even know about my date with Gretchen! In less than twenty-four hours!

Or that I'll have to miss Quaker Steak for it. Quaker Steak is Jill's sanctuary, our regular hangout outside of town. Just over the Pennsylvania border, it claims America's best wings, and is well enough away from Jill's dad and the rest of the police force that we go every Sunday for a break. Jill's treat.

We don't skip it, and we don't take dates.

Maybe Jill will make an exception for Gretchen.

We're at my house this afternoon, because Jill's brothers and parents have converted her house into a medieval battlefield, complete with armor and weapons. Jill and I settle into the ancient metal glider on my questionably safe back deck. How can I tell her I'm bailing on Quaker Steak without sounding like an asshole?

In my defense, I am very new at the whole dating thing. In my further defense, this is Gretchen, so shifting around my schedule for this epic occasion is completely justified. Still, weaseling out of Sunday night Quaker Steak will be infinitely more difficult than getting the date itself.

And that took four years. Crap.

Hoping Jill's excitement will eclipse her anger, I draw a herculean breath, and blurt, "I need to bail on Quaker tomorrow."

"Grounded again?"

"No." I wait a beat for dramatic effect. "I have a date with Gretchen."

Jill pulls the latest teen zombie novel from her bag. "Yeah, I know."

"How do you know?"

"I had coffee with Gretchen yesterday. She says you two are going out. And I had to act all nonchalant when she apologized for keeping you from our Sunday tradition."

"I'm sorry."

"You should be. I don't know why you two can't spend a couple hours making out and then come to Quaker Steak together. We always go together."

I hadn't considered that. "Maybe we could!"

"Just don't be an ass about it, okay, Xander? The two of you shouldn't disappear from everything just because you're going out. Nothing needs to change."

"You disappeared for a while when you dated that football player from Howland who expressly requested number 69 on his jersey."

"Yeah, but did you really want him around all the time?"

Point taken. "I promise to behave."

Jill scrapes the filling from an Oreo and piles it on her knee. Munching the chocolate cookies, she reaches for another. She repeats this several times before rolling the sizable mound of lardy filling into a ball, smashing it like a pancake, and shoving it in her mouth.

She's done this since the day I met her. I still find it repulsive, but who cares? I'm off the hook for Quaker Steak!

Today is the perfect segue into summer. Jill will have free evenings after babysitting her brothers, and I only have twenty hours a week at the batting cages, so this will be awesome. Hanging out, eating junk, and plotting dates.

Infinite Summer, here at last!

Well, one graduation speech, then here at last! Starting with Gretchen. Tomorrow!

Jill has read my mind. "So where are you taking her?"

"I have no idea."

"Xander, she's just a girl."

"Yeah, but it's not like hanging out with you," I say. "This is a real date. I need something that will impress her."

"Oh, I get it." Jill pulls out her bookmark and presses her book open.

"You get what?"

She refuses to look at me. "You want to get into her pants."

"What? No!" Okay, that's exactly what I have in mind, but I am about three bases shy of a home run with anyone. Plus, that's the sort of thing you don't say aloud. "I just want to have a great date."

"Too bad."

"What? You have some foolproof way to ease a girl's seat into full recline?"

Jill jabs me with her fist. She has spent more than her fair share of dates in full recline. And on several of those occasions, she was half naked.

"Xander, just start with what you like about her and go from there."

"I like everything about her."

"No."

"I really like kissing?"

Jill straightens up. "No. That's generic. She'll want to hear the things you like about her, specifically. You can't just say you like kissing."

I can dissect the "everything" I like about Gretchen. Easy. "She's strong; I could watch her play soccer all day. I like her stories and the way she tells them. I like watching her try to pronounce *schlüessel* and *frühling* and *München*. Her freckles. I love her hair."

"Never." Jill forces eye contact. "Never use the word *love* about anything, because if you say you love her, it will freak her out. But if you say you love other things—U2 or my mother's perfect crispy bacon or that ratty periodic table T-shirt—that makes you seem like you're slutting the word around."

This T-shirt isn't ratty. It's a little faded, but none of the atomic numbers have cracked. It's just old enough that it's super, super soft.

"Gretchen would get it, Jill. She also loves U2."

"Whatever."

"Okay. I'm done talking about this. I'm going to shut up and work on a soundtrack for my date. You read."

Jill puts in earbuds while I create the best-ever mix of music for the girl who either is my girlfriend or soon will be.

I've pared down the collection to fifty-three songs when Mom shouts out the kitchen window two hours later. "I'm home!" She pokes her nose into the screen. "Hi Jilly, you staying for dinner? Tacos! And I remembered the limes."

I thumb toward the window and mouth, "Dinner?"

Jill rips out her earbuds. "Yes, please! I need to be home and dressed by 5:15."

"No problem. You line up at 5:45, right?"

Jill nods. "Hey, Helen, I got *The Zombie's Attaché*, book 3!"

She flashes the cover at Mom, who says, "I want that when you're done. And Xander? I'm feeling gracious today. Yes, you may borrow my car tomorrow."

"Mom! Thanks!" I throw open the sliding glass door, run through the dining room, and give her a huge, huge hug that lifts her off the ground.

"Hot stove," she says.

She stirs the beef, staring intently as it browns. Quieter, she says, "And, look, some things are private, but I understand why you did what you did last night. That was a pretty mature thing to do, even though you did it in a really puerile way."

"I'm so mad at him right now. This is supposed to be a happy time, and instead he's pissing in my cornflakes."

"Language." Mom scratches her fingers through my hair the way she has since I was five. "I know you were trying to protect that woman, but you also were angry. You wanted to hurt Gary, and no good can come of that. Acting in anger will lead to a lifetime of regret. Think of it this way: I act out of love and comfort. Gary acts out of anger.

47

You're half him and half me, and you get to choose which is the better way to live."

Her point made, she nods. "You're a better person than he is, Xander. Remember that at Tulane."

Mom tears up a little, and I look away. She wasn't thrilled when I chose Tulane, but I've been jonesing for warm weather as long as I can remember. I mean, visiting all fifty states is on my bucket list for sure, but I only want to live where it's warm. Every single school on my list was well south of the Mason-Dixon line.

Tulane was my third choice, but together I'm smart enough, Mom's broke enough, and Tulane admissions is still hurting enough from Hurricane Katrina that they're giving me several significant scholarships. Kick. Ass.

Mom thinks school eleven hundred miles away is less kickass, but she promises to love me anyway.

Maybe she's thinking about that when she digs in her purse and presses three twenties—*three*—into my hand.

"This isn't a loan, and it's not an advance. Consider it a graduation present for you and Gretchen, okay?" She's tearing up again and I can't really look at her. "We made it through. You and me. We did okay, right?"

Mom's fingers smell of cilantro when she cradles my face in her hands. I hate it when she does this, but she's so sincere.

And a little sappy.

And sixty dollars.

"You did great, Mom."

She stretches her face really long and wipes her eyes with her thumbs. "You made it happen, kid. Even in the rough years—and god, were they rough!—even in the rough years, you made it totally worth it."

She hugs me again—one of those hugs that's so tight and so long that I'm glad Jill is outside.

"I am so proud of you, College Man!"

"Almost."

"Okay, Mr. Almost. Dinner in about twenty minutes, and then we'll get changed for the big night."

The scent of generic dryer sheets wafts up through the deck as I settle back on the glider next to Jill. She glances at me and I mime a steering wheel and a thumbs up.

She gives me a high five and I go back to my playlist.

I've been working on it maybe ten minutes when a car tears down the street and screeches to a halt. A moment later, someone pounds on our flimsy front screen.

"Where is fucking Alexander?"

Gary. I freeze.

Ours is a split-entry house, so he can see right up to the kitchen from the front door.

"It's just me in the kitchen!" Mom sounds carefree. How has she shed her fear of him while I hold onto mine with every atom of my being?

The front screen slams and Gary's voice is closer. "You're lying, Helen. Where is that motherfucking kid? I'm gonna send his head through plaster."

I tug on Jill's earbud cord and cover her mouth before she can protest. "Gary's here."

Silently, we move off the glider and tuck ourselves under the kitchen window where there's a blind spot that will hide us. Toe to toe, our hips right up against the vinyl siding, we rest our heads on the house. Jill hugs her knees.

Gary yells, "You put him up to it, didn't you, Helen? I'm gonna take care of you both at once. Where is that little fucker?"

Mom is only slightly flustered. "It's graduation weekend. He could be just about anywhere."

I learned my lawyer's answers from her, clearly.

A thud rattles the house and I wonder whether our kitchen has a new hole in the wall.

Mom is cool. "Get out. Of my. House."

Gary's not cool. "You poisoned his mind. I am so tired of you people fucking with my life."

"Well, you fucked with ours for years." Swearing means Mom is either really pissed or really scared. Her voice, at least, is nonchalant. "I guess payback is a bitch, Gary. Now get out."

The funny thing about a punch is that it sounds remarkably like any old thud. I've heard enough punches in my life to know that Mom just got one. Gary curses and I can hear them wrestling. The commotion wakes a hurt deep within me, and my wounds start to throb. The back of my head, where Gary first shoved me into plaster, pulses. My left arm, long since healed, throbs just like on that day six years ago, when I cradled it until Mom came home and took me to the emergency room. All the pain returns to my body as though this beating, too, is on me.

I hold my shins tighter and push my closed eyes into my knees so hard that I see white spots. I'm five years old again. I can't control my breathing.

I can't believe this is happening.

Gary's timing is freaking impeccable. Mom is going to be all bruised at graduation. She'll be back in long sleeves, for sure, and it will take months for her to be as happy and whole as she was last night at dinner. I am so tired of my parents' shit. Let them duke it out.

Why does this keep happening to us? Why can't we have a normal life?

Gary bangs the wall and snarls. "I have had enough of your bullshit and that kid's bullshit and I swear to god I will kill him for this. He has fucked with my life one too many times. *I* deserve to be happy."

Mom makes a squeaky sort of sound and something pounds furiously against the wall.

"Do you hear me? Do you have anything to say, Helen? I am going to wipe him off the face of the earth. *I* deserve to be happy. *I deserve to be happy.*"

Mom is probably curled up on the floor at this point. The best defense is making Gary believe he's won.

"Oh, goddammit," Gary says, and the house is quiet.

Jill stares at my hands, which grip hers so tightly my knuckles are white.

I am not in the mood to clean up my mother's wounds today. I am not in the mood for drama when I am meant to be graduating and moving—

Jill presses herself to the back of the house, wide-eyed.

I hear it, too: Gary's breathing is so heavy and close that I hold my own breath. He's looking out onto the deck, just a few feet above our heads. I look up and see only my mom's window boxes, the poppies' petals spilling over the edge.

Please don't see us. Please.

Jill's book lays fanned open in full sun. She cries silently and I mouth the words, "I'm sorry."

"Me, too," she mouths back. She is brave enough not to run down the deck stairs and back to her own home.

A minute later, we can no longer hear Gary's breathing.

When his engine rumbles, Jill starts sobbing. "I thought it was over!" She still grips my hands in terror.

I wish it were over.

"What if he had found us?" she asks.

I don't know. Gary must know that Jill's family is aware of the abuse already, but he would have freaked if Jill saw him in action. Or maybe he wouldn't have hit Mom at all if he'd known we were there. Jill, at least. If he'd seen me, I'd have had my share, for sure. He wouldn't really kill me, would he? He's just pissed.

Jill stands up and peeks into the kitchen. "What can I do to help?"

Mom will be mortified that Jill was around for this.

"You know, it's going to take a while to get Mom ready for tonight. I can handle this. You go home and read and calm down before it's time to go. I'll see you at the music hall."

Jill peeks into the kitchen again, unsure. "She might need moral support."

"I can handle it. I'll bandage her body and galvanize her spirits for graduation. You go home and let music put you in the right mood for the night."

Halfway to the steps, Jill says, "I want the computer back by five."

"Roger."

Jill runs down the back staircase, crosses through our neighbor's backyard, and heads into her own house.

Better Jill than Gretchen, because there are some things I would never in a million years share with a girlfriend.

I am so beyond the bullshit of my parents' relationship. At least we aren't lying about it anymore. For years, Mom totally bought into Gary's excuse that he beat her because he loved her, and he beat me to keep me in line. We don't accept his lame apologies anymore. We just acknowledge that he's a jerk and leave it at that.

So, this changes our plans for the evening. I'll offer to accompany her to the hospital and she'll refuse. She'll sit through my speech in extreme pain—pain that will forever be attached to her memory of this night—and afterward we'll spend the night in the boring confines of the emergency room. I say a silent prayer she won't require stitches this time.

I want to move forward—with Gretchen, with this summer, with school a thousand miles away—and Gary has just set my mind back ten years.

Here I am again, cleaning up a mess my parents made. No one else has to put up with this shit.

Heaving a huge sigh, I slide the screen door open. Inside the dining room, I bend to work on a hangnail and think about how I want to play this. I need to strike the right tone or she'll rescind the sixty bucks and car offer. I need to come off as light. Maybe: *I guess Renee spilled the beans, huh?* Mom is always talking like that: spill the beans, Bob's your uncle, don't teach your grandma to suck eggs.

Instead, I say, "He probably only needs one ticket for graduation, now, huh?" I turn to find Mom lying face-up on the fake linoleum tile, her eyes wide open.

What am I supposed to do? I grab her wrist. Do I use my thumb or absolutely not use my thumb to check for a pulse? I can't remember. I use my fingers on her neck instead, but feel nothing.

53

Must be the wrong spot.

I run my fingers up and down her neck and finally yank down her T-shirt and lay my ear over her bare chest.

Nothing.

Seventh-grade CPR was ages ago. Something about ABCs?

Pushing on her chest, I'm terrified I will break her.

Blow into Mom's mouth and I swear I feel air leave her lungs.

I blow again. Nothing.

"Somebody help me!" My scream incites a sense of urgency and I pull out my cheap phone to dial 9-1-1.

Balancing the stupid phone on my shoulder, I get instructions for real CPR: straight arms, full weight behind each thrust.

Her ribs don't crack.

I tilt her head, plug her nose—*of course! Plug the nose!*— and force air into her lungs.

My phone falls and lands on Mom's face as I beg her heart to respond.

The dispatcher tells me to keep the rhythm of "Staying Alive" and she starts singing it. Mom raised me on disco, so I don't need the help. I sing under my breath as I press and press and press and press and press and press and press and pray.

Someone yells through the front screen: "EMT!"

I yell down. "Here!"

Huge hands reach for my mother's wrist. He doesn't use his thumb. "I'll take it from here, Alex."

That's not my name. I don't correct him. I keep pounding on Mom's chest. "Come on! Come on! Come on."

Another EMT—a woman—touches my shoulder and says, "He does a good job. Let him work."

I sit back on my heels as he starts compressions. He is much stronger than I am. More confident, too.

"Helen?" Jill's mom hollers through the screen door.

SEVEN

Jill's mom, Janice, follows the ambulance at a brisk pace.

I've ridden this stretch of Route 46 dozens of times, hundreds. Every time we go to the courthouse or the good library or the Hot Dog Shoppe.

Right now nothing is registering. "He was looking for me," I say about a thousand times.

Janice keeps her eyes on the road as we speed. "*Gary* was looking for you?"

"Yeah, Gary. He said he wanted to kill me. Mom told him I wasn't there and they fought. He hit her, I think? Maybe he punched her out? Maybe that's why she's unconscious?"

———

The EMT from the house sits with us in the waiting area. Janice recognizes him as Derrick Rhymes. She colors his mother's hair and has heard his whole life story in monthly installments.

Derrick holds Janice's hand.

Derrick asks how I am.

Derrick keeps Janice talking about anything outside this hospital.

And every time I ask him to, he walks through the swinging STAFF ONLY doors and inquires about Mom. He swears he got a faint pulse out of her on the drive to the hospital. He promises doctors are doing everything they can. He says there's a chance she'll pull through.

She doesn't.

Eight

An hour after Jill walked across the stage to accept her diploma, police officers interrogate the two of us relentlessly. Separately, they ask us hundreds of questions to nail down our story and recreate a timeline.

Mom's gone.

I sound like a coward. Every time I tell the story—and I'm on Retelling Number Seven right now—the person asking the questions says the same thing: You heard them fighting, but you stayed outside?

I sound like a coward *and* an asshole.

Some squat, balding police officer who reeks of tobacco repeats the question twice.

"Yes. I stayed outside. I didn't see anything."

He wants to know why I hung out in a seated fetal position for a few minutes after Gary had gone and why I sauntered into the house and gave myself a pedicure while my mother died on the floor.

My mother died on the floor.

Coward.

But what can I say? That I was too disgusted with my parents? That I wanted to pretend it wasn't happening? That I was terrified?

The thing is, I never—not in a million years—thought he was killing her. I thought it was just another fight. He could have beaten her or beaten us both, and I didn't want that. Not on graduation day. Not when I was going to stand in front of my entire graduating class and everyone else I've ever met. I couldn't do that with a black eye and newly broken bones.

So, yes, I was craven. But I didn't know he was going to kill her.

He killed her. Forever. She's gone forever.

We now know that Gary strangled my mother after—presumably after—inflicting a few final scrapes on the left side of her face. I've had several run-ins with his gargantuan class ring before, so I'm guessing it was that. And at some point—either by Gary's doing, or on her way to the floor after she stopped breathing—her left wrist was broken. This time her bones won't heal.

After enduring a half dozen interviews, I don't want to talk to anyone. About anything. Fact is, they still have that thick file about my family's domestic violence. What more can anyone say?

Instead of waiting for the hospital to release Mom, I'm waiting for the police to release me. I excuse myself to the hospital bathroom, which is far down a sterile, white corridor. Lucky me, it's empty.

I can't even look in the mirror. Coward!

The handicapped door is swung open next to the sinks. I push it out of my way and it swings open again. It hurts when I punch it, but the hurt is good. I punch it again and again, dozens of times, until I'm so close that it can't open anymore. The door is closed and I keep punching and the pain feels so good. So real.

I'm alive. My hand aches, but I can't stop. I am alive.

When I have nothing left, I slide to the floor in a puddle.

It starts in my belly—a long, low wail.

Deep breath. Wail.

Deep breath. Wail.

It builds until I am screaming at the top of my lungs, "You killed my mother! You freaking coward!"

My hand throbs. Damn, it hurts. And I'm crying. Not for my hand. For my mother. For my stupid fucking family. For my life, which never started at all.

For Mom.

For Mom.

My mom.

————

The whole thing is my fault. He flat-out said he was looking for me. And he was looking for me because Renee had emptied their apartment an hour after I shared all those gruesome pictures of my mother.

My fault.

Hell, it's my fault my parents were together in the first place. They married in February and I was born that August; I've done the math.

If you look at it that way, the marriage, the beatings, and the murder are all my fault.

There's no one else to blame, really.

What am I going to do without her?

————

Planning a funeral is like one of those ridiculous ice-breaker exercises: if you were a tree, which species would you be? Except the trees in question have been carved into coffins. I choose poplar because it's the cheapest. The tall, lanky guy at the funeral home, who looks just like Ichabod Crane, tells me to call it a casket.

It's a coffin.

Next icebreaker: if you could wear only one outfit for the rest of your life, what would you wear?

Ichabod Crane says we're choosing clothes for Mom's "final rest." Someone else should be doing this. Mom's parents have been estranged for years, but I'm pretty sure they're alive and out there somewhere. Choosing clothes for all eternity should be their job.

Except it's not. It's mine. I am my mother's next-of-kin, so I take a huge dose of grow-the-fuck-up and choose Mom's green dress. It's not exactly clean, but maybe she would have appreciated the faint Olive Garden scent.

Mom loved those breadsticks. She loved this dress. It made her feel beautiful. It made her sashay. How can something so annoying three days ago now seem charming? Between her divorce from Gary and her death at his hands, Mom had a little peace and happiness, a sliver of light in her otherwise gray life.

I smell the shoulder of the dress. It's not just Olive Garden; it's Mom. She always smelled faintly of sawed-apart cardboard from the warehouse. And Ivory soap—the white bars, always the white bars. And something else that's distinctly Mom. Her skin.

That skin doesn't exist anymore. Well, not alive. It's cold and rigid now instead of soft and squishy. Mom's hugs are soft and squishy. Were.

She won't cradle my face in her hands ever again. I hated that so much, but I want it so badly. I just want to go back.

Nine

Jill's parents, Janice and Dale, are letting me stay indefinitely. We've rolled out a sleeping bag—not *that* one—on Jill's bedroom floor.

And Jill is amazing. She holds my hand through the whole blur of events. I'm doing it all with a police escort because everyone is pretty scared for my life.

Janice rarely leaves us alone, and when she does it's to buy me a black suit for the funeral or drop off the obituary at *The Vindicator* or pick up donuts for breakfast even though I don't want donuts.

I don't want anything.

They think Gary will steer clear of calling hours and the funeral, but there's a huge police presence anyway. At the funeral home, I stand by a closed coffin that allegedly has my mother in it. Why was her outfit so important if no one will see it?

It feels like I'm watching an underwater movie of my life, on mute; everything moves in slow motion, and I can't hear a sound.

Lots of people hug and kiss me.

Where's Gary?

Every time I close my eyes, I hear him breathing out the kitchen window. I'm still cowering beneath it.

I can't close my eyes anymore.

The nights are long, and my brain is just as bad when I'm awake. Dinner with Renee runs over and over in my head. I shouldn't have done it. My parents' last argument plays on continuous loop. I should have run in. I could have saved her.

Or we both could be dead, I guess.

There was no way for us to win against Gary. One or both of us was bound to lose.

Where is he?

Is he coming?

When?

———

Some of Dale's officers are here for Wednesday dinner. Just, you know, casually.

"You haven't touched your pasta," the fat smoker cop says.

"Full." Grief and dread have permeated every last cell in my body. I am so full that my stomach can't take on any food right now. Also, I'm not hungry.

Despite not having any more questions for me or Jill, the cops hang around, keeping watch. After years of Dale's police stories, all I can think is *You're welcome for the overtime,* because this is ridiculous. Gary won't come after me when I'm surrounded by friends.

Dale and Janice forbid us to leave windows open, though the weather is perfect. They pile on more rules:

No dates outside the house. No errands without an adult. No trip to the Adirondacks.

Nothing that can put my life in danger.

Privately, Jill and I refer to our captivity as Dale Jail.

Still, this is a million times better than the emotional imprisonment of the Gary years. And this time, I have a cellmate.

———

Two days after the funeral, Mom is a mere anecdote to everyone else: just another ancestor gone, no big deal.

Jill says the whole thing is surreal, but it's not surreal to me. I was there. I saw my mother. I tried to revive her.

It's almost too freaking real.

Janice is sort of force-feeding me a few bites a day, but I'm really not hungry. It's as if my body stopped when Mom died. My belly is full. My days are empty. I am full and empty. My life is one big dichotomy.

The only thing heavier than Mom's death is my own imminent danger. Gary is out there, waiting. I can't leave the house without panicking, so here we sit. Jill and I used to spend long summer hours inside the house listening to music, but that was by choice. Now we're imprisoned.

Jill still tries to escape. "Movies, Mom? The new Spiderman opened today."

Janice sighs. "We've been over this. I don't want to sit around somewhere. I want to go do what we need to do and come back home. It's the safest place for Xander right now."

I hate that she blames me. "Maybe today you two can go, and I'll stay here. No danger for you."

Janice shakes her head. "I can't leave you here alone."

"Who's alone? There's a cop on the front porch. Gary isn't sitting across the street with a sniper rifle or something."

The second it comes out of my mouth, I realize he could be. He could be hiding in the neighborhood. That would take balls the size of watermelons, but I wouldn't put it past him.

Our little Olive Garden encounter really spooked Renee. The life she and Gary were building together evaporated so, really, Gary now has nothing to lose. Maybe he's on the run. I sure as hell would run if I were him. Gary could be anywhere in the world right now, but I'm betting he's still here. He's never really been anywhere else.

At night, I lock Jill's bedroom door. I know the house is secure, but I still can't sleep. I run to the window every time a car drives up the street.

"It freaks me out when you do that," Jill says.

"I just have to check. I need to be sure it's not him."

"Just be quiet about it, okay?"

———

Friday, three days after the funeral, I finally find sleep.

I also find dreams.

Scenes from my past are warped: Mom and Gary are fighting in the next room and my door has become a wall, so I can't run in to save her. Gary's throwing knives at my mother again, but now she's strapped to a magician's spinning wheel of death. Gary pushes me down a waterslide, and I've forgotten how to swim. He looks like the deviant elves from *A Christmas Story*: "Ho. Ho. Ho." And down I go.

The garage door's groan jolts me awake.

My entire body is tense; every muscle flexed at once, with nowhere to go. *Only dreams.* I will never sleep again.

I creep close to Jill's door as Dale climbs the stairs.

"Another miss," he says to Janice. "Youngstown this time. Two sightings, reputable witnesses."

Youngstown is seventeen miles away.

"Do you think it was really Gary?" Janice sounds tired.

"Sure sounds like it was him. I left Clyde on our front porch."

"But you're home. Don't you think you're enough?"

Dale's pissed. "I don't even want him to think of coming here. We're keeping a cruiser or two at our house at all times. Someone will be posted at the door 24/7 until we catch him."

"It's been six days. I wonder what he's doing in Youngstown?"

"Being stupid. We just have to wait for him to raise his rotten head."

Janice is quiet for a while. "You don't think he'd come after the rest of us, do you?"

Dale's pause stretches out forever. "I don't know what he'd do at this point."

"Did we do the right thing bringing him here?"

"It's the safest place for him, Jan."

I press my ear to the door during the pregnant pause. There has to be more. I need to hear it.

Finally, she says, "But having him here makes it unsafe for the rest of us."

Janice has a very good point.

Ten

Sunday afternoon, Jill has arranged a sort of date for Gretchen and me. It's exactly two weeks after what was supposed to be our first date. Gretchen's body and our mini-forest seem a world away and absolutely unappealing, but Jill begs me to host one night of normalcy.

Everyone makes a big deal about it. When the doorbell chimes, Janice hustles the little boys upstairs for a night of new video games and junk food.

Jill opens the door to a huge hug from Gretchen. My hands are firmly in my pockets, but I tilt my head a little. "Hey."

We're standing here—them trying desperately to make normal conversation and me staring at the walls—waiting for Tucker and Grant Blakely. We had anticipated a much bigger gathering, but no one else is coming. Some parents won't let their kids anywhere near me.

To her credit, Jill screamed, "Screw your mother!" into her phone more than once while she was inviting people.

I'm being punished again. Wasn't the murder enough? Hell, wasn't my childhood enough? This is exactly why I never told anyone what was going on in my house. Well, the embarrassment, and the fact that I didn't want people to be scared to hang out with me.

Tucker, who is closest to his normal self, shows up with Oreos and orange soda. "Glad to see you alive, buddy."

I manage a half-smile.

Grant Blakely is close behind him with three giant pizza boxes.

In the kitchen, they all dig into the pies. Jill serves me a huge slice. "Here, Xander, you need to eat."

I sit at the kitchen table, because everyone's at the kitchen table, but I'm still full. Or not hungry.

Gretchen is watching me. She's quieter than I've ever seen her. "I thought sausage and onion was your favorite?"

Is it? This party was a terrible idea. It's too soon for all of this. It will always be too soon.

A year ago, I would have savored this moment. Hell, sixteen days ago, I would have been elated about our little fivesome.

Mom has been gone fifteen days, and now my life is divided: with her and without. Before and after.

My friends—these people—make small talk as they devour pizza.

Afterward, Jill says, "Okay. How about a few hands of euchre to get us back into the swing of things?"

"Sure," Gretchen says, much to my surprise. Since her parents taught her to play bridge, she's had nothing good to say about euchre. Desperate times, I guess.

I bow out of the game but sit near the table. Jill keeps the conversation afloat and I feel like I'm sitting outside of life. Things are moving on, but I can't go on with them.

Moving on would mean I accept what has happened. Moving on would mean I no longer have a mother.

Deputy Nolton tips an invisible hat when he comes inside to use the toilet.

"He's the one who sits down to pee," Jill whispers. "Quietest pees ever."

Tucker lays down outside the bathroom, peeking beneath the door to confirm that Nolton's feet face away from the toilet. Unless the guy is biologically backward, he pees sitting down. This is hilarious to everyone but Gretchen, who looks at me with big, sad eyes while everyone else snickers.

Tucker scrambles back to his seat when the toilet flushes. Nolton emerges, tips his not-hat again, collects a Mountain Dew from the fridge, and is out the front door.

"What kind of dude pees sitting down?" Tucker says.

Jill laughs. "One who's used to sitting on his ass outside my house all day?"

Play continues and Gretchen turns her focus to me. "How are you doing cooped up in the house for days and days?"

I shrug.

"We call it Dale Jail," Jill says, and Tucker laughs. "No, seriously. I'm thinking of mocking up some orange shirts with inmate numbers and everything."

Jill has other plans, too, of course. For an hour, she fills in details about the road trip to the Adirondacks: the pack list, the emergency kit, the route, and the menus. Every miniscule detail is planned, except that tiny factor of getting out of Dale Jail.

Being here is more than unsafe. I'm ruining everything. I can't do much about my life, but Jill's would be a lot better if it weren't for me.

"I think I'm ready to call it a night," I say, and everyone's eyes shift toward me.

Gretchen reaches across the table toward my hands, which are instantly in my lap. "Xander, what can we do for you?"

"I'm fine."

She's very quiet. Infinitely calm. "We know you're not fine. No one expects you to be fine. How are you really?"

"I'm fine." I look at Gretchen, who looks at Jill, who looks at Tucker, who studies his cards.

Grant Blakely looks at me. "I'm sorry, man, I don't know what to say either."

"I'm just tired," I lie.

Gretchen says, "We're all here for you, Xander. We want to help."

"And what does that entail, exactly?"

Gretchen wraps her arms around her waist and stares at her lap. I feel bad, but I can't exactly apologize. These people can do nothing for me.

When I stand, Grant Blakely jumps right in front of me. "Listen, I kind of know how you're feeling."

He won't let me get around him.

"Just hear me out," he says, and I'm still. "Did you know my uncle died two years ago?"

"Not the same."

His eyes soften a little. "You're right, it's not the same, but hear me out. He had two young kids—really young, like two and three—and my aunt had to deal with this and them all together. She says life will never be normal again."

He's said it, the thing everyone else has been too stupid or too afraid to admit.

And Grant Blakely has more. "She says all they have is the new normal, which is marred with this huge void left by his death. So what she did—the only thing she said that worked—was to pretend she was going on with life. She took the boys to school. She made dinners and resumed the routine and put up a Christmas tree in December. Balloons and streamers for birthdays. She made herself go through the motions until it became the new normal. But, yeah, it'll never be the same."

The honesty helps, it really does. Grant Blakely just gave me permission to accept that nothing will ever be the same. I'm not ready for a new normal, though; I might never be ready. This is one of those times for baby steps. The best I can muster is a whisper. "Maybe a movie."

Their bodies relax in unison.

Grant Blakely pats me on the shoulder. "It's worth a shot."

Jill leads us into the living room. Gretchen saves the smaller couch—the one Mom referred to as a love seat—for us. Jill rushes back to the kitchen for Oreos and we round-robin veto movies before settling on a stupid Ben Stiller comedy.

Tucker reaches for an Oreo and Jill snatches it back. "Get your own."

Twenty minutes into the film, Grant Blakely turns off the lights and Gretchen rests her head on my shoulder. A moment later, she lifts her mouth to my ear and whispers, "I've missed you."

I can't say anything to that. I haven't exactly been focused on Gretchen for the last two weeks. I wish I could go back to that place where my only concern was shrinking a playlist to a suitable size.

Something flickers outside the sliding glass doors, and I hop off the couch to close the curtains.

I can't sit back down with Gretchen. I can't just pick up where we left off. The thought of wrapping my arms around Gretchen seems sacrilegious when I will never again wrap my arms around my mom.

I retreat to the bathroom and close the door.

I usually avoid mirrors because, come on, my hair does what it wants anyway. But I can't help looking now. Scratching my hair, I try to move it around into something presentable. Probably, if I let it grow, it would be curly. It has the course texture of a curly-haired person's hair. Like Mom's. Mom's hair was wavy.

It's gone.

Mom's eyes are gone, too, and with them the sorrow and fear that lived there. I'll never be judged by them again. I won't see disappointment or pride in them. Never again. Mom had the palest blue eyes.

Mine are Gary's eyes—a deep, dark brown. Looking into them now, a huge sob rises from my gut and I reach for a towel.

Dropping to my knees, I heave sobs into the stupid, pink, embroidered towel. Why is this happening to me? Why am I alone in the world?

I want to lie curled up on this floor forever and create a world in my mind. A world where Mom is outside the door and everything is fine and graduation is still ahead of me. And I will have a date with Gretchen tomorrow, and everything will be fine. If I could wind back the clock and live in that moment, I would never leave this bathroom, I swear. *I promise.*

Sobbing, I promise a thousand times that I would give anything—anything!—for everything to go back to normal.

After a million promises and a forever of relentless sobbing, I'm done, apparently. And, as much as I want my old life—my life before Mom died—on the other side of the door, I know I can't have it. I know I have to make something of this new normal.

I wash my face and study my reflection again. I can't stay in this bathroom, no matter how much I wish I could.

I turn the knob and crack the door. Thank god Grant Blakely turned off the lights; if I return to the movie with more food, maybe no one will realize how long I've been gone. When I grab a Coke and a bag of Cheetos from the counter, Gretchen joins me in the kitchen.

She's very quiet. "You okay?"

"Yeah. Fine! Just hungry, I think?"

"I'm so sorry about all of this." She wraps her arms around my neck, and her warmth radiates through our clothes again. Closing my eyes, I conjure our mini-forest in my mind. I just want to go backward. Just seventeen days back to that forest.

Gretchen is staring at me when I open my eyes. We stare for a long time, but there's no silent conversation between us. There's nothing to say, really. She licks her lips and my stomach does a little flip to signal either excitement or impending vomit.

Without thinking, I close my eyes and we kiss quietly. I know what I'm doing this time, and for a second my mind is free. For maybe the first time ever, I am literally thinking about nothing.

When Gretchen tousles my hair, Mom springs to mind.

I pull back. "I'm sorry, Gretchen. I just can't do this right now."

I can't take it back, don't want to, so I hustle up the stairs and lock myself in Jill's bedroom.

My life is over. My mother is dead. A killer is after me. I just blew off the most amazing girl I've ever known. I am alone in the world.

I have nothing to lose anymore.

Eleven

Janice serves us french toast and bacon for breakfast. Yesterday was pancakes. Saturday, waffles. They're all my favorite things, which is a testament to the fact that, really, I am full.

Jill picks through my breakfast after Janice leaves for work.

She's munching my bacon when the phone rings. We've had two hang ups in the last fifteen minutes. This annoys the hell out of Jill, the girl who spent half of eighth grade pranking everyone we knew.

This time I answer. "Bernards."

This time Gary answers back. "Just give me five minutes with you, Alexander."

I can't speak. I can hardly breathe.

"Same assholes?" Jill asks lightly. She turns to find me clutching the phone and her face falls. "No. No!" she screams, running for the front porch.

Seconds later, Jill is back with Deputy Nolton. He reaches toward the phone, and I press it into my ear. The line is dead.

The world swirls around me: Nolton making calls on his cell and Jill frantically begging her mother to come back home. She closes all the blinds before bawling on the kitchen floor.

Minutes later, when Janice and Dale return, I'm still holding the phone in the kitchen.

What would Gary do with five minutes? It took less than that to break my clavicle. Three seconds to kick me down the stairs. With five minutes, he could actually kill me.

He's going to kill me.

Jill maniacally repeats, "Trace the call, trace the call, trace the call," and Dale demands to know what Gary said.

Once I've repeated Gary's eight words a dozen times, Dale gets to work, converting the kitchen to a makeshift command center where five cops discuss how to proceed. One is talking with the phone company, one with the police station, one with a judge downtown.

Jill cries in her mother's lap on the love seat. She'd made progress on breaking out of Dale Jail, but this will set us back several days.

The cops are done with me, so I creep down to the basement, where the cold concrete floor and cinderblock walls better suit my mood. I can hear everything down here. Jill screams at her father. "Just do your damn job and catch him!"

Janice uses the world's loudest coffee maker and takes a cup to the cop on the front porch.

It's going to be a long day.

And maybe a short life. Gary knows exactly where I am, and there's nowhere to hide. And nowhere else to go, either. My grandparents didn't even come to Mom's funeral. They disowned her years ago, and I guess that applies to me, too.

Among my friends' houses, Jill's is my safest bet. But even here, I'm at risk. And staying means Jill also is in danger. She's been looking forward to Infinite Summer for ages, and now she's imprisoned.

I have to escape. I need to go somewhere no one will ever look for me.

Twelve

I plot my escape in the wee hours.

During the really bad years, when Gary spent our money on god-knows-what and Mom often went to bed without supper, I thought Mom could make it on her own if she didn't also have to provide for me. Gary always complained that I was eating too much or that I grew out of clothes too fast. And he went apeshit once when I lost my gym shoes on a field trip. I desperately wanted to start a new life devoid of name-calling and those thumps on the wall and the constant screaming.

But then they divorced, and life improved, and I didn't feel like running away anymore.

Until now.

I'm robbing Jill of her summer. Everything is on hold until Gary is found. If Gary finds me, he'll kill me. I'm sure of it. The whole state knows he murdered my mother, so he has nothing left to lose. They need to find him before he finds me.

And while he's watching this house waiting for his *five minutes,* I know just where I can hide out.

Like everyone else, I spent junior year poring over hundreds of college brochures, dreaming of the life that awaited me. The University of Vermont sits above the snow belt, so it was never on my short list, but one photo from their stunning brochure sticks with me: the Burlington Youth Hostel, where students in their hospitality program have the option to work.

Hostels are cheap.

Burlington also is one of the most educated cities in America, with high levels of reading. I like reading. And Burlington is in the opposite direction of where anyone will look for me. I can disappear there for a while.

I let the thought marinate, weighing the pros and cons against other options.

The only other option is to stay here and rot.

This is totally above board: I'm not a suspect, I'm not under arrest if you don't count Dale Jail, and I don't *legally* have to stay in Laurel.

I crawl over to Jill's bed to rouse her. She sleeps through her name three times, but startles when I say, "Are you naked under there?"

"What the hell, Xander?"

"Sorry. I was trying to be funny. Remember? You used to wake me up like that."

Jill is groggy. "That was a long time ago."

It was three weeks ago, but that was Life Before. This is Life After.

"Jill, I don't think Dale Jail is going to get any better."

"They have to let us leave the house sooner or later." Her silhouette appears over the side of her bed. "We just have to wait it out."

"I don't think I can. I think they're right: if I leave the house, he'll kill me." My face contorts into a cry again. I'm getting used to it. "You aren't safe with me here. And Dale Jail sucks. I just need to go away until they catch him."

"This isn't some pre-teen escape-plan fantasy, Xander." Jill also remembers our Youngstown Escape Plan. "This is real life."

And real death. She's forgetting the death part.

"I can't see any other way out," I say. "For either of us."

Back in my sleeping bag, I can't get comfortable. The idea is out there now. I can elude my minders, get to the bus station, tell Jill I'm going somewhere, and head in the opposite direction.

Dale will lift Jill's house arrest while I lay low in Burlington. Holed up in the hostel, I won't have to watch my back. And when Gary is captured, I can return to Laurel and Infinite Summer will commence. Simple.

An hour of silence later, Jill says, "So, what's our plan?"

"I thought you were asleep."

She sighs. "Nah, it's too fun to think about."

Fun? Nothing will ever be fun again.

"So, where are you going?"

I hem and haw for a minute. I don't want to tell her.

"Come on! This is me, Xander."

It just comes out: "New York."

It's sort of the truth. I mean, in the messed-up route map that is Greyhound, I do have to pass through New York to get to Burlington. I guess it's sort of a lawyer's answer, but it's definitely the first time I have lied to Jill in a big, big way.

"Alright then." Jill flips on the light and pulls two pads of paper from her drawer. "What's the plan?"

Thirteen

Standing on the threshold of my house for the first time in seventeen days, I'm having trouble focusing. From the landing inside the door, I have to choose: six steps down to the basement and laundry, or eight steps up to bedrooms, bathrooms, living room . . . and kitchen.

As a kid, I used to hold my breath while I ran to the basement for a clean pair of jeans. If I made the trip without releasing or drawing a breath, I was safe. Safe from what, I'm not sure. In my experience, real people are more dangerous than whatever supernatural horrors could be concealed in my basement.

Today I have no interest in heading upstairs, either. Some part of my brain believes Mom is still lying on the kitchen floor, just at the top of the stairs.

Deputy Nolton, who walked us to my house to get more of my stuff, keeps watch on the porch while Jill steps into my house.

She bounds upstairs. Nothing improves her mood like hijinks. "You coming?"

Do I have a choice? On my slow ascent, I focus on Jill's feet and turn the corner at the top of the stairs without looking into the kitchen. She follows me down the hall.

In my bedroom, Jill touches my shoulder. "You okay?"

"Yup, fine."

Jill disappears back down the hall while I survey my room. It really is kind of a sty. I find my black duffel and empty the dirty clothes—oops—before filling it with non-distinct ones: cargo shorts and plain T-shirts. Nothing with a Laurel Woods Lions logo. Nothing about Ohio. Nothing that remotely stands out.

Jill darts in and out of my bedroom, dropping off things from her list: extra contact solution, toiletries, clean under-wear from the dryer.

The dryer. Where Mom put them shortly before she died. I hold them gingerly, as though they're art instead of Fruit of the Loom. These are some of the last things Mom ever touched. I wish I could reach into my underwear and back through time.

I close my eyes and wish it again.

"You okay?"

I lie to Jill and keep packing. My copy of *On the Road* goes into the backpack with other stuff to keep my brain busy. Again, nothing that screams Xander. If Gary starts asking around about me—at the bus station, for instance—I don't want anyone to remember me.

Jill returns with diet granola bars, which I reject.

"Are those the shoes you're taking?"

My brown Teva knockoffs seem fine to me. It's summer.

"For traveling, and for walking around New York, you need real shoes." Jill pulls my grungy Chucks from the closet. "Closed toe. More support. Trust me."

I add them—and some clean tube socks—to my duffel. I'm almost done.

Looking to supplement the sixty bucks from Mom, I raid her favorite cubby holes: inside the toilet paper cylinder, the gap behind the tall bathroom towel case, and between twin copies of her favorite novel, *Midwives*.

With nearly three hundred dollars cash in hand, I bid a silent thanks to my mother's distrust of banks.

It's not stealing, right? Even when I was hard up for cash, I never touched my mom's stash. Never. But if she's dead, all her money is mine, right? Mom would want me to be safe and far from Gary. Pooling our cash is crucial. That's what people do in emergencies.

Mom's whole freaking life was an emergency. If she hadn't wound up pregnant at nineteen, she wouldn't have married Gary. And she wouldn't be dead now. Of course, that means I wouldn't be alive now, but let's put that aside. Any way you slice it, her life was over the second she became pregnant with me. That's a lot of guilt to put on a guy.

I launch my duffel from the top of the stairs to the landing at the front door. Jill is back in the basement, so I'm up here alone. Steeling myself, I close my eyes and turn toward the kitchen.

Deep breaths.

I open just one eye.

And the kitchen is normal. Quiet. No scent of cilantro. No ghosts. No chalk outline or little evidence tents. Laurel Woods cops aren't *CSI*, after all. When I muster the courage to step onto the linoleum, nothing happens.

I am in my kitchen alone. Mom is gone.

Fourteen

Dale and Janice have left us alone in the house with a cop on the front porch. Six hours before departure, Jill and I sneak into the garage. Dale thought Neapolitan was too conspicuous, and taking a squad car seemed ridiculous, so tonight we're driving Dale's civilian vehicle to Pittsburgh for a concert. He's sending a deputy to babysit us.

I dump my duffel and backpack in Dale's trunk. I'm ready. "Saturday, 7:30. Pizza Works. You'll be there, right?"

Jill rolls her eyes. The Pizza Works pay phone was part of our old plan, the one so practiced that it forms the fabric of our childhood. YEP.

"This is serious, Jill. I need you to promise me you'll be at the phone."

"I promise." She combs her fingers through her hair. A wad of bubblegum would make her the quintessential teenaged girl. "What?"

"You're not taking this seriously. Write it on your hand or set an email reminder or something. Say something. Wish me luck. Tell me I'll be safe. Tell me everything is gonna be okay."

Another eye roll, and I totally get why Mom was so irritated by that response.

Jill whispers, "You're safer here."

"In Dale Jail, right? Jill, I might not be safe anywhere! He wants five minutes to finish me off! That day, if I'd been in the house—if I'd gone in for a snack, or if I'd been too hot, or if I had finished my playlist early—I would have been inside, and we wouldn't be having this conversation."

"Your parents had a long and sordid history. He has no reason to come kill you."

Now I'm screaming. "Since when did Gary need a reason?"

We stare at each other for a minute and I try not to cry. Jill doesn't even try. She wipes her nose on her T-shirt.

"I'm sorry, Jill. I'm trying to save my own life here!"

She glares. "Dad says Gary can't get to you here."

"Yeah, well, I know just how much your dad's protection helped my mother. I can't put my life in his hands anymore."

She stares for a moment before thrusting a heavy paper bag toward me. "Okay, if you're really doing this, I have a couple things for you. Here's a bunch of food and some apples."

"Is it mostly Oreos?"

"No. I kept those to console myself." She piles on a few more prizes. "A present: *Masterful Sudoku*, which ought to last you an hour. On loan: my copy of the US Atlas, since you'll be off the grid. And, until you get back, I'll swap your mp3 player. Mine's all loaded up."

Hers is a 128G touch-screen loaded with ten thousand songs and dozens of games. Mine is a vintage knock-off Mom found on eBay.

Jill cries harder.

"Wow, you're really upset about that iPod."

She hugs me. "Keep it in airplane mode. Wireless and Bluetooth off, just in case."

"Why just in case?"

"It's registered in my name. Gary knows me, he knows us. He could trace it."

"Do you really believe that? Even if he doesn't know you own it?"

"I don't know, but just in case, okay?" Jill puts my Columbus Crew hat on her own head and yanks another one—god, Seattle Mariners—from her bag. "This will help you be incognito once you get to New York. And there's this."

I unfurl a strip of leather to find four beads: W, W, J & D. WWJD? More like WTF?

I chortle. "Did you just get religion?"

"The 'J' is for Jill. I'm hoping you don't do anything stupid or daring. Just ask yourself what I would do."

I love how she claims the moral high ground. "You're always doing stupid and daring shit."

"Right, but just ask yourself, okay? You have to come back in one piece. Alive."

I tuck the bracelet next to Gretchen's Labello lip balm in my backpack's tiniest pocket.

Jill fills the cooler with ice and the two-liters Tucker brought over this morning. I love that he's not asking questions. *Hey Tucker, could you bring us half a dozen two-liters? Hey, Tucker, could you buy me some super laxatives? Hey, Tucker, could you exchange these two-liters for Mountain Dew?*

Tucker always says yes when Jill's doing the asking.

Thank god she abandoned the laxative idea already. Drugging a cop, even with over-the-counter stuff, is an actual crime. I'm trying to stay above the law here.

Jill's phone rings. "It's Tucker. Can you finish bagging up this stuff?"

She races back into the house, leaving me alone in the garage.

Quickly, I prop up the tallest ladder and climb toward the gray box on the highest shelf in the garage. I couldn't figure out a way to get a gun, especially in this house, but Dale's tackle box has lots of knives. I definitely need one that folds and isn't rusted. That leaves two options. The one with the longer blade is smooth and engraved, definitely something he would miss if I took it.

Strictly speaking, I need it more than he does, though. I slip it into my shorts pocket, close the box, and replace the ladder.

Now I'm armed. It's just a knife, but still.

FIFTEEN

The fake plan is on. Jill and I have dragged Tucker and our police escort to Pittsburgh under guise of attending a concert. We have tickets, and they're not selling more at the door, which is the only reason Dale let us come. In the parking lot, Jill catches my eye over the sedan's roof. Half the Mountain Dew is gone. It's nearly dusk. We're right on schedule.

This has to work.

Jill leaves the car unlocked and the four of us file into the building with hundreds of other people. Once we've found our section, Nolton says, "I need to use the can," and a big, goofy grin spreads across Jill's face.

Seconds later, Nolton disappears and it's Go Time.

Handing over my cheap red flip phone officially takes me off the grid. No phone, no email, no social networking, no digital trail. Jill's face contorts into a cry and I hug her.

I hug Tucker, too. "I have to get out of here."

Tuck is pissed. "You're leaving? Why did we drive to Steeler Nation to hear a band with a stupid name and shit music?"

"I'm taking a bow, Tucker. I'm leaving you two here."

"He's running away from home," Jill says.

"I am excusing myself from the media circus and Gary's ever-cooling trail."

Tuck is not amused. "You're an idiot."

"What's your plan then, Tucker? Gary is now an experienced murderer and I'm a sitting duck! Should I just hole up in Jill's house all summer? Will you bring all your dates to her couch, too, so it can be doubly awkward? Or are you going to track down Gary Fife yourself?"

He doesn't move.

"Then shut up."

Jill hugs me for the ten millionth time. "You have to take care of yourself. You're the best friend I've ever had, and I can't just be stuck here with Tucker for the rest of my life."

"Nice," Tuck says.

I hand over my house keys. "I promise. Take copious notes, okay? I want to hear about everything that happens in my absence."

Tucker is incredulous. "You're just leaving?"

"If I stay, I'm dead. You know it, and I know it. I'm just going into hiding. I'm not a truant or a deviant or a criminal. As soon as Gary's in custody, I will come back to Laurel. I'll be back in, like, five days. Tops."

"You're enjoying this, aren't you?" Tucker crosses his arms.

Jill glares at him. "I realize that mortal peril is a foreign concept to a guy whose biggest concern is finding a summer girlfriend, but your friend here is coping with some seriously heavy shit."

I will not miss the push-pull tension-laced drama between these two.

"Okay, you two can bicker on the way home. Ready? Here is the last thing I'm saying to you. Forget everything else here and just remember this."

Tucker pulls out his wallet. "Wait, do you need money?"

I'm looking around for Nolton, who must be about done in the john by now. "Thanks, no. Now, quickly. Ready?"

They nod.

"If I stay in Laurel, I'm as good as dead. I'm just going to blend into the background somewhere else until Gary turns up. Don't try to follow me. It will be easier to disappear if I'm alone."

We stare at one another for a few seconds—almost too long. Thank god Nolton is a sitter.

After two more quick hugs, I slip out of the building into open air.

Without police protection and absolutely alone, I feel okay. And I have a weapon, or I will in a minute. Dale's blade is tucked into my backpack. I couldn't risk losing it if the arena had metal detectors. And I don't need it yet anyway.

No one followed us here—Nolton checked—and there is a window, I think, before Gary catches on to the plan. There also is a very small window between when Nolton realizes I am gone and when he checks the parking lot.

I grab my stuff from Dale's sedan and lock it. "So long," I whisper before heading toward the Greyhound station.

———

Five hours in, my plan doesn't look so hot. Gary wasn't at the station, and he's not on my bus. Since Pittsburgh, there's been no sign of him. I've studied every car on the road. No Mustangs at all. I suppose a smart person traveling incognito would ditch his own car, but is Gary smart, really?

Tucked into the last seat on the bus, studying my Graham Bel(l) ID, I wonder what the hell I'm doing.

I'm traveling, which is the one thing I have always wanted to do, but it turns out traveling with someone on your tail isn't actually fun. If he hasn't followed me this far, Gary isn't going to miraculously show up at this instant. In fact, I can probably take out my contacts. Wearing them for twenty hours has dried them out, and surely I have earned a break from surveillance.

Eyes out and earbuds in, I move Jill's mp3 player near and far from my face to find the perfect reading distance. Jill has dozens of playlists, including the one I was making for Gretchen. It's like a farewell as I drift further and further from Xander Fife. Farewell, Jill. Farewell, Laurel Woods. Farewell, Gretchen.

People say *we'll always have Paris,* and, for sure, Gretchen and I will always have our mini-forest. That moment is mine, forever.

Actually, lots of things are mine forever, like Mom swishing in her dress. Sashaying. And that day she got the good job. And her laugh. Mom's laughter was rare, but so pure.

I can't believe she's gone. The warehouse is looking for a new manager already. Mom's lawyer says he'll handle the sale of the house. Another family will move in, and it will be like we never existed. Like she never existed, I guess, since I'm still alive.

Living without Mom doesn't seem right. I've never been without her. How does life just go on without her?

How do I go on without her?

That's a problem for Future Xander. I can't think about it right now. Right now, I need to figure out how, exactly, Graham Bel will survive in Burlington.

Sixteen

Ten minutes before we disembark in New York, I still don't have a plan. And now I can't find my glasses. My eyes aren't terrible, but they're not great either. And I don't want my first New York trip to be a mass of blurs.

But a blur it will be because my glasses are gone.

The Burlington bus leaves in three hours, and I can't resist stepping out of the Port Authority to taste New York City's air. It's a tiny reward for making it this far.

Gretchen raves about New York; *love* doesn't even begin to cover it. But all her talk about shopping and Broadway-with-a-capital-B and the Met were just stories until now.

Forty-eight hours ago, I knew nothing, but laying a digital trail to New York forced me into lots of research. Now I know celebrities are as common in New York as cows in Laurel. In New York, old men sell street food in a hundred languages, and the skyscrapers stretch on for miles. The food and the lights and the girls and the sub-ways of endless possibility are really freaking tempting.

If I had time to dick around, I would head straight for Strawberry Fields in Central Park. Or the New York Public Library or Gretchen's beloved Metropolitan Museum of

Art. I might also poke around her favorite neighborhood, Greenwich Village, which is hard to poke at online when you spell it phonetically. I want to visit all the places that make her light up like Christmas.

I just don't have that kind of time.

Times Square is a fifteen-minute walk from Port Authority and I feel safe enough to make it. If Gary is following me, there's no way he's gotten this far yet.

I pull Jill's Mariners cap over my face and gather my bags. Just another tourist. Nothing distinct about me. Nearly nine million people live in New York. It's probably the easiest place in the world to get lost in the crowd.

Outside the station, the city is pulsing . . . at six o'clock on a Friday morning. I can almost literally feel a pull toward Times Square. Maybe I should have considered colleges here. Winters be damned.

A huge glass front window reflects the shops across the street, and Mom is in my head. When I was very little, she constantly washed the sliding glass door to remove my fingerprints and the smudges Jill left with her Chapstick. Smooch Smudges. That's what mom called them. By the time we were seven, she gave up. And—

Someone is there. Someone's reflection is several paces behind my own. He's looking right at me. In sunglasses at 6 a.m.

I pick up the pace, like one of those Olympic walkers who always look like they need to pee.

The guy is still behind me, clad in white from head to toe, hat pulled down over his face, just like me. But I'm trying to hide. Is he trying to hide? He's built like Gary. It could be Gary in a weird outfit. It could be one of Gary's friends. Does Gary have friends?

What the hell was I thinking? I need the knife; it belongs in my pocket at all times.

I sort of run and look back to see the guy also sort of running. He has something small and black in his hand. A knife? A gun?

Why isn't anyone else paying attention to the guy with the weapon? I break into a full-out run, inasmuch as you can run with an overfull duffel bag. Crossing a street against traffic doesn't shake him.

Why didn't I put my contacts back in when I got to New York? Shit.

I run up a street of tall buildings, duck into an alley, and slither past a malodorous garbage truck. Peeking from beneath the truck, I see the guy's shoes trot by. He's breathless.

"Almost there. Cross your legs and call the midwife."

A phone makes infinitely more sense than a weapon in broad daylight. Panting, I lean against the cold, gray building and look skyward at the thin sliver of blue, stories and stories above me.

The garbage truck turns onto the street and I'm alone in the alley.

Cross your legs and call the midwife.

Laughing and crying are so similar. It's like shitting your pants when you want to fart. One minute I'm laughing at the not-Gary guy, whose whole life is about to explode. A second later, I burst into sobs because I just had a near-death experience. Or thought I did.

Laughing at the misunderstanding, in tears because, really, what the hell am I doing? This isn't an adventure. My first time out of Ohio, yes, but I'm not here for fun.

Did Mom feel this panic? I don't think she knew Gary was going to kill her. For her, it was just another day in their relationship, not her last day on Earth.

I hope she blacked out and never realized it was almost over.

Someone interrupts my laughing-crying fit. "Sleeping here."

She's curled up next to a garbage bin, propped up in the corner like a rag doll. Everything about her—clothes, shins, face, hair—is a drab gray-brown.

It strikes me that the garbage truck's stench didn't leave with it; the foulness is hers. Jill's obese grandmother always smells slightly of rancid cheese. This woman smells exponentially worse.

Do not plug your nose. Do not plug your nose.

"Sorry," I say.

"I bet." She spits and closes her eyes.

Backing away from her, I turn to face the street again. At my first opportunity, which happens to be a McDonald's, I slip into the bathroom. First the knife into my pocket, then the contacts into my eyes. I am so not ready for this.

I hope my glasses are in the bottom of my backpack. No use looking now; if the glasses aren't there, there's nothing I can do about it.

I can do something about breakfast, though. After inhaling hotcakes and sausage, I say a silent apology to Janice for my loss of appetite at her house.

From my perch, I can see New York City through floor-to-ceiling windows. This is it: I am traveling. And already I'm doing it wrong: a breakfast I could buy anywhere in America. Anywhere in the world.

Hundreds of miles from home, I'm just watching the world walk by. New York City, with its bustle and business, could be a movie to me. I need to go out there.

Am I being a coward again? Is my cowardice self-preservation, or still the wrong thing? I have no idea.

Times Square could be my reward for all those hours on the bus. And my last hurrah before I really go into hiding.

Gary wouldn't kill me in Times Square. He's not even here. Not yet. I would have seen him on the highway. He would have caught up with me by now. It's going to take him a while to realize I'm gone, and then a while to figure out where I went. And with any luck, he'll be caught in the meantime.

This morning, Times Square should be safe. Just twenty minutes.

Right?

What would Jill do? She'd rush right out there. But, again, she's prone to stupid and daring shit.

Tucker? He would never have come this far in the first place. He has a dozen relatives who would take him in at a moment's notice.

What would Mom do? I don't know. I hate doing exactly as she tells me, but there's still value in consulting her. Or there was. I could use her advice right now.

Fact is: if Gary is in New York, I'm toast. And I would rather die in Times Square than in McDonald's.

It's a moot point. I keep coming back to this: *Gary is not here yet.* But I am, and Times Square is right there. Mom has never been there.

She'll never go, either. And she'll never nag me about cleaning my room again. Or deny me the car again or buy the wrong shaving cream again or nose her way into the basement when I have friends over again. And she'll never ask embarrassing questions about my date with Gretchen, if there ever is a date with Gretchen. There are so many things she will never do. And things we'll never do together.

But I'm still here. I get to keep having new experiences and doing the things I want to do.

I dart out of McDonald's and head toward Times Square. I hear it before I reach it—the loudest intersection ever. Times Square is also visually loud: ads everywhere, news feeds, cameras, food carts, street performers. Coffee for five bucks. People requesting spare change. Lots and lots of long New York legs, even before eight in the morning.

The allure of this place makes me feel closer than ever to Gretchen. Does she know yet, that I'm gone? I wish I could tell her what I was seeing. I wish she could tell me where to go and what to do and how to make my time here count.

The street performers are unreal. This enormous dude—he must be nearly seven feet tall—twists his arms behind his body in inhuman ways. Then a brief pause and he moves like water across the concrete. This is art unlike any I've ever seen.

With all of Times Square at my disposal, I can't take my eyes off these dancers. I spend half an hour—backed against a wall so I can see all the other passersby—awed by this guy and his whole troop of friends.

The hubbub emboldens me: I really could just disappear, right here. Embrace the fake plan and hunker down in New York's youth hostel—for surely there must be one, somewhere—and bide my time until I can return to Laurel.

I defuse the idea almost immediately. New York is too expensive. Even if I could afford a couple nights in a hostel, I probably couldn't also feed myself. Getting anywhere in New York requires cabs or subways, and I don't have change to spare. Plus, if Jill spills the beans, people will come looking for me in New York. I need to bounce.

I'll come back once this whole mess is over. Maybe with Gretchen. Jill and Tucker, too. Hell, we could have our big adventure here instead of the Adirondacks.

Now that's a plan.

In the Port Authority bathroom, I change into jeans and a T-shirt and pull Jill's ball cap over my hair. Jill suggested I chuck my old T-shirt and shorts in the trash at the station but that seems unnecessarily drastic. Only murderers and people being hunted by the police toss their clothes in the trash.

Plus, I only have so many pairs of shorts.

Tucking my fake ID into the front of my wallet, I am now nineteen-year-old Georgia resident Graham Bel.

I used this ID last month to get into *Easier with Practice*, an uneven if not wholly intolerable NC-17 film. I flashed it at the door, but this is different. This is semi-permanent. I'm not Xander anymore, not for the foreseeable future. Being Graham for more than five seconds is weird.

That movie was a celebration for Tucker's eighteenth birthday. Will I be home for my eighteenth birthday? Do I still get to celebrate if I'm Graham?

That's another problem for Future Xander. Or Future Graham, as the case may be.

I stuff my Alexander Fife ID into my backpack's tiniest pocket with Gretchen's lip balm and WWJD. With a formal and upright posture befitting one Alexander Graham Bell, I step up to the Greyhound window. "One ticket to Burlington, Vermont?"

The guy doesn't even compare my face to the awesome fake. He types in my name, hands over my ticket, and directs me toward the staircase with grace, like it's some game show instead of my actual life.

Door number three! A Greyhound bus! Bound for the dreary north!

Jill has been with me up until this point. She knew when I left Pittsburgh and when I arrived in New York. Knowing her, she even tracked my bus online. And she knows I was eager to see Times Square. But she doesn't know what's next, or that there *is* a next.

When I step onto this bus, no one in the world will know where I am or how to reach me. It's equal parts freaky and freeing. Eight minutes before we're scheduled to depart, nausea seeps in again. I'm about to jump off a cliff into oblivion.

Seventeen

After hundreds of miles, Burlington looks an awful lot like Pittsburgh. It smells a whole lot better than the bus, though. These people reek. I've been traveling for twenty-four hours, but some passengers have been traveling for days. The stench is almost unbearable.

Round concrete planters of happy flowers dot Greyhound's sidewalks, and a constant stream of airplanes roars overhead. Only slightly cooler than Laurel, but far cooler than New York City, this parking lot could be early summer almost anywhere.

Burlington has to be right. Vermont is the one detail of my escape plan firmly affixed in my head. It has to be right.

Jill was right about *Masterful Sudoku*: it lasted as long as I needed it to. I toss it into the nearest recycling bin and wait for my bags a few yards away from everyone else's stench. Rocking between my feet, I cultivate the appearance of an unapproachable person. Hat over my face, hands in pockets, I'm broadcasting an image: *Disaffected teen. Disaffected teen. Stay away.*

The driver unloads some crazy stuff, including a huge empty birdcage. Several passengers, including one enormous woman whose foot fat extends over the edges of her flip-flops, have military-issue camouflage duffel bags.

A worn, middle-aged woman pulls two huge birds from her trench coat and releases them into the cage. Her stench has an excuse, apparently, and I cringe thinking about the inside of that jacket.

A tiny old lady claims a crate of oranges and a striped yellow backpack embroidered with the word MUMS and a huge heart.

My own duffel is full to bursting, and I'm carrying it into the vast unknown.

At least I hope it's vast.

What am I waiting for? I still get to live, whatever that means now.

This is the tricky part. I have done a *lot* of research about New York City, but I didn't dare research Burlington's geography, in case there was some tricky way for Gary to track Jill's computer traffic. In Burlington, I know nothing but the hostel.

I score a free map and two brochures from the station's information desk. The hostel is less than three miles away, and I have literally nothing else to do. Satisfied that Gary hasn't trailed me this far yet, I heave my duffel over my shoulder and head west on foot.

————

An hour later, drenched in sweat and Burlington's humidity, I'm not impressed. The hostel's glass door, complete with press-on sticker letters, is sandwiched between a Salvation

Army and a repair shop. The T is half missing, so looks like a Hos⁻el with a really high hyphen. Through the door, I see only a narrow, tall staircase.

It is remarkably quiet. I almost feel like I shouldn't be here, like I've entered someone's house uninvited. At the top of the stairs, a pock-faced receptionist is absorbed in her magazine.

Here we go.

I open my wallet and put my cash on the counter. "Hello?"

She doesn't look up. "Do you have a reservation?" Her British accent gives me flashbacks to *Doctor Who* marathons with Jill.

"I don't."

"I'm sorry to say we're booked full tonight."

She keeps talking, but I don't hear a word of it. Shit. Shitshitshit. What Would Jill Do?

"Excuse me? Sir?" Now she's looking at me.

Shitshitshit. "Sorry. I missed that?"

"I would be happy to call one of our hotel partners if you'd like."

"Yes. Sure. Yes, please."

Half an hour later, the gist is that every available room is too expensive. If I only needed one night, no big deal, but I can't exactly drop two hundred bucks on a bed for a single night. Because what will I do if I need a second night in Burlington? Sleep in the street?

This girl is apologetic. "It's this jazz festival. Loads of places are booked up." She looks at her computer. "Now, if you have a relation who can host you tonight, we have a bed available tomorrow night."

I have literally no relations, let alone one in Burlington. What can I do for the next twenty-four hours? This is a special kind of insult—when I finally have the money to do what I want to do, that thing still isn't available to me.

She cranes toward me, her eyebrows raised in hope. "Sound good?"

I guess. I mean, I should take that bed before someone gets it, too. "Yes. Yes, please."

"Name?"

"Xan—Graham? Graham Bel! One 'l' in Bel."

"You got the last bed for a week, mate."

That's okay. My call to Jill is tomorrow night. If all is well and Gary is caught, I can leave Sunday morning anyway.

"Oh, wait," she says.

I don't want to Oh Wait.

"We have a cancellation."

Oh, thank god.

"For Sunday night. Will you still be in Burlington then?"

God, I hope not. "Maybe? I'm not sure. It depends?"

Check-in is not multiple choice. She says, "Let's book you in, and you can cancel if your plans change."

"Thanks."

"No worries."

In minutes, we've sorted the paperwork and I'm on my way again.

———

Heading down the stairs to the great outdoors, I convince myself this is okay. Gary is a close-range weapon kind of guy: knives, skewers, his own hands. He doesn't own a gun.

I don't think he owns a gun.

Shit.

No, it has to be true. For Gary to kill me, he will have to get close. *Very* close. I'll see him coming. As long as I stay out in broad daylight in the company of other people, I will be safe.

But I'll stay inside as much as possible.

Stay in public places. Don't let him get close.

About three thousand silent repetitions later, I push open the door and walk into the world. Burlington is very, very busy.

It's nine o'clock. I'm very, very hungry.

Curt's Deli, where the girl at the desk recommended I have dinner, is just three doors east of the hostel. I hope her recommendation is based on food and not mere convenience. If I'm not spending money on a bed, I might as well splurge on dinner.

The clean-cut guy behind the counter tips his chin upward. "Sup?" He's not much older than I am. Maybe twenty-two, tops. Where would he stay tonight if he were me?

"Hi!"

"Hiya. I'm Curt. Wicked hot out there still? Heard it's supposed to be even hotter tomorrow. What do you hear?"

I hate small talk. "I need a minute."

"Sure. Everything's fresh. Everything's local. Everything's good."

That is their shtick; it's printed on every sign and menu in the place. Menus over and behind the counter look like chalkboards, with words meticulously painted to look like chalk. Curt's apron is black, as is his hair. And the back of the deli case.

I can't tell whether it's hipster or sincere, but judging by the sandwich Curt passes over the deli case to another customer, his sandwiches are sincerely enormous. I order a Reuben with extra Thousand Island.

Curt nods. "Excellent choice. Name?"

"Graham?"

"Sure about that?"

"Graham. Yes. I'm Graham." I'm Graham.

Curt hands over my change, which is over by nineteen bucks.

I hand back a twenty. "I think you had a twenty in your ones drawer. You owed me $3.97, but you gave me $22.97. See?" I hold out the cash toward him.

He swaps the twenty for a single. "Thanks, man."

Curt says dinner will come to my table. Sitting alone at a table for two, I realize I've never gone anywhere alone before. Even *not* talking to Jill while we waited for sandwiches felt normal. Sitting alone feels ridiculous, like some part of me is missing. Digging in my backpack for something to do, I find my glasses at the very bottom, very misshapen.

Gretchen's lip balm is still in the front pocket. I slide my finger across the tube and run my finger over my lips. Gretchen. I'm not ready to think about Gretchen, so I shove the lip balm way down in the front pocket. How can a lip balm make me feel so crummy? Jill's bracelet is right here, too.

What Would Jill Do? A fine question. I don't freaking know. Would she blow almost two hundred bucks on a bed for one night? If I have to stay here longer, I won't be able to afford a second night at two hundred bucks a pop. It seems pretty likely I'll be here at least two nights. The math just won't work out in my favor. I have to find somewhere less legit.

Jill would make friends quickly and couch surf, but that's easier for girls. And for Jill, specifically. She's couch surfed a lot.

A balding, cranky old guy delivers my Reuben with extra Thousand Island, chips so thick I can tell they're not from a bag, the biggest dill pickle I have ever seen, and a root beer. It's the good stuff, too, in a bottle.

The dressing is tangy, and the rye is toasted. Probably a bit too much sauerkraut, but I can scrape it off with my fork. This may be the best sandwich in the history of the world.

In the history of the world, there must have been loads of people like me: wayward travelers who needed somewhere to stay. What did they do?

Curt passes me on the way to another table.

"Curt?"

"Yeah, man?"

"Any idea where a guy could find a bed for the night?"

"Hotels are mostly booked for Jazz Fest, aren't they? Best advice I have for everyone: try the hostel. Three doors down, excellent staff, and free waffles for breakfast."

"Yeah, thanks," I say.

Now what?

Curt's closes at ten, and I'm the last person out the door.

"Come again," Curt says, and I promise I'll be back.

EIGHTEEN

Everything is different in the dark. Shadows have fallen over everything, making Burlington really freaking creepy. Ten paces past exhausted, I feel super vulnerable. Hat pulled over my eyes, shifting my gaze every which way, I must look like a criminal. No sign of Gary, though, so there's that.

For real, if I were Gary, I would be hunting me at night. But then, if Gary were here, he would have made his move by now, probably.

Okay, so what's my next move?

Bed. Or sleep, at least.

For maybe an hour, I poke around the University of Vermont looking for a spot. My best bet for the night is a bench that butts right up to a brick building. It's somewhat obscured by large trees, which cast enough shadow for me to stay hidden. Kick the duffel under the bench, tuck the backpack under my head, rub a little of Gretchen's Labello on my lips—*good night, Gretchen*—and close my eyes.

It's almost comfortable. Almost. And I'm so on edge, I'll hear anyone approaching.

As it turns out, I don't.

"You can't sleep here."

I startle to find a cop, wide awake and surly, standing right next to my bench. His uniform suggests he isn't even a cop, but some second-rate security officer.

"Sorry, I—I must have dozed off."

Holding a handle stuck into his utility belt, he's threatening without threatening. "Well, move along, then."

"Sure."

It's well after midnight. Oh my god, so tired.

"Bags up," he says. "I'll walk you off campus."

"It's okay, I can make it on my own."

"I wouldn't want you to get lost, son." He guides me to a sidewalk at the edge of campus. "Have a good night, then."

I have nothing to lose to the fake cop. "Any idea where I can sleep?"

"Try the hostel on Main."

"They're booked."

Heaving a huge sigh, he recites, "Spectrum Center for Homeless Youth if you're under twenty-two. Emergency Shelter on North Street. COTS shelters a couple of places."

Shelters? "I'm not homeless."

"Then go sleep at home."

Touché. "Anything else?"

"If you're not homeless and not in need, go to a hotel. Bunk with a friend. Call someone. But you can't sleep on campus. Anywhere on campus."

"Thanks."

"Any time."

How many times a night does he run that script?

"Thanks," I say again.

"Any. Time."

"Bye, then."

I head down Main Street, in the opposite direction from the hostel. This morning's high has vanished. The homeless shelter is not an option. I keep smelling that woman in the New York alley, and I am not her. My life has lots of gray areas, but I am not one of them.

There's that twenty-four-hour Price Chopper store I saw on my walk from the station, but what am I going to do, shop all night? I need a bed.

I desperately, desperately need to turn on Jill's Wi-Fi and find somewhere to go. How likely is it that Gary could track it?

I already lied to Jill about New York. I can't also break my promise about the Wi-Fi. Plus, I'm out of the commercial district now, so if I want to break my promise, I also have to steal the Wi-Fi from someone's house.

Lies? Sometimes okay. Broken promises, maybe. But stealing is one step further than I'm willing to go.

The knife is borrowed, not stolen. I'm not going to steal Wi-Fi.

Next to a brown fence—residential, for sure—I sit on my duffel, contemplating my options.

I just need a break. Where do normal people sleep? Normal people without a house or a friend's house? Or money for a hotel? People who need to sleep elsewhere, where do they sleep?

I would do anything for a bed at this point. Well, not anything. A homeless shelter surely has beds, but that's just . . . embarrassing. I'm only without a bed for a single night, not forever. This is temporary homelessness. Tomorrow I get the hostel for two nights.

What if Gary isn't caught? Then what? Then where? *Am I homeless?* No. Homeless people are dirty and sickly and old. There aren't many in Laurel, but I saw a few in New York. I am not one of them. Am I?

The inky sky holds no answers. Nor does the uneven sidewalk. A brown landmark sign points down the street directly opposite my perch. White letters read COSLEY WOODS.

Woods sound promising. My last foray into the woods was a huge success. And even without Gretchen, how bad can it be, really? Burlington is too urban for bears, and I've been battling the herd of mosquitoes since my arrival. Things can't get worse.

I look up and down Main Street, but no one else is here, let alone tailing me. The brown sign's road is dark, its residents tucked in for the night.

A forever walk away, far at the end of the street, is the entrance to Cosley Woods. I don't see a sign prohibiting pedestrians, but then, I can't see much. The mere sliver of moon hardly helps. At the edge of the parking lot, I spot a huge kiosk like the ones on Laurel's fitness circuit. I'm sure there's valuable information here—stuff that has nothing to do with chin-ups or lunges—but I can't make out the writing.

It's just one large flat surface without enough contrast for reading. Maybe the kiosk includes instructions or disallows sleeping overnight, but I won't know until morning and, frankly, I don't care.

Behind the kiosk is another, smaller sign. A giant arrow, etched about a half-inch deep, directs me into the forest. At its mouth, the trail is quite wide. Two people could walk abreast without touching each other or the trees. Soon, it tapers to a narrower path.

If anyone noticed me heading into Cosley Woods, they might follow to investigate, so I pick up the pace.

This isn't my thing. The canopy is so thick I can hardly see. Walking with my arms outstretched like Frankenstein's monster, I stumble over something and bang into a tree. I hate nature.

The quiet is good, but the darkness is unnerving. What else is out here, roaming around?

I hate this. I hate it so hard. The moon sliver peeks through the canopy, and I use the light to get off the path and walk deep into the woods. Far enough away that morning joggers won't see me, I drop my stuff on the ground. Bedtime. Finally. Jill's iPod tells me it's nearly 2 a.m. The night is half over.

Also, I'm an idiot, because iPods make great flashlights.

My sweatshirt is a little toasty, but will help keep the mosquitoes at bay. Weather that's too hot for Curt feels just right to me. I tuck myself in the middle of some trees and lie on my back. It's not remotely comfortable, but my body is too exhausted to care. It's only one night. Tomorrow at two, I'll be safe in the hostel for two whole days.

Last time I tried to catapult myself forward a few hours, the shit hit the fan. This time I'll be patient. The future will come, either way.

How far into the future did Mom dream? How old did she think she would live to be? She accepted the beatings from Gary, but it wasn't until she thought her life was over that she left him. How long did she expect to live?

She absolutely thought she would make it to my graduation. And to drive me to college. I might have to take another Greyhound to Tulane. Maybe Janice will drive me? She didn't exactly ask to take on another son, though.

Mom said we had made it, but she was wrong. She didn't make it . . . and I may not make it. Mom will never visit Tulane for Parents' Weekend. I'll never know how she would have decorated her empty nest. For months, Mom had promised to live vicariously through my college years. And now? She's going to miss everything.

Something cracks in the distance, and I'm wide awake. It cracks again. Something is out here. Not bears, for sure not bears. Not bears. Crap. What types of animals are lurking out here?

Not Gary. Probably not Gary. Just a rabbit or something. Something nocturnal. A raccoon, maybe. Maybe not.

Clutching the knife, I open and close it several times. Sleeping with an open knife is a terrible idea, but if I need it, I want to know how to use it.

Open. Close. Open. Close.

No more creature noises.

Open. Close. Open. Close.

I close my eyes again. I'll be okay tonight, but what about tomorrow? I feel too vulnerable out in the open. I need to be inside, back against the wall, so I can maintain constant vigilance, on high alert, until the hostel opens. Somewhere free.

I'll figure it out in the morning. I'll make it be okay.

Sometime between sleep and sunrise, the rain starts. In minutes, my stuff is muddy and I'm soaked.

I fashion a face tent out of my backpack and rain jacket and try to find sleep again in the cold, wet darkness. Nature makes a lot of noise. I'll never fall asleep out here.

———

"Xander!"

Sun up. I am completely disoriented. Voice yells my name again and I sprint in the other direction before I even know I'm standing. I open the knife while I'm running. Thank god I practiced.

Louder, Voice calls again. I don't recognize it, but anyone calling my name in Burlington is bad news. And Voice is angry, impatient.

I sprint through trees in our reverse game of Marco Polo. My foot catches the bank of a stream and I'm flat on my belly. I right myself and take inventory as I run.

Nothing broken.

Just keep breathing.

Voice screams, "You can't run forever, Xander!"

I stumble over the stream twice more. I'm running in circles! Haven't seen the path. Haven't found the edge of the forest.

A dog barks, frantic.

Would they send dogs after me? Is it the police?

I am the dog, turning in circles between Voice and the barking. They're closing in on me.

But who are they?

I run again, away from Voice, who knows my name. Through the damned stream this time, soaking my Chucks, which make me even slower.

The dog, a stupid-happy golden who just wants love, finds me first. He licks my hand and rolls over in case I'm interested in rubbing his belly.

"No time for that, buddy." I run from Voice. The dog follows. We're running and running through the trees.

And then we're not. Turns out the edge is on a cul-de-sac. I hide the knife behind my back.

Some guy is watering his garden the morning after a downpour. Children play with Nerf bows and arrows. Running will make all these people suspicious.

Not running could kill me.

The dog licks my hand. I squat to pet him while I think of my next move. The moronic gardener waves timidly and I wave back. *No big deal. I'm just a guy, hanging out with my dog. Casually walking through the woods.*

Voice doesn't call again.

The dog's collar jingles when I scratch behind his ears. His tag is an enormous silver bone. One side reads, "If found . . ." and information about his owners. The other side is etched with his name: Sanders.

It all comes together.

What a stupid name for a dog.

His human yells again, "Sanders!"

"You'd better run," I tell him, and he bolts back through the trees.

Nineteen

It's almost eleven when I make my way out of the woods with all my crap. I'm starving.

At the trailhead, the kiosk tells me everything I need to know: no camping, no sleeping, stay on the trails. Also, leave no trace, and I actually abided that one since I can't afford to lose what little I have with me.

I'm so grateful to have a bed tonight. And a shower. My teeth feel like I've swallowed a cat, and the night's rain weighs down my bags.

After another Reuben from Curt's Deli, I beeline it to the Free Library, where I can sit and read in a corner for two whole hours before checking in at the hostel.

Though I'm traveling light, lugging everything everywhere is a pain. I wish I could leave my wet, stinky duffel outside the library door, but that would be even more suspicious than the guy who brushes his teeth in the library bathrooms.

Yeah, I do it. Slimy teeth are gross. And though I haven't showered in days, clean teeth make me feel human. Human-like, at least. I'm starting to smell less than human. Or *very* human, depending on how you look at it.

My clean teeth and I settle into a comfortable chair for the morning. The nonfiction section is wanting, but *The History of Science* has been on my list for months. Based on the bits I catch between regular surveillance of the area, it's downright fascinating.

Here's irony: it's called the Free Library, but you're only free to check out books if you have a Burlington address. At ten to two, I reshelve my book before hightailing it to the hostel.

The Hos⁻el. The stairs are brighter this afternoon. The girl—the same girl—is at the desk, and more attentive than yesterday. She reads aloud off my fake. "Graham Bel of Georgia. I haven't visited Georgia yet. How do you find it?"

Um . . . "Hotter than here?" I'm an idiot. Of course Georgia is hotter than Vermont. Desperate for nuggets about Georgia, my obsession with travel becomes an asset.

"American Stonehenge is in Georgia! And Savannah, which is allegedly the least friendly city in the whole country. And peaches! Peaches, peaches, peaches. Hey, you know, Georgia was one of the original thirteen colonies, so even though they were admitted to the union just three years before Vermont, Georgia has had it together fifty years longer than Vermont. So, one could say mine is a more American state than yours."

I'm a terrible liar. Just terrible. And pompous.

She isn't fazed. "I'm Welsh. My name is Mia, by the way."

Mia offers an information packet and tells me to vacate by 11 a.m. for the cleaning crew's mandatory checkout. "You can check back in tomorrow at two."

I seriously could have used some recon before this trip. Mandatory checkout? For three hours, thrust back into the world in plain site of . . . anyone?

Still, I have a place to breathe. Thanking Mia, I walk toward the dorm at the back of the building. The mixed dorm is big and bright with six empty beds. I can't tell whether this is better or worse than the dingy dorm room I expected.

I choose the bed closest to the window and dig through my bag for toiletries. All my clothes smell a little musty. I've been trying to separate the clean and dirty clothes but, well, I'm not trying that hard.

After a long, hot shower, I lie on my cot and settle into Jill's iPod. I'm not using the hostel's free Wi-Fi, but I'm thinking about it. Thinking about what everyone else is doing, and how much email they've sent me.

But I promised Jill I wouldn't, and it's her iPod, so I don't.

She has a million new games on here, including some college-prep educational stuff. Definitely no. The mushroom icon for "Save Ur Ash" is cool, but it turns out to be a nuclear apocalypse survival game. Dumb. On my first try, I see the bright flash of the mushroom cloud and I'm toast. On my second try, I miss the flash but can't find my way out of the street where I was standing when the bomb dropped. Ash falls and I'm radioactive.

Apparently, if you're not immediately dead, you have to run as far as possible to escape the impending ash shower. When I see the flash on my third try, I actually blurt out, "Screw you!"

But I don't stop playing. I let the mind-numbing app suck me in because, in the safety of the hostel, a numb mind is absolutely welcome.

Twenty

By 7:10, I'm still alone, still haven't won the stupid game, and still hungry. I swing by Curt's for another sandwich before my scheduled call with Jill.

Curt narrows his eyes and points at me. "Graham. Extra dressing, right?"

I fork over my cash, bemused that he remembered me. Maybe he knows everyone in here. One old lady in slippers and a gnarled, curly wig is literally licking her plate clean. No one pays her any attention. It's normal life.

"Hey, Curt, do you know where I can find a pay phone?"

"No idea. Haven't seen one in years."

Crap.

He surveys the other customers, who shrug and shake their heads.

My internal panic alarm pings. "I need to make a phone call in ten minutes."

"Try mine." Curt unlocks it and hands me an open browser. A quick Google search finds hundreds of phones in Burlington, but their addresses mean nothing to me. I'm on Main Street and the library's on College, but I don't know anything else.

I shine the phone in Curt's direction. "Which one of these is closest?"

"Just use my phone, man."

Oh. That makes sense.

Curt studies the list in his browser. "I mean, if you want privacy, probably . . . probably this one on Union is closest."

I don't know what I want. The security of staying right here sounds good, but I'm expecting some heavy shit on this particular call. Privacy trumps security today.

"I'll try Union Street. Thanks, man. See you tomorrow."

Even a sprint gets me to the phone five minutes late. I dial the ever-important *67 first.

It rings thirteen times before I hang up.

Jill has forgotten. My oldest friend, my single confidante, my only lifeline has forgotten our date.

Desperate for news, I can't very well order *The Vindicator* way up here, not that it covers intimate details of our tiny town anyway. Maybe I could do some Internet searches without naming my town or my father . . . and still find out whether I can go home.

What if I can never go home?

Two minutes later, I try again. Seventeen rings with no answer.

Maybe she's sick. Maybe Gary got to her. No. She's on a date, more likely. *Goddammit, Jill! This is important!*

At exactly 7:40, it doesn't even ring once before Jill says, "Um. Hi?"

"Oh, thank god." Knowing Jill is there relaxes me slightly. Leaning against the brick wall, phone cord stretched taut, I can see the whole street while we talk.

"I can't believe this actually worked," she says. "How are you?"

"M'okay. Yeah, fine. Sorry I'm late. You first. How's Dale Jail?"

"Ha. Ha." Oh, her sarcasm. It's a nice taste of home. "It's getting better, actually. He let me go to the mall with Mom tonight."

"Good for you. What's happening?"

"Well, everything and nothing. My dad confiscated my computer and dug through the search history. He knows you're in New York."

He knows nothing.

"Dad said he can't really do anything about it, though. It's not like he can send the NYPD hunting all over the city, you know? He's pretty pissed at you. He's supremely pissed at me, but he'll get over it. I think he's more worried about you than anything else."

"But I'm not in trouble?"

Jill snorts. "No, you're not in trouble, Xander. As you said, you're not a deviant or a criminal. People are asking about you, though. I haven't said a word. Everyone is looking for Gary, but there's no sign of him, either."

Some invisible force sucks the air from my lungs. I really thought this would be over if I just gave Gary enough space to surface.

"Xander?"

"Yeah?"

She's quiet for too long. "We should maybe end the ruse, Xander. Folks who don't know better are saying things—awful things—about you."

"Like what?"

"You don't want to know."

She's probably right, but our conversation will deflate if I admit that. "Jill, I want to know everything. Spill."

"Well, some say you killed your mother. And some say you're dead, too. And—well, I guess those are the two theories. The news reported that you were the only witness, which makes it sound very suspicious. You wouldn't believe the people calling me: Tom Shultz—remember him? He called out of the blue to ask what's up. I told him not much had changed in the last two years, and he jumped right to you: are we still great friends? Have I heard from you? Do I think you're wrapped up in something bad? I asked him whether he even knew you, and he said of course he does, from the news."

"The news?"

"Yeah, Xander, you're still in the news. Lots of murders in Youngstown, but something out here in the township is rare. And there's not much else to report from here. So they keep posting Gary's picture, and one of your mom, and one of you. It's not a good one, either. From the junior yearbook in that horrible brown shirt. My mom won't let me send them a better one. I told her maybe you could get a few dates if I sent them the ones from your deck this spring—"

Her gargantuan pause is probably filled with memories from that deck just three weeks ago. We were so happy. Damn.

"Xander?"

"Yeah, sorry. What?"

"Are you ready to come home? Daddy says you'll have full protection, and who knows: with you here, Gary might resurface, and they can arrest him."

"Nope. I can't risk it. Plus, I'm fine right now. I'm recovering from what has heretofore been one fucked-up life." At least, I hope I'm recovering. I very badly want a normal, sane life, even if that means living (briefly) in the frigid northeast. It's not even frigid in June. Things here are fine.

A family of five bikes toward me—on the sidewalk, no less—and the parents try to keep two of the kids from falling off the curb and into the street. The youngest child, in a seat attached to his dad's bike, mimics an ambulance siren as they whoosh by.

"What the hell was that?" Jill says.

"A family just passed me on the street."

"You're living on the street?"

I chuckle. "Nope. I promise you: I have somewhere to stay." Lawyer Truth.

A recorded operator says, "*Please insert additional funds.*"

"Hold on. I need more quarters." I fumble through my pockets and push all my change through the slot. "I think I just bought us another five minutes."

Jill offers me cash, but wiring money to me would broadcast my whereabouts to a whole lot of people. I suspect that's her intent anyway, because when I refuse her offer, she starts needling for details.

I hate lying to Jill. "Jill, I can't give you any details about New York." Lawyer truth. Separate lawyer truth:

"Just know that I'm safe here. I won't stay a second too long, but I think it's safest to stay away until things settle down there."

"Fine." Her tone suggests it's anything but fine. "Can we talk again tomorrow?"

It's intense, standing here in full view with no crowd protection. Talking every day would be too much of a routine. I want to be scarce and inconsistent, just in case anyone is watching. "Actually, I was thinking in two days, and maybe at a different time?"

Jill sighs. "You're going to be gone two more days?"

That sinks in. I'm going to be gone two more days. At least. "I'm not coming back until I feel safe."

She's quiet, digging for something to compel me back. "Gretchen's not gonna wait forever, you know."

Low blow. "Have you seen her?"

"She comes over every day. She is dying for details, not that it matters since you're so secretive. I've hinted that you're somewhere you've never been before, but that doesn't exactly narrow it down, you know? And, if I'm being honest, you coming back wouldn't really fix things with Gretchen because her dad has forbidden her to see you. He thinks you're a fugitive."

Most parents love me, so being banned is a sort of trophy, in addition to a huge bummer. I press my finger into the outside of my backpack, right at the pocket. Gretchen's lip balm creates a little bulge from inside.

Jill says, "What if something happens tomorrow and you could be *home* by Wednesday?"

After a lot of back-and-forth, we agree I can use social media, but not from her iPod and only passively. No logging in, not even creating a fake account, because if Gary's really watching, he might catch on to some random person who starts following all my friends online.

If anything significant happens, Jill will post a photo of herself with a number somewhere in the photo. The number is the time I should call her at Pizza Works. If Gary is caught, she'll just post that he's caught, and I can call her cell.

"Please insert additional funds."

Crap. "Jill, I'm out of quarters. I'll call in two days—Monday afternoon, okay?"

"I think nine at night would be better."

"Nine p.m. Got it. Give your Mom a big hug for me . . . but maybe don't tell her it's from me, okay?"

"Yeah."

"Please insert additional funds."

I try to pull both our moods out of the mire with my tone. "Okay, I'll talk to you then! Bye Jill!"

My phone is halfway to the receiver when Jill shouts, "Xander?"

"Yeah?"

"I miss you."

"I miss you too, Jill," and I do. I want nothing more than to share Oreos, and harp on her music, and discuss the little problems of our small town. "Think of this as a trial. When I'm at Tulane and you're at Oberlin, we won't see each other ten times a day. This is like a test to see whether we can breathe without each other."

"Please insert additional funds."

"I guess."

She knows, as I do, that this isn't a trial. She can't call me. We can't talk every day, and there are no video chats. No instant messages, witty online quips, or loquacious emails. But this is the best I can do for now.

Jill says, "Okay. You have to be—"

Her end of the line goes dead, so I have no idea what I have to be.

Okay. If Jill really thinks I'm in New York, perhaps I can stay hidden for a while. Now, with a new lifeline. During tomorrow's kick out, I'm heading straight to the Internet so I can see what everyone else is talking about. That's awesome.

———

The dorm has come alive in my absence. Two guys are poring over a giant map, discussing route options. A three-some clusters together in the opposite corner: a tall, lanky guy in Birkenstocks strumming a guitar and humming occasionally, a guy with dreadlocks reading, and a third staring off into space.

The map boys swat mosquitoes every few seconds.

"Where you from?" Guitar asks.

"Georgia." The lie is no easier the second time around. "You?"

"Berkeley. Name's Bingham." He thrusts an enormous bony hand toward me.

I take it. "Graham Bel."

One of the map guys says, "Alexander Graham Bell! Thanks for the telephone, buddy." He might be drunk.

Hearing *Alexander* is unsettling. "I get that a lot. But I'm just Graham."

Everyone else chimes in. Brad. Paul. Oscar. Reed. Oscar and Reed are the map gawkers.

Bingham, the trio's ringleader, strums his guitar. "Hey, uh—"

"Graham?"

"Graham, right. What's your plan for tomorrow?"

Staying alive. "Not sure. I just came in from New York yesterday. I thought I'd poke around some tomorrow."

"We're headed to the beach in the morning. Try to find some locals. Want to come with?"

"I'll think about it." And just as it did when that phrase came out of Mom's mouth, it means no. Mia said I can stay here until eleven, so I'm staying here. Until eleven. No way am I spending a single second out there when I could be hidden in here.

"So what did you think of New York?" Bingham's interest is genuine.

"I loved it."

"Visit any museums?"

I will sound like an idiot if I confess I was there for less than three hours. So I lie. "The Metropolitan Museum of Art." I furiously pick around my brain, hunting for any other museum Gretchen has mentioned. All I come up with is Glockenspiel, and I know that's not it.

"Ah, the Met. We spent a whole day there and I still barely scratched the surface."

"Yeah."

"My family spent Christmas in New York last year— that's when we hit the Met—and I wound up going back to the Natural History Museum because it was so fascinating. Put me in front of a dinosaur, and I'm like six years old again."

"Yeah."

"That's kind of what we're doing this summer: searching for the fascinating bits of the country. It's a totally organic experience, you know? We're going wherever we want and just soaking stuff in. Soaking in the mountains, soaking in museums, soaking in the people we meet."

The only thing I'm soaking in is Bingham. I want a worldly life, and Bingham is actually living one. I want to know everything. "So what are you soaking in here?"

He strums for a minute. "We chartered a boat today, for fishing, but that was our only concrete plan. The experience won't really be organic if we plan the whole thing, you know? So, we'll check out the beach and the school. Maybe find some local people we like enough to hang out with.

"That's the important thing, you know? Find the local people so you're not really a tourist. Most people who live in New York City have never been to the Statue of Liberty, you know? But they can take you to a really chill bar. And the greatest used clothing joints. And a cup of coffee that's not burnt and doesn't cost eight bucks a cup. Real people sharing real lives."

Bingham is a real hippy, but I like him. What a brilliant way to travel! I want to do *that*. Jill would totally be down with meeting new people and living like a local.

Bingham plays the same melody a few dozen times, altering one particular note up and down with each iteration. He is creating new music right in front of me.

When he's happy with the riff, he says, "What's your story?"

I don't want to lie, but I don't want to tell my life story, either. Instead, I go with an infinitely relevant truth: "This is my first time traveling."

He stops strumming to study me. "Why's that?"

"It wasn't a priority, I guess." Complete lie—it has always been my dream. "Plus my family never really had the money." And there's the truth.

"You're doing it now," Bingham says. "That's what's important. And Paul can teach you how to do it on the cheap. He is a genius of frugality."

Bingham's fingers return to the strings. He's so good that he's exercising his fingers relentlessly while he fills my head with ideas about traveling on the cheap. I think I'm doing a pretty good job so far, but this is my first time, so what do I know? My bus ticket was cheap. Hostel is cheap, and includes breakfast. I'm sort of proud to be in my first sort-of-hotel.

For two days, at least.

This is cool. I can do this. The privacy of my dorm, Mia guarding the entrance, and Gary absolutely clueless to my whereabouts.

I hope he's clueless. And hundreds of miles away.

I can do this.

Bingham focuses on his guitar and I whip out "Save Ur Ash." I'm nowhere near winning, but I can't stop playing. The game isn't even that good! The edge of the radioactive zone is just out of reach. Two hours ago, I was within eleven miles of safety when my car ran out of fuel and the ash rained down. Maybe next time I'll make it.

One more try. One more mile. Once more, once more, once more.

Oscar-or-Reed stands up. "Mia will kill the lights in half an hour. I'm going out for a smoke. Anyone else?"

Brad follows Oscar-or-Reed out of the dorm while Reed-or-Oscar lies down on his cot with a coverless book. Either speed reading or seeking a really important passage, he flips a page every twenty seconds or so, and the constant flip, flip, flip is distracting. I can't get back into my game.

It's Saturday night, so Tucker is probably treating all our friends to homemade root beer floats. Or actual beer, hold the ice cream. If Jill is off house arrest, she's with him. Or with her girlfriends at the movies. Without me.

What's Gretchen doing, without me, at this very moment?

We sort of have a relationship, right? If you count the time between our first (horrible! I am such a moron!) kiss and the attempted kisses in Jill's kitchen, we dated for seventeen days ... which by her rules means she is already over the 10-percent mourning period. Ten percent is just 1.7 days less, if you count the actual hours between the first kiss and my lame I-can't-do-this exit.

Her warm mouth could be on someone else's this very instant. Someone else could be trying to decide exactly how her mouth tastes, a combination of pizza and beer and sweet Gretchen. Some other guy could be discovering those dimples above her perfect butt.

Is it sacrilegious to think about a girl's butt when my mother is very recently in the ground?

I reach into the front pouch of my backpack for the blue plastic lip balm. Smearing it on my lips, I wonder whether Gretchen is doing the same.

Maybe she's sharing a new tube with someone else.

What have I done? If I make it home alive, running away will be worth losing Gretchen. But if I can never go home again, I will have lost twice.

What have I done?

I should be grateful to be alive, with or without Gretchen. I should be grateful right now, but I guess abject fear is stronger than gratefulness. Paper covers rock.

So, what is scissors? What is greater than fear?

Pure exhaustion. Pure exhaustion is greater than fear, and finally I find dreamless sleep.

Twenty-one

An accented voice wakes me. "Halloo Halloo! Eleven o'clock!"

The dorm is empty, and I'm late.

"Sorry, so sorry!" I rip off my sheets and pick up my bags, stuffing papers and Jill's iPod into my backpack. Without a shower or the gratis waffles I was promised, I check my duffel at the desk.

The girl at the desk—not Mia—shames me for missing breakfast. I resist the urge to mention that a nice girl would have woken me for waffles. A bone fide hotel would have let me hole up all day. But then, that's someone else's road trip.

I check my bag with not-Mia, who is far too chipper for my taste.

"Have a great day, Mr. Bel."

"Yeah."

I head down the staircase. Almost out into the world, I spot the bright blue Mustang directly across the street.

I can't breathe, in or out. My body is suspended in space and time.

When the suspension ends, I suck in a thin line of air. I have nowhere to hide. I run back up the stairs, but not-Mia is not at the desk.

I fumble inside my backpack for the knife. Why isn't it in my pocket at all times? Haven't I had this conversation with myself before? I open the blade and position it in my pocket.

At this hour, the front door cannot be opened from the outside. Telling myself I'll just take a peek, I creep back down the stairs. The Mustang is parked and empty, so that's something.

Gary could be anywhere. He could nab me right outside this door. Or wait until I'm halfway down the block.

Ohmygod ohmygod ohmygod. I can't go out there.

I holler up the stairs. "Hello?"

A few seconds later, she looks down the stairs at me. "Yes, Mr. Bel?"

"What's your name again?"

"I'm Kiki."

"Kiki. Right, sorry." I'm panting now. "I can't. I—I can't go out there."

She steps down two stairs. "I'm sorry, Mr. Bel. Those are the rules. I need to clean up here, and you need to be out."

I plaster myself against the wall just inside the glass door. A giant, translucent sticker designed to block out the sun is peeling at all four edges. It offers zero protection. *Shit.*

Kiki glares at me. "If you don't clear off, you will be blackballed for life."

If I do clear off, I may not *have* a life.

"Out!"

Breathing is difficult, and talking is nearly impossible. "Could you—could you just do me one favor? One?" Leaving the knife in my pocket, I pull out my wallet and shove all my cash toward her, even the Gretchen Sixty, the cash from Mom I didn't want to spend on anything but us. This is desperation. "I'll pay you. I will give you everything if you just go out ahead of me. Can you poke your head out first?"

She comes halfway down the stairs, glances at the bulge in my pocket, and decides it is something innocuous, like a phone.

Please don't be afraid of me. Uttering the sentence aloud would have the opposite effect. I can't slow my breathing. I can't calm down. "I know. I know I sound like a nutjob. I know this is strange. It's just that—" *Deep breath.* Crap, what version do I give her? "Kiki, someone has been following me, and his car is right across the street. I promise you, if you poke your head out and see no one waiting, I will leave." And run to Curt's, where I can figure out what to do next.

Kiki's not buying it. "Calm down! Just relax!"

Why do people do that? Screaming "relax" pushes me the other way.

"Humor me?" I offer her the money again.

She's not going to crack, so I resort to begging. "Please. Please . . . please, I beg you."

My desperation makes an impression. Wiping her hands on her pants, Kiki stomps down the last few stairs, throws open the door, and walks out into the sunshine. She spins with outstretched arms, looking up and down the street.

"Nobody here," she says. "Now out."

Maybe he's hiding. Maybe he's waiting at Curt's! "I could help you today, Kiki. Free labor. I'll do anything you need me to do. Light bulbs? I'm tall. I'm strong, too. I can lift things. Anything, Kiki. Kiki, please."

She is infinitely calm. "Mr. Bel, if you do not vacate the premises by the count of five, you will be done with this establishment."

She's so professional! I don't know what to do.

I jump out onto the street and sprint to Curt's. Everyone inside stares as I pin myself to the wall just inside the door, desperately trying to catch my breath.

Smiling casually, I straighten my pants and mosey over to the window, where I can get a good look at the Mustang. Its license plate is green with a jagged white band at the top. Colorado.

I almost lost my housing over a car that's not even Gary's. I can't believe this. What are the odds? I have never *seen* another bright blue Mustang, let alone one parked right outside my tiny hostel in this small city in this tiny state in the northeast.

It's too coincidental. Maybe Gary stole some Colorado plates and is traveling incognito.

Backed next to the window, I part two blinds with my fingers so I can really study the car. The little red tassel Gary had attached to his antenna is missing, and the front grate is completely different.

This is no way to live.

Herds of cool people are roaming the sidewalks, chatting about professors and philosophy and parties, and I can't leave this block. Burlington is gloriously welcoming, and utterly unavailable to me.

On my way to the library after a slow and laborious lunch, I spot some nooks and crannies where I can hide if I need to. A pinewood at the edge of campus would be ideal for sur-reptitious people watching, but it's still not as safe as the library.

Not only can I not check out library books without a library card, I also can't use their Internet. The very nice, kind of goth librarian directs me to an Internet café where I can buy some time online.

If only I could use Burlington's pervasive Wi-Fi! It is literally everywhere, but I promised Jill I wouldn't, so now I need The Byte, a hysterically named Internet café.

It's on the other side of the hostel, so I'll read first, head to The Byte, and back to my hostel by two.

On the back corner of the library's second floor again, I score an overstuffed orange chair before realizing someone has checked out *The History of Science.*

Really? Today?

Instead, I arm myself with a thick tome about New York City and tuck into the giant chair. If Gary arrives, I'll see him coming.

———

Two hours later, The Byte is less Internet than café. Dozens of enticing pastries line a cloudy plastic case next to the counter. I wish I could justify a four-dollar peanut butter brownie.

A half-dozen guys crowd around a coffee table, playing a dice game. Baristas sing theatrically, sometimes into the enormous mirror behind the counter, and deliver coffee to the ancient computers that ring two huge tables far from the door.

Internet access costs twenty bucks for an hour. Twenty bucks! Since my fiscal responsibility is shot, I spring for another root beer, too. I flash my Graham Bel(l) ID and sit at the computer farthest from the huge picture book windows. Passersby parade down the sidewalk. I can see everything. Perfect.

I should have paid more attention when Gary claimed he knew exactly what I was doing online. He said he could find anyone anywhere if they weren't smart. I'm plenty smart, but I don't know exactly what that means online.

So what can he track? If Laurel's weekly newspaper can discern the origin of their Internet traffic, Burlington would be a dead giveaway. Half of Laurel doesn't give a rat's fart about the rag, and no one outside Laurel has reason to visit the site.

Except me, of course.

So. No tiny Laurel-related websites. No sites for any of Gary's known clients. In fact, I should just stick to the big social media sites that would never have hired him. A tiny list of my friends' usernames helps. Jill, Tuck, and Gretchen are first. Grant Blakely posts hilarious anecdotes about his family. I have a half hour before I can check into the hostel, so I jot down a few other people who provide online entertainment.

My barista is overly curious about my Internet activity, and I can't blame him. Wouldn't you expect the guy who shuffles to the back of the café to be looking at porn or something?

He's perky. "Do you need help getting started?"

"No, thank you."

"You know you're not on yet, right?"

I smile broadly. "I'm trying to maximize my time here by knowing exactly where I'm going. If I'm efficient about it, I can stretch my twenty-dollar token for several days."

He accepts this and walks away. A bright yellow backpack shakes in front of me as a girl giggles over The Onion. I can do better than that.

Logging on feels like Christmas. The Christmas in movies, I mean: so much to devour, and so much to see, and so much to celebrate!

Well, not that last one. Gary is nowhere to be found, but my people are here, in this thirteen-inch screen. Jill hasn't posted any photos with numbers in them, so we won't be talking until tomorrow. She has, however, gone into more detail than I needed about last night's dinner at Olive Garden.

Now there's something I can never do again. Mom used to crave Olive Garden, so now the whole restaurant chain is sort of the scene of the crime. No more bottomless baskets of under-baked breadsticks for me.

That's probably a good thing. But still, Jill should know better than to post about freaking Olive Garden. And also, no one needs to see photos of every meal she eats. At a dollar every three minutes online, I need to keep moving.

I devour Jill's happy life in 140-character bites. She babysat her brothers this morning and, apparently, had a fight with her mother last night. She didn't tag me in tonight's Quaker Steak details, and that hurts. Not that I'm posting or reading my personalized queue, but still. I get that she can leave her house now, but a collective mourning over my absence would be nice. Last night everyone gorged on contraband snacks at the movies. Or everyone *else* did. Jill, Tucker, Grant Blakely, Gretchen, and a dozen others.

I close my eyes for a second before opening Gretchen's page. Her profile photo is like a punch in the gut. She's in the middle of a huge belly laugh, her face caked with mud from the spring mudslides, mouth wide open and eyes squeezed shut. I run my index finger down her cheek. Gretchen is here, inside this computer, writing about her normal life. I take note of the books she's reading. She's off to New York again next week—so close, and yet so far from me. Would it be weird if I went back to New York to see her?

More stalker than weird, probably.

Everyone is busy online. Tucker is waxing poetic about love. Grant Blakely is, indeed, organizing pickup soccer multiple times this week. Everyone is obsessing over *Seven Versions,* which Google tells me is a summer replacement/spin-off TV show I have never heard of.

I feel like one of those people who sits alone at lunch.

Toggling between Jill, Tucker, Gretchen, and a few other profiles, I can reasonably piece together the last twenty-four hours. It's all typical summer stuff: Dairy Queen, cruising the mall, movies, and plans for more hanging out.

It's Infinite Summer. In Laurel, at least. Mine is an entirely different sort of infinity.

Damn.

Catching up online doesn't sate my hunger for friendship. Now I'm dying to open my email. Status updates and photos are great, but I need something personal, something to say they haven't forgotten me.

Are they thinking of me? Maybe they're sending lots of emails. I choose to believe my inbox is full, but settle for Reddit instead. Twenty minutes later, after enough cat pictures and trendy new memes to satisfy any junkie, I log off. Mostly, the Internet binge has made me homesick. And all the talk about Quaker Steak has left me hungry.

Time to check in at Curt's before checking back in with Kiki. Sunday is practically over. I'm one day closer to going home. I'll lock into the hostel with my sandwich and coast until lights out.

And Gary has no clue where I am. And I have Jill tomorrow at nine. Perfect.

Perfect except that I'll probably be sleeping in the woods again after, of course. Maybe Jill will have great news and I can head to the Greyhound station instead.

It's way after two when I climb the hostel stairs. Kudos to me for braving the world for an extra half hour. It feels too quiet. The empty dorm means I can blast some U2 and feel a little like my normal self, though.

One of Mom's frilly bookmarks falls out of *On the Road*, and for an instant I am pissed at her for reading my stuff. How petty am I, being pissed at her when she's dead? Why did we fight over books anyway?

Sometimes I was really crummy to her. She always said I would get my comeuppance when I was older, but I don't think she meant a month older. We're supposed to be bickering over stupid shit, still. She's supposed to tell me to eat something other than Reubens and tell me I need a shower. She doesn't get to tell me anything anymore.

I was a crap son. Maybe Gary was right: I am worthless. Maybe I did deserve what I got. Did he mean that? Did he mean I deserve to be orphaned from my mother and isolated from my friends?

If I had gone into the kitchen, Mom would be alive. I would have given my stupid graduation speech, and I still would have never left Ohio. I got exactly what I wanted: road trip, no speech, no curfews. I did this to myself.

This continuous Mom-Gary-fault loop is agonizing, but I can't stop. No matter how fast I run from radioactive ash, or how loudly I blast the iPod, my mind is filled with Mom.

I try to focus on "Save Ur Ash," though. I'm not sure how nuclear holocaust compares to my current situation, but at least the game can be beaten. Unlike Mom's absence, the game has an end. And I'm so close.

––––––

I still haven't won, and the dorm is full.

Tonight Brad, Bingham, Paul, and I are joined by Bridget and AnneMarie. Brad suggests card games that the girls have never heard of.

Bridget dismisses euchre outright. "Too complicated."

Gretchen is two levels of complicated removed from this girl.

Brad runs through a dozen other card games, most of which I don't know, before they settle on schwanz. *Schwanz* is German for "tail."

"You look interested," Brad says.

I hate getting caught staring. "Sorry, I don't know schwanz."

"Want to learn?"

I literally have nothing better to do. "Sure."

Brad launches into a brief explanation of the game, and play begins. Schwanz is awesome, but it makes me ache for Jill. Euchre over lunch. Euchre as we wait for Mr. Tucker to make dinner. Euchre because it's our favorite thing to do. We always needed a fourth, so we were constantly teaching Tuck's Girlfriend of the Day how to play.

Jill would love schwanz, and I can't even call her to share.

I just want to be there. Home. I'm safer here than in Laurel, but I can't stay away indefinitely. If Jill's parents have loosened her leash, she has been gallivanting all over Ohio.

I want to gallivant. I'm riding the new friendship wave with Bingham—hearing his best stories and marveling at our differences. There are worse ways to spend my time, but I miss *my* people. With a bit of luck, I can head home tomorrow.

Twenty-two

Today has been a low-profile carbon copy of yesterday: exit hostel—but without the Mustang freakout and accompanying embarrassment—Curt's, library, The Byte Café.

And now, on the cusp of my homecoming call, I'm ready to be done with this little adventure. I want to go home to Laurel. Mom won't be there anymore, so it's not truly home, but I want to be where she was. I want to do the things we used to do. Normal things.

Or normal for me. I've never been *normal* normal, and it won't be normal to have a father in prison—provided they ever actually find him. A trial won't be *normal*. Life without Mom won't be *normal*.

But there will be something. If Gary is caught, I'll have twenty-four Greyhound hours to figure out that tiny detail of a new normal. As soon as tomorrow, I can hear about everything I've missed—especially Gretchen's cryptic lovelorn posts—and ease back into life.

By the time I dial Jill, I'm grinning like an idiot. Missing two weeks of summer was a small price to pay for freedom from Gary forever. Forever!

"Uh, hi?"

My entire body relaxes at the sound of Jill's voice. "Hi, Jill."

"Xander! How are you?"

"Great, now that I'm talking to you! I have an entire roll of quarters in my hand and all the time in the world. Tell me everything."

"You're not gonna like the news," Jill says, and I know I'm not going home tomorrow. Maybe ever. "Last night, some rinky-dink cop in Columbiana County picked up Gary and let him go."

"What? How?"

"He was on a county road doing eighty-five and the cop called in his plate and didn't wait to hear from command. So they chatted and—get this—your dad had a *Hustler* open in his passenger seat."

"Gross." Who keeps his porn in his car?

"Yeah, so the cop got all chummy with him and they talked about the centerfold and the guy let your dad off with a warning. To hear him tell it—and this is third-hand now, from his sheriff to Dad to Mom last night after they thought I was in bed."

That's my girl.

"The cop—quote—relieved himself in the field—endquote—before he got back to the radio. And I think both of us know what he relieved himself of. By the time he was back in his cruiser, Gary was long gone."

I was so right not to trust the police. "Tell me again where this was."

"County Road 421 in Columbiana."

At least Gary was headed in the wrong direction. "That's near where his mother lives!" I am a better sleuth than all of those cops. We haven't seen Ethel Fife for years, but Mom saved everything. "Her address is in my mom's red Christmas letter book."

"They thought of that. Ethel is long dead."

Damn. My family is tumbling like dominoes.

"Natural causes," Jill says. "Three years ago."

That's embarrassing. I haven't seen Gary's mom for years, but I should at least be able to place her on the right side of death's door.

Okay. Okay, okay. "What's the new plan?"

Jill's sigh takes the wind out of my sails from hundreds of miles away.

"Jill?"

"There is no new plan, Xander. They're looking as hard as they can. My dad comes home for a few hours every night and goes back in to work. He says he's culpable. He was home that day, did you know? He was home napping and Gary was two doors away, and Dad did nothing."

It sounds kind of bad, but nowhere near as bad as my having actually caused the whole thing. Or being three feet away when Gary killed Mom. "Tell him it's not his fault."

She's quiet. "Well, he feels like it is. Last night I leaned on his guilty conscience enough that he let me go out with Tucker. Now that the police have made a huge production about you being gone, Dad feels like we're safe. He *is* sort of getting suspicious about my recent appetite for Pizza Works, though. And he's watching my email. He's worried about you. We all are. Can't you just come home?"

I wish. "I will when it's all over, I promise."

"You're entering paranoid territory, Xander. No one can find you on a trail that is a week cold. I think you maybe need to let the conspiracy theory die."

This from the champion of the conspiracy theory. She's right, though: *Xander Fife* isn't in Burlington, nor is his phone or anything else that would point Gary here.

Okay, but even as we assume Gary isn't after me at this very moment, we also agree that I wouldn't exactly be safe in Laurel, either. This is an endless loop. I might spend the rest of my life kicking around as Graham Bel, just because Gary is only halfheartedly interested in finding me.

We should have laid a trap for him instead.

I'm done talking about this. "Enough, Jill. I'm not coming home until I feel safe."

"Sightseeing, right?"

"Actually, I'm trying to lay low and keep out of sight."

"That doesn't sound like the Xander I know."

"I'm Graham, though, right? This isn't exactly an adventure."

"It's pretty hard to believe that you're not touring the Empire State Building or seeing the Statue of Liberty or playing soccer in the Central Park."

"Central Park, no 'the,' and I promise I have done none of those things. I want to remain unseen. Like a shadow."

"Or a ninja."

"Yes, but less violent."

Jill giggles and I ache for home. "You know, if you tell me where you are in New York, I could arrange an accidental meeting with Gretchen."

I should have stayed in New York. Gretchen is just the slice of home I need right now. And she's exactly what I want. "Jill, for many reasons, that won't work. And don't you dare tell her I'm in New York."

"Oh-kay. So when should we talk? I have a new curfew—ten o'clock every day—so we can't really move it later."

"How about nine in two days—Wednesday?"

"How about afternoon instead?" She's thinking of her mom's working hours.

"Noon on the nose."

"Sure. And remember there are other perils in the big city. Take care of yourself."

"You take care too, Jilly."

I haven't called her Jilly in years. I wish we were nine again, marching through the woods behind my house and making pacts with neighbors and inviting half the class to sleepovers in her basement and freezing Tucker's—Tucker!

"Wait—wait, Jill, wait!" I scream into the phone.

"Yeah?"

"You said your dad just let you go out with Tucker? What's that all about?"

Her gargantuan pause discloses the entire story. Holy. Crap.

"We may be having a date or two, to test the waters."

"Damn, Jill, you *lead* with that. You lead with my two best friends getting it on."

Her laugh is another warm hug from the old normal. "Your priorities never cease to amaze me."

"Wow. Well, keep me posted on that, too. No naked details though, okay?"

"Yeah." She laughs again. "Xander, if we're veering into this territory, I think you should also know that we saw Gretchen at the Mocha House with Evan."

Damn. Closing my eyes I envision Gretchen making out with smartass Evan, captain of the speech team. I guess that ship has sailed, and rightly so. Gretchen can't just pine away for me while I'm stuck up here in mosquito country. It would be nice if she pined a little, though.

"That's okay."

Jill knows it's not okay. "I'm sure it's nothing. I'll ask her about it tomorrow."

"Jill, who knows how long I'll be here? Gretchen deserves to be happy."

"Maybe you should remove that particular phrase from your lexicon."

"Duly noted."

"Night, Xander."

"Good night."

My friends are marching forward while I'm walking in place. I guess I wouldn't have been hanging out with Tucker and Jill this summer anyway. Perhaps they've been waiting years for me to be out of the picture.

I guess it makes sense. They do have tons in common, and they already know how to put up with each others' pain-in-the-assedness. Maybe the tension between them was fueled with desire. Sexual tension. I can't really think about that, but good for them, I guess.

Pushing the idea from my head, I pull my cap over my face, and tug Gretchen's lip balm from my backpack. I want to go back to Tucker's backyard party, when everything was fine and life was good and Gretchen was warm. I want to live there again.

If I'm going to live in Burlington much longer, I need cash. And a job.

Back at The Byte—because, really, I'm not eager to go back to the woods—I stuff my duffel under my chair and dig into the Internet.

It turns out job sites are for professional people who have degrees and work experience and stuff. I buy another hour on the web, but the extra time does me no good.

I am so screwed. I am so without a bed and so without a job. And so screwed.

And sleeping in the woods again.

And screwed.

Twenty-three

Tuesday morning, I have $56.87 in my wallet, which means I've already started digging into my Gretchen Sixty. Desperate times, I guess. Sixty bucks would be enough for two nights at the hostel but is nowhere near enough for one night anywhere else in Burlington.

Just as well, because two nights at the hostel would have left me with no money for food. There must be cheaper food in Burlington, but I don't know where it is, and Curt's is like a second home now.

"Back again?" Curt says. "I gotta recommend something else today. Man cannot live on Reubens alone! How about a meatball sandwich? Rolled the meatballs myself this morning."

"Okay." I hand over my cash, but it's not okay. A Reuben is my thing. It's the (very distant) next best thing to eating at home. And life in Laurel isn't even that good! Jill and Tucker and Gretchen, yes, but my family life was total crap. And school is school wherever. Why am I so eager to go back when it wasn't so great in the first place?

I am deep into pathetic, self-loathing territory when Curt delivers my sandwich. "So what was that all about the other day?"

My mind is as blank as my face.

"You? Peeking through the blinds."

Oh. Right. "Long story."

Leaning in close, Curt whispers, "You playing the spy game with the rising seniors?"

What the hell does that mean? "I thought I saw someone I didn't want to see. Someone I didn't want to see *me*."

A half-grin suggests Curt's been there. "Some girl hunting you down?"

"Something like that."

"Gotta mix it up! If you eat here every day, she'll catch on."

"I was staying at the hostel? Up the street? They sent me here and I love your Reubens."

He hands over my plate. "Sorry about the meatballs."

"No problem." I try a bite to prove that it's no problem, but the meatballs are huge, and already the sauce has permeated all but the very crustiest bits of the bun. It *is* a problem. With sauce all over my fingers, I shrug in a way that I hope conveys *no problem*.

"So, why you in town?" Curt asks.

"I needed a break. My family is sort of out of control."

"Parents?"

"Yeah."

Curt thinks he understands my emotional abyss. "It gets better. You're what? Eighteen? Nineteen?"

I could pass for one of those.

"Tell me about it," Curt says. "My parents were a nightmare when I was in high school. I moved out. They got divorced. Everything got better."

He has an inkling, so I throw him a bone. "Divorce definitely helped."

"Yeah. Helps everyone. My dad is the Curt who owns the deli, so now I work with him almost every day."

The only guy old enough to be his dad is the balding dude who knows everyone. "The grumpy guy?"

"You've seen him? Yeah. So I work with him. Mom moved in with me after the divorce. It's complicated, but honestly? It's a lot easier. It will get easier for you, too. How long can you stay away?"

"Not sure." That's the truth. "I'm going to, uh, Tulane University? In the fall?"

"Never heard of it."

"It's in New Orleans."

Curt's eyes shine at the very idea. "Rockin'. I've been to Mardi Gras twice. Nice way to lose yourself. Complete with lots and lots of girls. You won't even remember whatsherface who was chasing you Sunday."

It takes me a minute to catch his drift. I already forgot I had let him believe a girl was after me.

Curt chuckles. "Here I am thinking this summer is the hottest ever, and it's only June! But you're headed into the hottest, steamiest place on the face of the earth."

"Yep. And I can hardly wait."

We're swapping stories now, or Curt is filling me up with his. Why does everyone go straight to Mardi Gras? There are fifty-one other weeks in a New Orleans year, but everyone wants to talk about the party.

Curt has a lot of experience with the party. "I'm jealous, man. How long you kicking around here?"

"I might be going back home as early as tomorrow. I am really, really missing my friends right now. You know, summer and all that. Tulane doesn't start until August."

"Well, I hope you can endure the family life. Know what really helped me? Moved out of their house at eighteen. When I really, really didn't need them anymore, I felt better about being around them. When Mom moved in with me, it was on my terms, and I know I can take care of her."

Well, there's that.

The old, balding Curt calls my Curt into the kitchen.

"Hey, sorry I scared you off the Reuben if that's your last sandwich from us. If you stick around, come on back, okay?"

"You got it."

Curt hustles back to the kitchen and I feel . . . fine. I have just divulged about as much as I am willing to share, without having to lie or use a lawyer's answer.

On some level, Curt gets it. I can almost breathe again. We have a connection. Maybe Curt could give me a job? I need one off the record. Mom used to call it being paid under the table, but you can't exactly Google for that. If Curt has work that needs to be done and I'm right here . . .

I've never started this kind of conversation. On Curt's next trip through the dining room, I flag him down. "So, Curt, it seems like you and your dad are crazy busy back there."

"Luck of the draw, I guess. Everyone wanted the same two weeks off. No big deal. Things'll slow down soon."

"Do you need help now?"

"Nah, I'm fine."

Wrong answer. I try another tack. "I meant to ask whether you need employees? If I stick around Burlington a bit longer, I could use a job."

He studies the ceiling so long that I glance up to be sure nothing's written up there. "You'd have to ask my dad about that. He's in a mood today. Let me talk to him. We can always use a hand for a few things, particularly with a couple of our guys on vacation. Come back after the dinner rush?"

"Awesome. That would be awesome. I will do anything you need. Wash dishes, clear tables, chop meat, whatever."

"Slow down, man. Let me talk to him and I'll let you know."

I actually shake his hand like I'm a businessman or something. He doesn't mind.

I'm full of courage today. "Curt? One more thing."

"Yeah?"

"Do you have any idea where I can stay on the cheap? The hostel girls—the hostile girls! Ha!—they threw me out on my ear."

"Not these days. Month ago, you could have found a thousand kids around here'd let you sleep on their dorm floors for a little beer money. Not now. Place is a friggin' resort. B&Bs are full and tourists have taken over."

"Yeah."

He eyes me again, in an almost fatherly way. "I can ask around if you want."

"Yes! Thanks."

He pulls out his notepad. "Man, I didn't know things were that dire. Tell you what, I'll talk to some friends and see whether anyone has a room or something, okay? I'll call you if anything turns up."

My admission that I don't have a phone ushers in a lot of confusion; Curt has seen me with Jill's iPod, which looks a lot like a phone. Also, he's dubious about anyone who doesn't have a phone.

We compromise: I'll check in with him tonight, about the job *and* the bed.

"Thanks. Thanks, Curt."

He nods and starts bussing tables.

On my way to the library, I'm floating, even under the weight of my duffel. Curt is like a guardian angel or something: cheap room to rent and a job off the books? Things are turning around.

And maybe Jill is right. Maybe I can just walk around like a normal person. That would change things. I could be cautious without being paranoid.

I take off the stupid Mariners hat and raise my head in full sun. Who's hiding?

———

Hours later, after eking out every last second at the library, I'm making my way very slowly to the deli, trying to compose myself for meeting Curt's dad. I have seen Big Curt a lot, but I've never talked to him. I hope he can see in me whatever it is he likes in employees.

I desperately need that job.

And I hope Curt has found a bed. I hope I'm not being a nag. I mean, he offered. I hate asking for things. I hate being the guy who needs things—a bed, a job. But even if there's only a 5-percent chance he's found something, I can be that needy guy.

I'm all tied up in knots over this.

And it's all in vain, because Curt's is closed.

A sign on the door reads CLOSED FOR A FEW DUE TO EMERGENCY.

Really? Really. Would he have closed the deli early to avoid talking to me? Maybe he thinks I'm a pariah. Closed for a few could mean I should wait to see whether they open again tonight. Should I? The convenience store down the street has lots of options. I buy the biggest jar of crunchy peanut butter and a loaf of the cheapest bread and shove both into my backpack.

I head back to Curt's to see whether the "few" is over, but it's still closed.

Shit. Now what? Without new income, my quickly diminishing wad of cash needs to stretch as far as possible.

At least I'm not hiding anymore. There's that. Life is half normal again. Except that Mom is still dead. And I am still away. And my friends are just carrying on like nothing has changed.

Everything has changed. I'm living in the woods.

Settled into a new campsite, I realize that a smart person would have picked up a plastic butter knife from the convenience store. My stolen fish knife will do in a pinch, I guess. *Sorry, Dale.*

A peanut butter sandwich is a fine idea—protein, and all that—but washing it down with saliva is just stupid. I can't shake the feeling that a little bit of sandwich is stuck in my throat. As I sleep, that little bit of sandwich becomes Gary trying to strangle me, and Oreos stifling my breathing, and Mom's casket dancing in my windpipe.

Twenty-four

I still hate mornings. I drag my ass to Curt's, which is still closed.

Whatever. My convenience store carries tall bottles of water, and I practically down one in a single gulp. Totally worth the money, since I can keep refilling it in the library sink as long as my camping life lasts.

Convenience store bacon, egg, and cheese bagels cost three bucks, so this is my new lunch place. I'm starting over. Again.

The bagel puts me below the Greyhound Threshold; I can't even afford a bus home. What the hell am I doing?

I'm not hiding anymore, but I am carrying a load of crap, and I'm starting to stink. Not a good recipe for going full-on tourist. Between the convenience store and the library, I spy exactly one HELP WANTED sign—at a boutique where my help is absolutely not wanted.

Ten minutes before the library closes, I slip into the bathroom. A tube sock makes a surprisingly good washcloth, though library soap smells like Froot Loops.

Someone comes into the bathroom as I'm scrubbing my left pit with my sock. Clamping my arm down to hold the washcloth, I do a pretty decent impression of checking out my zits in the mirror. I have lots of zits now.

"Can I help you?" He's wearing a Free Library name tag.

The tube sock soaks my shirt and dribbles onto my shorts. "I'm fine, thanks!"

"We're closing. I need to escort you out."

"Of the bathroom?"

His smile is a sneer, for sure. "We escort out anyone we think might *accidentally* get locked in overnight."

Who does he think I am? I'm a guy who smells like Froot Loops. Still, Froot Loops are better than BO. I follow the guy out of the john and straight out the front door.

My convenience store marks down food when it's a little stale, so for a buck fifty I get to choke down a ham and cheese sandwich. For a buck fifty, I can handle slimy ham and sweaty lettuce. And I'll be Frooty fresh for my call with Jill.

———

That sandwich is a rock in my stomach as heat rises in my chest again. It's ridiculous to hold out hope for something impossible, but I hold out a little anyway.

Jill has no news. There may never be news. Well, no news on Gary. Next Tuesday, Jill is hosting a huge birthday party at a tapas restaurant in the Flats, where I've never been and have always wanted to go, but that is neither here nor there.

Jill prattles about food and music and dancing and I don't care about any of this. Honestly, if there isn't news about Gary, she could spare me the details about all my friends having an awesome time while I'm stuck in alleged-New York.

Jill recaps her recent dates with Tucker, sparing me most of the details. "But apparently Tucker's toilet didn't actually flush the condom down all the way and now his dad wants to know why he was having sex with someone in his basement when he's supposed to be dating me. I swear, the man thinks two plus two equals five."

Two plus two *does* equal five, for large values of two. Gretchen could tell her that.

"And, for future reference," she said, "don't try to hide a condom from your parents by flushing it."

Ouch. "Obviously, that won't be a problem for me."

Her voice is tiny. "Oh my god, I'm sorry."

"Whatever. You know, Jill, what I really want is news. Could you tell people to send me some newsy emails?"

"No way. We agreed that email wasn't safe."

"Look, I really don't think he can track me if I just log on to check."

"He probably can't, but I wouldn't chance it."

Of course she wouldn't. She's too busy having parties and enjoying Infinite Summer.

"I think Gary has gone into hiding."

"Well, then, if he's in hiding, he's not going to come out of hiding to go on a wild goose chase looking for me."

Actually, if Jill is right, and Gary *has* gone into hiding, *I* should be going to her party. I should be trying to talk Gretchen into another date. Or a first date. Not getting pushed around by fake cops and sleeping in the woods and eating stale sandwiches and being desperate for a not-job job.

Jill says, "So?"

"So, you can't have it both ways. Either he's looking for me, in which case I need to be scared shitless, or he's not looking for me, in which case, I should be able to come back to Laurel without being put back in Dale Jail."

"That's not my decision. It's Dad's."

"Well, then, what do you want? Me in Dale Jail with you, or you without me, enjoying your summer?"

She's silent.

"I should go," I say.

"But we've hardly talked!"

"I just need to get going is all. Jill, I hope you have a really happy birthday."

"Uh, thanks?"

"Bye."

Hanging up without the typical I-miss-you and lament means Jill's moving on. I feel lamer than lame. And really pissed. If there is any silver lining here, it's that I know where I'm sleeping tonight.

And now I have the perfect excuse to beg off the freaking Adirondacks trip. I've had enough camping, thankyouverymuch.

I head back to the woods. They're my woods now, really. Halfway there, I realize Jill and I didn't set a time for our next call. Whatever. At least I don't feel like a common criminal anymore. No more hat over my face, just me in the air.

Huddled down in my nest—which is probably nowhere near last night's nest, but who can tell in the dark?—I stuff my darkest clothes under me. It's a reasonable facsimile of a pillow, but I can't convince myself this is a reasonable facsimile of a life.

TWENTY-FIVE

Day ten in Burlington, my new routine is on repeat: peanut butter on bread for breakfast, no Internet summons from Jill, quick check at the deli (closed for the fifth day), find a quick gross lunch, check bulletin boards for jobs and cheap places to stay (none), hole up at the library until closing, and back to the forest at dusk for peanut butter on dry bread. Peanut butter gets really old after a while.

Even though I'm out of hiding, I still look out of place, wearing the same four outfits and hauling around my duffel of crap.

I can't go on like this. Not least of which because I can't keep walking around town unshaven and stinking.

I've resorted to bird baths in the library stalls so I don't get caught bathing in public again. Today, someone has left a plastic cup on the floor, so I also can fix the unshaven thing. I splash some water on my face and take the cup—filled with warm water—into a stall.

I can't recommend shaving without a mirror. Now my stuff is still dank, I kind of reek, and my face is all carved up. I am the homeless guy, and I smell way worse than Froot Loops, no matter how hard I scrub.

I need something.

I've been thinking: it's probably safe to check my email. If I don't send anything, checking can't really hurt, right? If I *send* mail, there will be some kind of electronic stamp or something. But if I check, nothing bad can happen, I think.

Sitting in front of my computer at The Byte, behind the yellow backpack girl again, I am ready. I have eleven minutes left on my voucher, so I have to get online and hop right off.

I'm reasonably certain this will be okay.

A few genuine emails lay among hundreds of crap messages. Dozens from people I have never met, but they're real messages. People wish me well and want to help me and blah, blah, blah.

Several emails from Gary.

Deep breaths.

I thought I was past the whole Gary thing.

He's not in Burlington. I am safe. *Not here. Safe.* The mantra helps regulate my breathing.

These are definitely from Gary, though each one is from a different email address. It's like a trail of bread crumbs. He knows for sure that I'm gone, because the first subject is *You Didn't Need To Run Away*.

He sent it two days after my departure. Creepy. A few days later, the subject is *I Know You're Not Staying With Friends*. Okay, so he definitely checked that. Some subjects are questions, like *Do You Need Anything?* What, like I'm going to email him a shopping list or ask for cash?

Stay Safe.

That sounds like a threat. Maybe it includes suggestions for how to remain safe on the lam. I'm not opening it. It could just as likely include threats to my safety.

The subject from the last one, dated yesterday, reads *We Really Need to Talk*.

What could he possibly want to say to me? I know he killed Mom. He knows I know he killed her. End of story. His words can't change anything about anything. Screw him.

I don't know what I expected from email—some sort of relief, or lottery winnings, or something good. More than that, I want something that makes me feel normal. Something obnoxious from Tucker. He knows I'm underground, but he could at least drop a line. Jill could send me something hilarious. Grant Blakely should be sending me notices about midnight soccer.

I want something sweet from Gretchen.

She did send me three messages, none of them sweet. The first two basically say she's worried about me. That's sweet, sort of. The third message, from three days ago, is bad: *Dear Xander, Even though Jill won't tell me anything, I know you've been talking to her. I know you two are totally platonic, but I also know we were way more than platonic, so I want to remind you that I'm here, too. I can be a good platonic friend to you, too. Please tell me how I can help. I hope you are well, my friend. And I hope you're home safe soon. <3 Gretchen.*

That little heart is good. She said we were more than platonic friends, thank god, but the past tense sours the whole message. We were more than platonic, but what are we now? I want to be more than platonic friends. I want both from her. I want everything from her, but replying is one step beyond safety.

It seems like Gary isn't trailing me physically. But electronically? I don't know. Maybe he's waiting for me to send an email to someone and then he'll pounce.

Replying is too risky. And calling her phone is way out of the question.

I have other messages to read. One from Bingham in Pittsburgh, where he found some other people who play euchre. I wish I could send him to Jill's house, or point him toward Quaker Steak, but that will have to wait for next time.

Every one of my relationships is on hold, indefinitely.

And those messages from Gary. What the hell could he want to talk about? Why would I want to talk to him ever again? Deleting all his messages, unread, empowers me. Screw him.

In fact, screw this whole thing. In the café bathroom, I dump my duffel and start soaking my clothes in the sink. Ignoring customers who knock on the door, I methodically wash my socks and shirts and underwear. With almond-and-honey soap, which is a nice change.

Just as I'm finishing up, someone knocks loudly and shouts, "Manager!"

The door swings open and I waltz out of the bathroom, my arms full of wet laundry. "Have a great day!"

On campus, a group of people have just finished playing soccer. I hang my clothes over a bench in full sun and lie next to them in the grass. Maybe I can join them for pick-up tomorrow.

———

Once my clothes are dry and packed, I swing by the deli. Finally—finally!—it's open again. I am jonesing for one of Curt's Reubens, even if I have to spend my last seven bucks to get it.

It's been six days since he blew me off and closed the shop, but now that I have Cosley Woods, I don't need anything but a sandwich from him.

But boy, do I need one.

I order from some other guy behind the counter.

"Oh, man." Curt rushes out to greet me. "Graham, man! Did you find somewhere to stay?"

Like he's concerned.

"I did. I'm fine."

"I'm so glad, man. My grandpa died. Like ten seconds after you walked out of here, my grandma called, and we all packed up and got on a plane to Montana."

I am such an asshole. "I'm so sorry."

Curt asks the guys in the back to hold down the fort and sits down with a giant mug of coffee. Between sips, he spews the whole story about his family and the funeral and the resulting drama. His grandfather's secretary showed up and cried all over his grandfather's body.

"All my grandma can say is, 'What a cliché.' Can you believe that? 'What a cliché,' like it's no big deal her husband of sixty years has been snaking it to somebody else."

"I'm so sorry. You must have been embarrassed."

"Me? No! I'm not my grandfather's boneheaded decisions. Feel bad for my grandma, though. She was embarrassed. Frankly, she's always been a bit of a witch. Abrasive, you know. So I'm not surprised. I mean, good on him for getting some action in his eighties. Most men are dead by then."

Curt is awfully glib for someone who just tossed some deep family secrets to a guy he's known all of five seconds.

"So, where are you sleeping, Graham?"

"I found somewhere here in Burlington." Truth—100 percent truth.

Curt mulls that for a minute. He's sharp. "But that night I left, where did you sleep? You seemed pretty hard up."

"I slept outside." One thing about the actual truth: I don't even have to try it on for size.

"No way."

I'm almost proud of myself. "Yeah. Cosley Woods?"

His laugh is huge, boisterous. "No way. Where'd you get a tent?"

"No tent. No sleeping bag. Just me and my duffel."

He laughs again. "Good on you."

He's right: good on me. I'm still waiting out Gary—and that's a little piece of family history Curt doesn't need to know—but I've made my way five hundred miles from home (or seven hundred if you count actual miles traveled), and now am enduring what I hope is a brief stint as a homeless guy.

Good on me.

Curt doesn't ask where I'm sleeping tonight, and I don't tell him.

"Well, Graham, wish I could have found you and given you my couch for a couple nights."

"Thanks. I appreciate that."

He says, "Coulda used your help with my ma and her caregiver while I was in Montana, too."

"Oh. What did she do while you were gone?"

"I played to the sympathies of my ex-fiancée. My ma needs a lot of help, and we have a caregiver, but it's never quite enough. My ex was happy to help."

I've been thinking of Curt as just a little older than me, but having an ex-fiancée relegates him straight to adulthood. Double adult, even.

I don't want him to see me as a kid. "I'm glad for your ex-fiancée. I mean, not that she's your ex. Unless you like that she's your ex, then that's fine. I mean, sorry."

Man, am I an ass!

Curt tips his mug to drain it. "No worries. We're friends. She didn't realize until after we were engaged that she was a lesbian. So, it wasn't really her fault."

Curt drops these bombs like they're no big deal. Dead grandfather, BOOM. Grandfather's mistress, BOOM. Bitchy Grandma, BOOM! Lesbian ex-fiancée, BOOM, BOOM!

Here I've been burying all my secrets, and Curt just lays them out for the world to see, like there's nothing to be embarrassed about.

Regarding his ex-fiancée, he says, "She even set up a blog to post stories about what they did while I was gone. It automatically pulled photos and locations from her phone, too, so I knew exactly what they did every day."

Someone who set up such a fancy blog probably knows about other stuff, like Internet tracking. It's worth a shot. "Do you think I could meet your ex-fiancée?"

"Why would you want to do that?"

It's almost a relief to tell him. Curt gets an (admittedly abridged) version of my story. I skip the whole abuse section and don't mention Mom's murder, and after I admit that my estranged father may be tracking me online, Curt is intrigued.

"That's like secret spy stuff."

"I know! I'm also still looking for a more permanent place to stay, if you know anyone."

"I'll keep an ear out," he says, in a way that means he wasn't ready to change the subject. "My ex isn't that kind of computer person—she's just a blogger—but I know there's no way to track where email is checked. If he's hacked into your email, he would know that you're reading your email, but there's no way to know from where. And there's probably a way you could send email, too. Probably."

Curt studies the ceiling for a minute while I have a little mental party: I probably can send mail!

Dear Gretchen: I hope we still are more than platonic.

No. *Dear Gretchen: I miss you a lot.*

No. *Dear Gretchen: I think of our mini-forest all the time and can't wait to wrap my arms around you again.*

Curt, who isn't privy to this very important email draft, interrupts my train of thought. "How sophisticated is he? Could he hack into your friends' emails? Because if he can get into their email boxes, he could get your IP address here."

Well, that sucks. Gary definitely knows Jill. And if he has hacked into her email, he could know about almost anyone else. If I were Gary, and Jill and Gretchen were emailing about me, I would hack into Gretchen's email next.

So, yeah. No reply for Gretchen.

Curt cuts into my thoughts. "Hey, my dad said you can at least fill in for a week or two."

The boulder weighing me down shrinks slightly. "Thanks, man. That's awesome."

Curt shakes his head. "Don't thank me until you've heard the details: sinks and toilets. Toilets are always the job of the newest person, so that would be you. Sinks are all the dirty dishes. Grace, that woman who licks the ketchup off her plate every day? Somebody has to clear and wash it."

Gross. Money, but gross. "I'm on it. I can handle it."

"Pays minimum wage, in cash. Anyone asks, you say you're just helping the family out while you're in town. Free. You can't tell anyone we paid you anything, or we all get in trouble."

Who would I tell? "Got it."

"I'll put you to work after your sandwich, if you want." He returns my cash. "Meals are on the house when you're working."

Curt clearly doesn't understand what a huge deal this is; his offer has reversed my cash flow.

Only after I scrub my very first toilet do I realize that I got the shit end of this deal, literally. It's not just about toilets, because people pee everywhere. There is shit on one of the seats. Pee on the walls, on the floor, in the sinks—really, people?

I mean, washing laundry is one thing, but pissing in a sink is just wrong.

Curt gives me a quick overview of the dishwasher and back of the kitchen. I'll be handling the dirty part of the assembly line, since you can't very well handle the clean end after you've handled the toilets.

At closing, Big Curt inspects the toilet, consults his son, and hands me thirty bucks from the register. That's easily ten lunches from the convenience store, but still not a hotel room.

While Curt's locking up, he says, "See you in the morning for more of the same. Ten o'clock."

I desperately want a bed, but I'm too grateful for the money to ask for one more favor.

I just can't sleep outside again. With an actual job now, earning actual money, I'm not really so hard up anymore. And I need a shower. I can suck it up and go to the shelter for a shower.

————

In this situation, Mom would say she put on her big girl panties, but there's no appropriate analogy for guys. Manning up or growing a set would work, except sleeping at a shelter feels more like a cowardly move.

The walk from Curt's is short, but I am a whole different person when I reach the shelter. Small. Sad. Defeated. This whole thing is surreal.

All the surreal moments of my life are cringeworthy. Like that night in sleeping bags on my parents' floor. Or banging on Mom's chest in our kitchen. Pulling away from Gretchen's kisses at Jill's house.

The first time Gretchen kissed also me was surreal, but totally pleasurable.

Walking into the shelter is not.

The upbeat staff can probably tell it's my first time. Mom and I never wound up at one of those battered women's shelters, even though we definitely belonged. Unfortunately—or brilliantly, depending on how you look at it—Gary volunteered as one of the good Samaritans who showed up with his car and his muscles when a woman needed to leave her home. The shelter called him a protector.

There's no irony at the Burlington shelter. I actually, legally, belong here. Seven people form a line toward the processing table, where two men are asking questions and passing out forms. Encouraging posters and twelve-step pamphlets paper the walls between naked light bulbs.

The guy in front of me is wearing a freaking suit, for god's sake. His pants are shorter than they should be, but he's clean shaven in a suit. Two people have cool spinner suitcases and are far, far better groomed than I am.

These are decent people. Why are they here? No one remotely resembles the stinking woman in New York City. No one except me, of course.

After a scuffle about my not being a Vermont resident and my repeated assurance that I have nowhere else to go, the guy behind the table asks where I've been sleeping. It's not a trick question.

Shudder. I may have had company in those woods. A normal person would opt to stay in a homeless shelter instead of staying outside where a number of unsavory things could happen. I'm not normal. And not the new normal, either.

Using my Graham Bel ID is convenient. Intake paperwork includes lots of embarrassing questions I can evade because I'm Graham. For example, *Are you the victim of abuse?*

Nope. Graham's life is peachy. Georgia peachy.

In the end, Graham Bel is my undoing. They don't have any beds. Burlington's only available beds are for under-18s:

runaways and youth-in-crisis. And at this point, I can't very well whip out seventeen-year-old Alexander Fife's ID.

Why didn't I know about that before I became Graham Bel? I could have been staying here since landing in Burlington. Nice.

I can't win. My real self would have been fine in this situation. As Graham, I'm screwed. What the hell?

Can't they tell that I need a bed and shower more than Mr. Suit and The Suitcases? An adult with a suit or suitcase obviously has resources, whereas I have nothing.

I need to catch a break.

I mean, another one.

An hour later, deep in the forest, I wish on a star for the first time in years: *please, no rain tonight*.

Twenty-six

For the first time in maybe forever, my wish comes true: the rain holds off until morning. I am so famished that one peanut butter sandwich doesn't do it. I tear another slice of bread in half and slather on the peanut butter. I'll need a new jar tomorrow or the next day.

If I ever get out of here, I'm never eating peanut butter again.

Plenty of real food is just two hours away at work. I strap on my backpack. I've made it through another night undiscovered.

Twigs break in a walking rhythm, and they're getting louder. I pick up the knife, caked with peanut butter, and hide behind the biggest tree I can find.

I'm not undiscovered at all.

"Hello?" His hello knows I'm within earshot.

I peek from beyond my tree to see a guy in a black uniform. A cop, facing away from me. I scamper to a tree even farther from my campsite.

What kind of trouble am I in? I know there's no camping, but that's what? A misdemeanor?

I need to get out of here. I don't want to leave all my stuff, but I don't exactly have a choice. I can't get involved with the cops.

Knife in hand, I drop to my knees and crawl in the general direction of the path until brush and trees stand between us.

Far enough from the campsite that he can't hear me, I break into a run.

Shit. What about all my clothes? What about that peanut butter?

I do a mental inventory: knife, iPod, IDs, books, Labello, bracelet. The important stuff is on my back. I can come back for the rest later. Jogging toward the trailhead, I fold the knife in my hand.

I emerge from the woods to find a tiny police officer leaning against her cruiser in the parking lot.

She draws her gun. "Lower your weapon."

I do, in the most literal way: I drop it straight onto the ground.

"Stay where you are, with your hands where I can see them."

I raise my hands toward the sky and she pulls out a tiny walkie-talkie.

"I've got him, Walt."

Walt's response is garbled.

I got too comfortable. And there's no sense running from this girl. I'm out of shape, my lousy backpack is weighing me down, and she looks like she's fresh out of the police academy; I don't stand a chance.

She knows it, too. "Why are you running around with a weapon?"

"I thought someone was after me. Protection. Just that, I swear."

"You the guy who's been sneaking around here after hours? Lots of complaints from the neighborhood."

One very important thing I learned from Chief Dale Bernard at a very young age: don't talk too much. I've already talked too much, so I wait for her to ask a genuine question.

"How long have you been sleeping here?"

Do not shrug. "A couple nights."

"You have ID on you?"

"I do."

We stare at each other for a minute before she reaches toward me. No words, just an outstretched hand. She thinks I'm being a smartass, but I'm really, really not. This is a make-or-break moment. Jill's dad once locked up a guy for thumbing his nose.

I can't go to jail. It would be all over the news.

This cop is eager. "ID please?"

Another very important thing I learned from Dale? Never lie to cops.

Ever.

My fingers brush quickly over Gretchen's Labello as I dig in the tiny pocket of my backpack. And here I am, Xander Fife, surfacing in Burlington.

The cop looks at my driver's license and opens the back door of her cruiser, inviting me in. It's more demand than invitation. Climbing inside feels very final.

She studies my knife, pulling out the blade and smelling it before folding it again. She calls someone on her cell phone, but takes the call outside the cruiser. It's practically soundproof in here, and she's facing away from me.

A few minutes later, her partner—Walt?—emerges with my duffel. Is it evidence now?

Why was I so casual this morning? How could I let Jill convince me to let my guard down? Yeah, maybe Gary's not on my tail, but I am breaking laws here.

And now I'm going to jail. Prison! I'm a criminal. And if they put out a news release or something, Gary will know exactly where I am.

I'm being paranoid.

I'm *probably* being paranoid. I'm—

"We have to take you to the station." My cop is off her phone climbing into the cruiser.

It takes us five seconds to get there. God, Burlington is small.

I don't remember anything else Dale taught me about dealing with the police. No one has read me my rights.

"Am I under arrest? I believe if I'm not under arrest I do not have to submit to questioning."

She eyes me in the rearview mirror, hops out of the cruiser, and gets on her phone again. Walt stays in the front seat, rubbing his temples. The cop turns around to look at me twice.

Something is happening. She returns the phone to her holster, glances at the sky, and opens my door.

"Sorry about this." She reaches toward me and, in a hot second, I'm splayed across the cruiser's trunk. She's not rough, but she handcuffs me before god and country and *oh my god, I am so screwed.*

My chin rests on the cruiser's roof while she cuffs me. "Am I under arrest?"

"You got skittish. I think you're a flight risk."

Shit. What can I say to that? "I have no money to fly with."

She's unimpressed.

Walt says, "Amy," and my cop has a name. "What about his bag?"

Officer Amy says, "Bring it in."

Inside the police station, which is easily five times the size of Laurel's, Officer Amy introduces me to her captain, Mack Davies. Irritable and hurried, he sizes me up before returning to his office. In the bare hall outside the captain's office, Amy makes me sit with my hands still cuffed behind me. Through his huge office windows, I watch Davies dig inside his nose and pick up his phone.

It's all very *Glengarry Glen Ross* with the phones and shenanigans and I really just need a break. I desperately need a break. Like right now.

He approaches the door, antique corded phone in hand. "Yeah, one of my guys found him." He slams the door. Silence.

Who is he talking to? *Who the hell is he talking to?*

He bites his cuticles while he's on the phone, so I can't even read his lips. It's probably one of the nosy neighbors near Cosley Woods. He could be calling Laurel. That seems unlikely, but then, so does my being handcuffed and sitting in a narrow hallway on a cheap plastic chair in freaking Burlington, Vermont. All for sleeping in a park.

What if they put me in jail? I don't want a shower *that* badly.

The captain keeps staring at me through his smudged window, and once even stands up to study me. After twenty minutes of toying with his rubbery face, he gets off the phone and calls Officer Amy into his office.

They talk very near each other, with the door closed again, and Officer Amy keeps turning to look at me. They're trying to decide what to do with me, and my get-out-of-jail free card, Dale Bernard, is nowhere near here.

Shit.

Another million years later, Officer Amy emerges from the office. "Follow me."

Standing up while handcuffed is tricky.

All the little warning bells in my head start going off when she takes me to a tiny interrogation room. She closes the door and unlocks my cuffs.

I have to do one big stretch, even though I wasn't restrained for long. It's just what you do.

She eyes me like I'm nuts. "Okay. First off, no more sleeping in the woods. You have a written warning for that. Drawing a weapon on an officer is against the law, but you weren't actually brandishing the knife, so, uh, it's a gray area. We're going to let you off with a warning but we, uh, we have to release you into the custody of an adult. Someone local. Do you know any adults here?"

Well, yes and no. I can think of only one person in all of Burlington who might pick me up. And he won't be ashamed to do it, probably.

"If I can call Curt's Deli, I can get someone to pick me up."

Dropping her shoulders, she grins. "Curt Danley will pick you up?"

"Yeah. The younger Curt?"

"Little Curt? Alrighty. That'll work." She dials and hands the ringing phone to me.

"Hey, is Curt there? The one . . . with hair?"

An eternity later, he says, "Curt."

Officer Amy is right here. I turn my back to her and whisper, "It's Graham."

"Hey, I was wondering where you were. I was expecting you fifteen minutes ago."

"I'm at . . . the police station?"

Behind me, Officer Amy says, "North Avenue. He knows the place."

"On North Avenue? Could you, um, could you come get me? I'll explain everything, I swear. They need to release me into someone's custody and you're sort of the only person I know here."

"Yeah, sure, give me a minute."

I hand the phone back to Amy. "He's coming."

She walks me back to the hallway. "Sit while you wait, Mr. Fife."

I'm not handcuffed or anything. I could walk out of here and avoid the unpleasant conversation I'm about to have with Curt. Davies looks at me through his office window, but he looks old and slow.

I could run and hide.

Then again, that hasn't been working so far.

Curt and his winning smile arrive, so I'm out of options. He shakes hands with Officer Amy before half-hugging her.

"There's a story *here*, isn't there?" he asks.

She shrugs. "How's your dad?"

"Alright. Headed back to Montana next weekend to pack up my grandmother. She's moving in with him."

Amy's guffaw suggests there's a story there, too. She says, "Talk to Mack for a minute," and I'm stuck twiddling my thumbs again while Curt ducks into the captain's office.

Amy brings my bags from around the counter and hands me my blade. Dale's blade.

Curt glances back at me a few times during their chat. He shakes hands with the captain before opening the door.

How bad is it?

"Okay, man, let's go."

He doesn't say anything for a few blocks. "You said you had sorted out your living situation, man."

I never actually said that. I lawyer-answered him. It was kind of a shitty thing to do. "Look, Curt, you were being so generous with the job, and I didn't want to ask for anything else. I was running out of money, and I figured making some money would get me partway to finding somewhere to stay."

He shakes his head and is quiet the rest of the way. Steps from the deli, he says, "Look, you can crash at my place until we figure out something else. Just don't say anything about this to my dad, okay? He has enough going on right now. We don't need him freaking out about you. Just be cool."

"Thank you."

"No worries," Curt says. "Hey, you okay?"

"I don't even know anymore."

To his credit, he doesn't press further. I follow him inside, grab my scrubby brushes, and get to work on the toilets.

Twenty-seven

Slimy, wet kale turns my stomach, and the deli uses a lot of it: kale in salads, kale on the side, kale chips, kale, kale, kale.

Kale Jail. I have to laugh. Worlds away from Dale Jail, I'm still captive. An hour before close, while shaking a plate of soggy kale chips into the trash, the plate slips from my fingers. Thousands of ceramic shards scatter.

For a moment, the only sounds are running water and the fryer's distinct sizzle.

"Oh, God. Oh, God. I'm sorry. I'm so sorry! It just slipped. I'll pay for it. I will work extra hours to make up for it." My heart races while I sweep the pieces into a dustpan. It's over: job, gone. Bed, gone.

The kitchen starts up again and Curt slaps me on the back. "No worries, man. It's just a dish. Why dwell?"

Because it costs money? Because I was careless? Because I am a worthless idiot?

But then, those are my father's answers, not mine.

They aren't the answers of any normal person in the world. People break plates. Stuff happens. Maybe I can stop beating myself up over it . . . so to speak. It'll take some getting used to.

After the customers have gone, I load the last batch of dishes, clean the toilets, and mop the floor.

Curt finally talks to me about something other than cleaning and toilet brushes. "I'm going to put you on my couch."

"Thanks, Curt, really. Thanks. I'll find a place as soon as I can."

He locks up the deli and we start the trek back to his house.

"Right. Look: this is a little complicated. Don't tell my ma you're working at the deli. And don't, under any circumstances, tell Dad you're staying at my house. They know what they need to know, and they would be suspicious if they knew both things."

"Suspicious of what?"

"Just . . . suspicious," he says. "Trust me, they won't be talking to each other. Just keep your mouth shut."

I don't know what they would be suspicious of. And if *they* would be suspicious of something, why isn't Curt? He's acting suspiciously himself, turning around every five seconds like someone might be following us. Maybe he's looking out for the girl he mentioned during the other-Mustang fiasco. Maybe he's more paranoid than I am!

Near the end of a cu-de-sac, Curt's house is just one floor, and eerily quiet.

Inside the back door, he says, "Ma is already asleep. Otherwise, Kat would be at the kitchen table. Kat is her caretaker most days. So, quick tour: living room, kitchen, bathroom, bedrooms."

We don't move during the tour. We don't need to.

"Okay. Take a shower. Wash all your clothes, too. Laundry's in the bathroom. Tomorrow, come out clean and fresh and shaven. The line for my mom is that you're visiting Burlington for a couple of weeks."

"Where will you be in the morning?"

Curt checks his watch. "Here with you. Tomorrow is Wednesday. I'm always off on Wednesdays. You're off with me tomorrow. But tonight I have a date. Watch TV. Surf the web if you want. Whatever."

Curt moves a wad of sheets from a tiny closet into my arms. "Couch is yours until the morning. Try to be quiet. Don't eat all the ice cream. See you in the morning."

And then he's gone.

Two weeks ago, I didn't know Curt. Now I work for him. And use his sheets in his tiny house with all the luxuries of home.

Obedient—and grateful!—I head for the shower. Heavenly. The second water hits my scalp, a whiff of my own stench overwhelms me. No wonder I have to shower before meeting Curt's mom. No wonder I'm assigned to toilets and dirties.

I wash my hair twice to get rid of the stench.

Shaving cream prevents any new cuts. And here, in the mirror, is Xander. I'm still here. Somewhere, some part of me feels normal. For some definition of normal, at least. I look older. Tired. My eyes look a lot like Mom's. Tired. Needful.

Lonely.

I'm almost happy while I shake out the sheets over Curt's squishy green couch. I have made it through a lot of shit. Good on me. I'm done sleeping outside! Good on me!

Curt left without giving me his computer password, but I'm happy to go for a run instead. The first glorious run since Mom died (unless you count my frantic run through Cosley Woods, which I don't).

Two miles from Curt's house, I feel alive again, for the first time in a month. It's quiet enough here that I can run in peace. (Dale's knife rests in the key pocket of my shorts. I'm not totally over the paranoia.) It feels almost a little bit normal, as much as running in Chucks is normal.

I feel so good. Running off the stress of the last several weeks takes a long time. Not marathon long, but well over an hour. Back in the house before midnight, I treat myself to another shower before switching on the TV. More normalcy in Curt's house.

By two, he still hasn't returned and I still can't shut off my brain. I miss home. Tonight I'm missing Jill's birthday party for the first time, ever.

The skate park is full. Movie theaters, too. The colorful town gossip continues, though now I'm part of the fodder. My boss is probably desperate to fill my job. Dairy Queen was probably hit pretty hard, too; most people lack my capacity to devour ice cream year-round.

Maybe Burlington has good ice cream.

Staring at the water-marked ceiling, I wonder where Gary is. Dozens, if not hundreds, of people are hunting for the man who killed my mother with his bare hands. Surely that's on my side.

This is a random house in a random city hundreds of miles from home. There are hundreds of millions of houses in America; no way is he coming to this one.

Does he have any idea where to search?

Has anyone spotted him again?

Is five hundred miles from home far enough away?

I just want to go home. To Jill. To Laurel Woods.

To Gretchen. Her Labello is nearly gone now, so I slide it carefully over my lips. *Good night, Gretchen. I hope to see you again someday.*

Still not tired. I need to be awake in a few hours. What the hell kind of date is Curt on until three in the morning?

Mom would be livid to know I'm still awake at three in the morning. She would never have let me sleep on the couch, either. She was always pretty adamant about bedtime.

Squeezing one of Curt's small pillows, I feel empty. This thing—this person—who has always been in my life, every single day for nearly eighteen years, is gone. Just gone. No transition, no good-bye. Happily prepping tacos one minute, dead on the floor the next.

It's so unnatural. So weird. This isn't how life is supposed to be. I want to believe that she's alive in some alternative universe. Maybe she has shifted to a different plane. Even that doesn't do me much good, since I can't get there from here.

I want her to be here. To tell me I will get through this—through Burlington, through the Gary hunt, through life after her. I need something.

I need my mom.

Twenty-eight

The morning feels like a whole new life, complete with washcloth and soap. Curt's decorative soaps smell like vanilla. Or maraschino cherries, I'm not sure which. Either way, the sweet scent reminds me of Jill's mom's kitchen, which exacerbates my ravenous hunger.

Curt is at the stove. He must live at the stove. "Morning, Graham! How did you sleep?"

"Great, thanks." I slide onto a bench at the kitchen table. A month ago, I might have said I'd slept like the dead, but I'm never using that expression again.

Curt tosses an omelet like a pro. I guess he is one. "Breakfast, Ma!" He makes cooking breakfast look like the greatest thing ever.

There's a low shuffle in the hall before she appears. Curt's mother's pale yellow shirtdress clings to her shoulders and falls over her body without otherwise touching her skin. My mom would have said this woman was swimming in her clothes.

"You needn't shout, love," she says, without so much as a glance in my direction.

"I know, Ma. Next time I'll come to you and speak civilly."

"Where have I heard that before?" She eases herself onto a seat across from me, holding tight to the kitchen table.

Curt slides an omelet in front of her. "Ma, this is Graham."

"Like the cracker?" She doesn't look at me.

"I guess so." It's difficult to ignore her bulbous knuckles and the distinct chill of her smooth skin when she grabs my hand. This is exactly how zombies feel, I just know it.

Her eyes are kind. "I'm Sophie Danley."

Curt says, "Graham will be sleeping on my couch for a few days, maybe a couple weeks."

"Well, Graham-like-the-cracker, I hope you will leave the sitting room tidy. My programs are on every afternoon, and I prefer an uncluttered space."

"Yes ma'am." Sophie seems like the ma'am type.

Sophie softens, suggesting I'm not alone in my discomfort here. "Please don't call me ma'am. We will use our given names."

No, we won't.

Sophie dissects her omelet with difficulty, torturing my empty stomach.

Between bites, Curt says, "Cereal's in the cabinet. I mean, feel free to make an omelet if you want, but cereal's in the cabinet if that's more your speed."

Curt's selection is more like Mom's—healthy tasteless crap—than Jill's yummy cereals. I thought Curt was cooler than that. Still, Special K is better than stale convenience-store bread.

Curt talks with his mouth full. "So, Ma, Graham is a Tulane student, in New Orleans. Every time I think of NOLA, I think of that day you, dad, and I tooled around the French Quarter hunting for the perfect muffuletta."

That must be like hunting heffalumps.

"Curt and Curt can really eat," Sophie says. Curt gets his smile from her.

"Central Grocery's the answer, Graham," Curt says. "Or it was during that trip. Haven't tried any other ones since, because why bother?"

"Sorry," I say. "What's a heffalotta?"

"Muffuletta. Kind of the city's signature sandwich. You, Mr. Reuben-with-extra-dressing, would love it."

Sophie cocks her head. "How can you not have had a muffuletta?"

"I'm just a freshman in August. I've never even been there yet."

"Well you are in for a treat." Sophie loads up a very calculated forkful of omelet. "So, New Orleans for college. What are you doing in Burlington?"

Let the games begin.

"I just felt like I needed a break. I've been in school or working for what seems like forever, you know? And my family's a little crazy," to say the least. To say the absolute least.

Sophie smiles. "Everyone says that about their families. My boys would tell you that our house was utter mayhem. I never had enough time to encourage them or focus on them individually or tell them how proud I was of the men they were becoming."

Curt interrupts. "No, Ma. You were always clear. I knew you were proud of me."

"And I am, Curtis." She turns to me. "Graham, even if your family is crazy, you are an important part of it. Does your mother tell you that? She must tell you she's proud of you for something, right?"

Not anymore, she doesn't. But maybe she mentioned it a few times, before she was mercilessly killed at my father's hands. While I cowered outside.

Sophie's family's craziness can't compete with mine. I don't have a civil answer for her. "My mother has told me she is proud of me, yes."

Her smile is wan. "So you wanted to get away from everything. Where is everything? Where are you from, originally?"

"Georgia." It's a practiced lie now. With a hasty fist pump, I add, "Go Falcons!"

Still a rotten liar.

Sophie opens her mouth to a small *o* shape. "How did you wind up here from Georgia? That's quite a journey for someone who just needed a break!" She looks toward Curt, incredulous.

Curt touches his mother's hand. "Okay, Ma, enough with the interrogation. It's Wednesday. How are you feeling?"

"Great. Do whatever you need to do. I'm fine here."

"You sure?"

"I'm sure."

"Alright. Love you, Ma." Curt shuffles the dishes into the dishwasher and turns to me. "Lots to do today. You ready, Graham?"

Guess we don't get a day off. "Just a sec." I rip the sheets off the couch and pile all my stuff in one corner of the living room.

In the car, Curt explains that Kat, the woman who takes care of his mother, has Wednesdays off. "So I take care of Ma on Wednesdays. When I asked how she was feeling, the best answer would have been that she was feeling great and wanted to come with us on errands. Worst answer: she needed me to stay with her today. I'll take the middle ground, frankly. Everything's faster without her."

He hands me a list and reverses out of the driveway. We'll be playing house today: picking up stuff from the cleaners, doing the grocery shopping, fetching a resoled pair of shoes, and retrieving Sophie's holds from the library, where they know me as a homeless guy.

The library! "Hey Curt? Do you think I can check out a few books on your card?"

"You are so weird, man. Gave you a job and a place to sleep, and the most excited I have ever seen you is over library books."

"They're like family to me." I look out the window at new parts of Burlington.

"Can't say no to that," he says, and life gets a tiny bit better.

———

Curt leaves me to his computer all afternoon. Jill has posted a photo of herself with a crown labeled FIVE! Thank goodness. I get through every single post on Jill's and Gretchen's pages, through all the social media, and catch up with all the trivial news.

An hour at the kitchen table with *All Fifty* feels like the best parts of home. The book is so good.

Books are like family, I meant that. But nothing compares to my friends, and I can hardly wait to talk to Jill in half an hour. Her page was full of cryptic stuff about drinking today. It must have been one hell of a birthday party.

Across the breakfast table, Sophie thumbs through a magazine. I think she just goes back and forth between here and my bed. Er, couch.

If I don't hurry, I'll be late to the phone again.

I yell in no particular direction, "Back in an hour, Curt."

"Graham!" Sophie eyes me sternly from the breakfast nook.

"Yes, Sophie?"

"We are not out in the wild. If you have something to say to Curtis, find him and say it civilly. There is no need to shout indoors, particularly in a house of this size."

I bite my lip a little. "Yes, Sophie."

Curtis is watching soccer in the living room. "Heard ya. Careful out there."

"Thanks."

A brisk walk lands me at my phone on time.

Jill picks up on the first ring. "Hi?"

"Hey, Jill."

"I just realized you've been gone two whole weeks."

No kidding. "Two weeks tomorrow. Does this mean there's no news again?"

A gargantuan pause. "Not exactly."

"Tell me."

"I don't know. I mean, I think something's going on. Dad is walking around like the cat that swallowed the canary, and I can't figure out why. He's, I dunno, giddy or something."

"That's weird."

"Yeah. And he won't tell me anything. Maybe there's a sting operation or something?"

Jill always thinks there's a sting operation. In her seventeen years, there has never been a single sting operation. Whatever. I'm dying to hear about the cryptic drinking instructions she posted online an hour ago. "What was all the beer-before-liquor stuff about?"

"Oh my god, Xander. You will never believe this. Grant Blakely is in a coma." Jill has all the details: alcohol and a swimming pool, ambulances, and arrests for underage drinking. That *never* happens in Laurel. Our police usually turn a blind eye to parties in people's houses. Because there is literally nothing else to do in our cow town.

And now Grant Blakely is in a coma.

"Oh my god."

"Yeah," Jill says. "It was touch-and-go for a while, but everyone is very hopeful."

"Shit."

"Yeah."

"And this was at your birthday party?"

She laughs. "My party was completely legal. No alcohol at all. The soccer team had a huge party after my party, and that's when it happened. He banged his head and fell into the pool and the drunks had a hard time fishing him out. Half the varsity team might be banned next year. I mean, it's a rumor, but maybe."

"And Grant Blakely is in a coma."

"An induced coma. They might bring him out of it tomorrow."

"Shit."

"Yeah."

I don't know what else to say. Grant Blakely is a really great guy. He's playing soccer at Ohio State next year. I mean, it's not football, but it's Big Ten athletics, and they recruited him. If he doesn't pull out of this . . . I don't even want to think about it.

Jill says, "You okay?"

"I don't know."

"Um, what have you been doing in New York?"

"I got some library books today."

"Really? I give you a life hanging in the balance and you give me library books?"

"I'm sort of speechless. The news about Grant sort of knocked the wind out of me."

"I'm sorry. I shouldn't have told you. Tucker told me not to tell you."

"Tell Tucker to fuck off. I want to know what's going on. Next time you see Grant, tell him I'm pulling for him."

"I will. I promise. Xander, how are *you*?"

"I got a job. And somewhere to sleep."

She lowers her voice. "Xander Fife, you promised me you weren't sleeping on the streets."

"Jill, I promise you I have not—not one single time— slept on the streets."

"My dad would kill you for that, you know. I mean, not literally. He would, you know, be pissed as hell if you were sleeping on the streets. He pretty much thinks I know something about where you are, but I don't think he knows we keep talking."

My stomach flips over. "Why do you think he knows something?"

"The questions he asks. He tries to do that interrogation thing with me, you know? He doesn't ask a yes/no question. He asks something else that would trip me up. Like 'What did Xander say about you going out with Tucker?' or 'Don't you think Xander would appreciate a slice in the mail?' over my birthday cake. He told me to figure out whether he should buy you a ticket for Mastodon next month. Like I'm going to tell him anything."

The answer is no. No Mastodon, even if they were passing out free beer and delivering Gary to the police on a silver platter. Okay, maybe for that.

Thank god Jill is keeping mum. "Do you think he's ever tailed you to Pizza Works?"

"Nope. And we've been scheduling when I know he's busy. Have you been dialing star-67?"

"Yeah, but . . ."

"But what?"

"I don't know. Maybe we should cool it with the calls for a while?"

"Xander, in the grand scheme of things, I think it's probably okay if my dad finds out where you are. He's not the one you have to worry about."

Who the hell knows what to worry about anymore?

"Also, I thought we agreed that Gary couldn't follow a cold trail, right?"

I never actually agreed to that. "He couldn't, but this is kind of a hot line, isn't it, Jill? It's not a cold trail if he suddenly figures out I've been calling Pizza Works from my very distinct area code."

"New York City isn't exactly small. And if you're using star-67, how exactly is he going to figure out New York in the first place?"

"I don't know! I just don't like it!"

"You don't like it, or you *do* like being all mysterious and going on adventures by yourself?"

That is low.

"Because, Xander, you could come home if you really wanted to. My dad will keep you safe. He said we could do things with an escort. I think he thinks the worst of this has passed. I think he thinks Gary has fled to Mexico or something. Why don't you just come home? Come on, come home."

Tempting. Home to Jill and Gretchen and Laurel. Home to Sunday dinners and pick-up soccer and Dairy Queen.

Home, where Gary would know exactly where to find me. "I can't."

"You can't? Or you won't. Why can't you?"

I don't know. Which is better: a cautious life at home overshadowed by constant fear, or freedom far away from friends? Then again, am I really free here? My hat is off and I'm not hiding anymore, but holing up inside every day isn't exactly freedom.

"I just can't, Jill. I'll come home when they find him, okay?"

Jill's pissed. "And what if they never find him?"

"We'll cross that bridge when we come to it."

"Listen to yourself. You're saying never. You're saying if they don't find him, you're never coming home. Really?"

I don't know. Really? "I don't know, Jill. Let me think about what I want to do, okay? I just need . . . I just need to think. Give me a few days. Talk Saturday? Five o'clock?"

"I leave for swim camp this Friday morning. No phones or electronics there, anyway. I'll be back next Friday. So, Friday?"

"Jill, that's nine days from now!"

"Well, I can't exactly come back from the lake to stand at Pizza Works to listen to you refuse to come home."

"That's just mean."

"It's true. For all we know, Gary is in Mexico! You are ruining Infinite Summer! And you're missing it. We're supposed to be doing this together."

"So, next Friday at nine is what I'm hearing from you."

"Friday at nine."

"Fine."

"Fine."

Twenty-nine

Only a really hard sleep makes me this sluggish. It's an interesting dichotomy: being well rested but feeling like the walking dead. On my way to the kitchen, the knocking begins: quiet at first, then quite loud.

Too groggy to register any paranoia, I ignore it. It's probably just that caretaker Curt mentioned. She's coming this morning.

"It's Kat," she yells from the other side of the door.

There ya go.

I holler toward the kitchen, "I've got it!" Shit. Yelling in the house again. Before opening the door, I whisper loudly, "Sorry, Sophie."

Kat looks like a lion. Not a lioness, but a genuine, big-cat lion. Her hair is that crazy naturally curly business that sticks out four inches all the way around her head. Her skin is a rich mahogany.

A John Lennon caricature is penned in Sharpie on her white T-shirt. Is she an artist?

She steps up into the house and is about half an inch taller than I am. Skin-tight denim shorts stretch across the tops of her long brown legs. She's barefoot.

And radiant.

"Hello?" she says when I've stared too long. "I'm Kat. Are you Graham?"

Sort of.

In my desperate search for an appropriate thought, my pause stretches so long that I also need an excuse for being speechless.

"I'm sorry. With the name Kat, I was expecting you to have green eyes." And something less than a smoking hot body, that's for sure.

Kat glows with a beauty that painters try to transcribe from imagination onto canvas.

"Excuse me?" She steps around me and into Curt's house.

That hair. Those legs. And like a dumbass, I'm standing here with my mouth hanging open. Curt didn't tell me that Kat was young and hot. And it's not a matter of opinion, either: clearly, she's hot.

Just outside the kitchen door, I hear Curt and Kat talking about what Sophie will eat, how she's been feeling, and what time Kat can expect Curt—us—home tonight.

Curt makes french toast for himself and offers some to Kat and me.

I scarf mine down while Curt debriefs Kat: whites are in the washer, lunch is chicken salad, count Sophie's Rituxan pills because he forgot yesterday and the prescription is nearly due for a refill.

"She'll want french toast. I'll leave out the custard so you can make her a few slices, okay?"

Kat nods and finishes her breakfast. When we leave, she's reading a textbook at the kitchen table. She doesn't say good-bye.

Images of Kat—those legs, that hair—consume me during work. What was she reading? She was enthralled, like shut-out-the-world-immersed in a huge tome.

Where has she been hiding out since I landed in Burlington? What does she do when she's not babysitting Sophie? And could I do it—whatever it is—with her? Who is she?

She is an almost total enigma who keeps my brain busy all day.

It's a relief to obsess over something else, frankly. In my brain, Kat is this new, fresh person running laps around Gary and Gretchen and Mom, who have been on continuous loop for weeks.

It's a nice change of pace . . . until the guilt seeps in.

I can't just trade in Gretchen for Kat, but I can be friendly. I should at least be friendly. I hope she's still at Curt's house when I get back.

Curt works late on Thursdays—how can he keep this schedule straight?—but he lets me leave after eight solid hours of work.

And she's still in the house, reading in the same space of this morning's not-good-bye. What do you say to a smoking hot girl you just met? In a town where you might have to live for the rest of your life?

"Hi, honey! I'm home!"

Kat's glare suggests I aimed too high. She goes back to her book.

"How was your day, Kat?"

"Fine, thanks."

She makes no move to leave. Maybe she also keeps track of Curt's wonky schedule.

I shake my white bag as little peace offering. "Want a sandwich from the deli? I brought Reubens."

"I ate, thanks."

Across from her in the breakfast nook, I plow through the first sandwich. Curt threw in some extra thousand island dressing, which is perfect for dipping the crusty bits. After chugging a root beer from the fridge, I start in on the second sandwich. My stomach suffers from refugee syndrome.

My brain suffers from insufficient data.

"What are you reading?"

Kat doesn't look up. "*Microeconomic Theory*, Mas-Colell et al, second edition."

"Why?" I read some dry stuff, but nothing that dry.

Finally, she looks up at me. "Graham, I need, like, twenty minutes. In twenty minutes, we'll talk."

Making like I need a snack, I look through the cupboards behind her and study the stack of books by her side. American lit, economics, and anatomy have almost nothing in common.

Not quite twenty minutes later, Kat slams the book shut and walks to the living room. I feel like a puppy following her down the short hall, but I can't not. She opens drawers and digs between the couch cushions of my bed.

"Do you know where the remote is? I would love to just veg out until Curt gets home."

"No idea."

She finds it beneath the ottoman and deftly navigates the cable menus. "Thursday night! Do you watch *So You Think You Can Dance*?"

"Definitely no."

"Sit."

On the first commercial break, I get part of Kat's story: she's staying late tonight because Sophie had a really rough day, and she doesn't want to leave until Curt is back, in case something goes wrong. Micro is one of the two classes she can afford, both time-wise and financially, at the university. The anatomy book is for fun.

On the second commercial break, she concedes, "I wasn't quite smart enough to get a full ride, but I was smart enough to get some scholarships. I promised to work with Sophie as long as I'm in school, as long as she's alive . . . so it all works out."

"That's a long time to wait for real life to begin."

She flinches. "What do you mean, real life?"

"You know: when you're done doing all the stuff you have to do before your real life starts."

Kat says, "Uh, this is it."

"This is what?"

"It's my real life. I've been living it for almost nineteen years."

The show is back on before I can rebut. This isn't real life. Real life is in college and out of college, doing real things.

Isn't it?

In the six seconds between the end of a routine and a judge's critique, I can't wait. "DVR has a pause button, you know. We could finish our conversation first."

"I'm an instant-gratification kind of girl," Kat says. "I like my TV in real time."

She can't be right. This isn't real life. Not for me. Maybe this is a pause in real life.

At the next commercial break, I pounce. "I'm a little younger than you. What I meant to say was that life begins when you move out of your parents' house."

She scowls. "Okay, so from birth to, what, eighteen? If that's not your life, what is it, exactly?"

"A prologue?"

Still scowling.

I can placate her. "Okay, I'll give you that. Real life, okay. But what if you take a break from your life, go away for a while. Two weeks, maybe? You leave everything—your people, your house, your things—leave it all behind for a while. What's that called?"

"It's still life, Graham. It's just your life in a different place. You take your life with you on vacation. You can slow down. You can abandon the sucky parts and start over, make it better, but all of it is your life. It's yours."

"No." I shake my head wildly. Hiding out in Burlington isn't part of my life story.

Kat says, "Don't obsess over it. Forget I said it. Can't we just enjoy?"

No, we can't. If she's right, then I'm wasting my life here. If I'm not hiding from anyone, then what am I doing holing up waiting for real life to begin? If this is real life, I need to get going.

I shake my head free of the thought and focus on the screen. Kat really enjoys introducing me to the show's nuance. By the time Curt gets home, Kat has explained how auditions work, detailed the dancers' life stories, and made an educated guess about who will win. It's not my jam, but I'm learning. For instance, the dancing I saw in Times Square was called bone breaking and liquid. It's almost as interesting as abstract impressionist art.

When Curt walks through the door, Kat becomes a different girl: all business, including many concerns about Sophie's lack of stamina.

Long after she's gone home, I can't stop thinking about what Kat said.

Do I want to waste my life biding my time in Burlington? Do I have a choice?

I need to get to real life as soon as possible. Or the thing formerly known as real life. Call it the next stage of my life already in progress.

For most of my life, I have focused on just getting through it. Get through the years we couldn't afford the luxury of Dairy Queen. Get through emergency room visits. Get through another hole Gary punched in the wall. Get through Mom being pissed off that she tried to fix the hole herself and couldn't get it right.

It feels like that's all I've ever done.

But this is life. Now. And getting through it isn't enough anymore. How do I take the reins?

Thirty

Monday morning, after our long weekend working at the deli, Curt says Kat has a family emergency. "She's stuck in New York, and I've exhausted my very short list of people who can take care of my ma. Can you?"

What's wrong with Kat?

Calm Curt is on edge. "Graham, can you hang out with my mother today? Sorry, I'm desperate. I'll pay time and a half what you get at the deli. Cash."

"Sure?" What else can I say?

Curt throws together a couple sandwiches while he runs me through Sophie's routine.

"It's just a really bad day for her. Wasn't expecting this." He puts his hands on my shoulders, like a concerned father might. "Listen: her mobility is limited, so assist her with everything. Make her respect her own limits. She can't stand up or sit down on her own. Her hands are useless, that sort of thing. I'm sorry I have to go, but Dad is doing estate stuff in Montana and it's our annual health inspection."

He explains Sophie's complicated thirty-five-compartment pillbox and hands me a schedule. "I'll be back when our manager comes on at four. Try to spend the day with her as much as you can, okay? Just . . . just call me if you need anything, okay?" He's out the door before I can answer.

Fifty percent more pay and no toilet brushes? Sounds like a good deal to me, and how hard can it be?

Peeking into Sophie's room, I find her lying supine in her bed. Well, sort of supine: her head is inclined on three pillows, her chin touching her chest. Morning sun floods through small bedroom windows. A dozen or so plastic prescription bottles litter her bedside table.

She could be dead, but for the rhythmic rise and fall of her cotton blanket. Why does she need a blanket when it's eighty degrees outside?

Sophie looks like she's dead. Mom looked like she was sleeping when I last saw her. Sophie is old and frail. Her face is like chicken skin—translucent and saggy. Mom was so happy and strong, with so much to do.

Mom is gone, but Sophie's still here. It makes no sense.

At precisely nine-thirty, I shake Sophie's shoulder to wake her. Her eyes snap open and she grabs my forearm to right herself.

Her voice is breathy. "Never. Never wake me by shaking. That is too much a jolt for me."

"I'm sorry, Sophie, I didn't know."

Her face softens. "I know, dear. I just want you to know for next time. Calling my name should suffice, I think." She tries to reposition herself but isn't strong enough. "When will Curt be back?"

"Before four, he said." I hand her the pill box labeled MONDAY 2. "This is your two-hours-before-lunch dose?"

Sophie tilts her head upward a bit, and between the two of us, we get the pill into her mouth and the water to her lips.

Now what? "What can I do for you?"

"I need to lie down for a spell," she says, despite the fact that she has been lying down for hours. She closes her eyes, which is my cue to leave.

I surf the web for two hours. No sign of Gary, no new email from Gretchen, no chance of going home any time soon. At least I have books.

At 11:45, I take Sophie her lunch, complete with a straw in her cup, because I am a genius.

She's right where I left her. "Sophie?" Raising the volume a little every time, I wake her on the fourth try.

"What time is it? When will Curt be back?" She is more hopeful than confused.

I offer my arm. "Around four, he said?"

Sophie holds tightly while I raise her to a seated position. She breathes slowly. "Graham, I am sorry about this, but I need to use the toilet."

"Sure."

"You know I need help to use the toilet."

"Sure. My whole thing here is to help you get around."

She enunciates pointedly. "I mean, I need help. With the whole . . . process."

The idea settles in my brain very slowly. *Shit*. I am not equipped to deal with this.

I reach for Sophie's elbow, but she jerks it out of reach.

"Grabbing my arm puts me off balance. When you're helping someone—when you're helping me—you let me take your arm and you shoulder the burden."

I swallow hard. "Yes ma'am."

She doesn't walk so much as slide one foot at a time through the worn carpet. What the hell has happened to her in the last twenty-eight hours?

In the bathroom, Sophie says, "Let's make this as painless as possible. Just look at my face." To herself, she mutters, "This is why I hired a girl."

She asks me to lift her dress, which is sort of okay. She holds onto my shoulders and asks me to pull down what she calls her knickers.

"Just look at my face, Graham."

I can't look her in the face, so I look down. But I can't look down without seeing her body.

Her skeleton, more like. Those soft parts that the rest of us have just . . . aren't there. Her *knickers* stretch between her hip bones like a trampoline with a huge gap next to her navel. There is no fat or pudgy belly to stretch the elastic. Sophie has almost no muscle. She doesn't really have thighs.

Skin and bones is a real thing, and her knobby knees are totally bereft of hair.

Is Sophie dying?

She tries to hold my elbows as I lower her onto the toilet.

She needs a nurse. Or, at the very least, someone more professional than a seventeen-year-old kid who has just seen his first naked woman and can't cope with her age. This is so beyond the scope of my job. Today is worth every penny that Curt offered, and more.

"Graham, it's a cruel fact of life: aging isn't for the faint of heart." She teeters on the toilet seat. "You can wait outside for this part."

Her bony butt could get stuck in the toilet bowl, and I can't afford to let her fall off the toilet, either. I also don't want to embarrass her. I reach for some levity. "Between all my friends and my parents, I've probably heard the worst bathroom noises ever."

Apparently we have not crossed the threshold of embarrassment. "This is something I would like to do in private."

"Okay. I'll wait right outside the door. Just call for me when you're ready."

Curt is not paying me enough for this. *How hard can it be?* Really freaking hard.

Every few minutes, I say, "You okay, Sophie?"

After the third time, she sing-songs, "Gra-ham! I can't get anything done in here with you talking. Get yourself a magazine or something."

Digging through my backpack, I snag Jill's bracelet. What Would Jill Do? Jill would probably bail. Taking care of people who are small—physically or otherwise—is her least favorite thing. What would Xander do?

He would support Sophie. Because that's who I am. I grab Bill Bryson from my stack of books and resume my bathroom watch.

But I can't read. Sophie has gone from walking around the neighborhood to practically bedridden in a matter of days. Getting old sucks. Sophie isn't even that old. Curt's in his early twenties, and he's her fourth child, which makes her mid-sixties at the oldest, right?

So Sophie is sixty-five, give or take a few years. She looks like she's a hundred. What the hell happened to her? I should have written down the name of her prescriptions so I could do a little research.

Sophie is right: aging is not for the faint of heart.

Or for the heartbroken, apparently. Mom won't get a chance to find out if aging was for her. She won't get a chance to joke about her ailing body. She'll never embarrass over some poor schlep dragging her to the john.

Maybe Mom was lucky to die in her thirties.

Only someone responsible for his mother's death would think that.

Mom will never have to age, but she lost everything else in exchange.

Her life is in a box now. Complete. Every thought, every day, every meal, every fight Mom ever had is packaged and ready to go. Nothing more to add to her life's contents. She is gone from me, yes, but her life is also gone from her.

I guess that's what she lost: a future.

What will happen to her clothes? And her books? And the rest of her stuff? She's wearing her green dress, but she has a closet full of clothes for all seasons. I guess they'll go to Goodwill, where many of them came from in the first place.

The battered women's shelter might take her clothes. Would that be weird? An abused woman accepting clothes from a woman who died at her ex-husband's hands?

"Graham?" Sophie's tone suggests it wasn't her first time calling my name. "Have you left me?"

I open the door. "I'm so sorry, Sophie. I was thinking about . . . aging?"

"Not for the faint of heart, but better than the alternative. Could you tear off some toilet tissue for me, please?"

Way, way, way, way above my pay grade.

Sophie knows it, too. "Don't worry, I will do the wiping myself."

Tearing off far more than she could need, I thrust it toward her.

Sophie mutters something about being reduced to this. "I raised my children, sent them out into the world, and now I am the child."

She excuses me back to my side of the door.

It's just too much. The first naked woman I have seen in person—other than Jill, who is practically my sister—is sixty-five years old. Frail and wrinkled. Tucker would have a field day with this.

Chuckling, I slide down the wall to sit on the floor.

"I can hear you, Graham."

I am mortified. Seeing another human naked is nothing compared to Sophie's issues. Losing her ability to function as a whole person must be demoralizing.

I can hear her straining. Her ring clangs on the bar next to the toilet.

"Sophie!" I push open the door. "Do not try to stand up by yourself."

"You cannot handle this," she says.

I can't get kicked out of this house. I can't get fired from my not job-job.

"Wait. Wait, Sophie." Only the truth can absolve me. "I was laughing at myself, not at you. I just realized this is the first time I have seen a woman ... unclothed ... the first time I have seen an unclothed woman. And my friends will have a field day with this."

Sophie freezes and I double back. "I mean, they would. If I ever told them, which I won't."

"No, you will not."

I put on my best commanding voice. "And you, Sophie, will not try to get off the toilet without help today. Curt told me to make you respect your limits."

She holds my elbows to steady herself again. "Keep your eyes on my face, put me back together, and flush without looking."

This time, I obey.

After we wash her hands, Sophie leads me back to the bed, where I lift her legs onto the mattress and tuck the blanket around them. In an eighty-degree room.

"It's just a bad day, is all," she says. "Tomorrow will be better."

I certainly hope so. "Right. Last week you were walking down the block. Tomorrow will be better."

"Thank you."

"No problem."

Sophie nods. "Tell your mother she has something new to be proud of."

No matter how hard I bite my lip, I can't stave off the tears. Sophie looks at me, expectantly, but I can't speak. Saltwater rolls down my face and my mouth is brackish with fresh blood and tears.

"Graham?"

I'm supposed to be taking care of Sophie. I was supposed to be taking care of my mom.

"Graham, what is it, son?"

Anything louder than a whisper would make me start wailing. "My mom died."

Sophie tilts her chin downward and slowly pats the edge of her mattress. When I shake my head, she nods and pats it again. She can't quite reach me, but I want her to. I want her to know. I want my mother. And in the absence of *my* mother, I want *a* mother. Someone to tell me I'm not alone. To lambaste my foolish decisions. A mother to promise there will be an end to this Burlington fiasco.

Instead, sitting beside Sophie, I get a mother's love. She strokes my back and says the right things—my mother loved me, she will always be with me, her love and her pride live in me—and Sophie knows. She knows not to ask, not to push. She knows how raw I feel, and she doesn't pretend anything will ever make it better.

And, by some divine miracle, Sophie doesn't tousle my hair. She just rubs my back until I run out of tears. And she doesn't chastise me for snotting on my sleeve.

Because mothers know when you are so low you just can't keep it together anymore.

Sophie is having difficulty keeping her eyes open. The room shifts, and again Sophie is the child. She claims she won't need anything else before Curt comes home and excuses me for the afternoon.

I would prefer to stay here, with the understanding of a mother, even though she isn't mine. I could close my eyes and, just for a minute, imagine that her hand is Mom's, rubbing slow circles around my back. Mom has done that a thousand times. Every time I vomited. Every time I was hurting from Gary. Every time we were the only thing each of us had in this world.

I would prefer to pretend with Sophie, but she's firm.

I close the door behind me, and I'm alone again.

THIRTY-ONE

Tuesday is another day off. Curt is stumbling through some vintage Mario game while I half-concentrate on my book. Someone bangs on our front door at about ten in the morning.

Curt focuses on Mario. "S'open!"

"I'm so sorry," Kat says about a thousand times, tripping over herself as she enters. Same short shorts. Another Sharpie shirt. Hair still amazing.

Curt hits pause. "I told you on the phone it was fine."

"I know, but I wanted to see Sophie and apologize to her, too. Is she up?"

"Probably awake in bed."

Kat disappears behind Sophie's door and I dive back into my book. I'm down to the last two pages when Kat rejoins us in the living room.

"Thanks, Curt. I needed to see her. I'm headed to the library now. Do either of you need anything?"

Without looking away from the TV, Curt says, "Take that one with you. No library card, and he goes through books like water."

My face feels hot, as if reading is an embarrassing hobby.

214

Kat sizes me up, literally, from head to toe. "Do you have a bike?"

"Mine's in the shed. Combination is 2-7-1-3. Go." Curt's Mario flies through the clouds.

Kat opens the shed, dusts off the bike, tests and inflates the tires, and adjusts the seat.

"I can do that, you know."

She keeps working. "Working helps my stress level. I'm so embarrassed. I have never missed a day of work. I'm never late. After yesterday, Sophie will always think I'm unreliable."

"I doubt that."

Kat points her bike toward the street and yells over her shoulder, "Stay close."

She's fast. Like, race fast. At the very end of the street, she levels her pedals and stands on them, shaking her head in the wind. This is summer.

Burlington is zipping past me, and I feel alive again. I could just as well be chasing Jill on our bikes, though we haven't ridden together since middle school.

Outside the library, Kat locks our bikes to a dull gray rack.

Fifteen minutes later, I have my typical stack of assorted nonfiction and she's checked out a pile of journals. I'm ready to mount my bike and head back, but Kat has other ideas.

"Want ice cream? Ben & Jerry's is a five-minute walk, tops."

Kat leads me down College Street. We could be in any small town in the world, just two friends, hanging out.

"So, you can tell me, Kat. Was it true? You had a family emergency?"

Kat stares at me, mouth agape. "Why would I make up something like that?"

"I dunno. Maybe so you didn't have to help Sophie use the bathroom?"

"Curt said you stayed with her. How was that for you?"

How can I put this nicely? "I don't think I could do your job, that's for sure. It seems like she needs more help than just you."

"We get by."

A pastel display of sweets beckons from a cupcake shop. I want to stop, but Kat's heart is set on ice cream. We turn on to Church Street, a brick thoroughfare that allows only pedestrian traffic. Shops and bistros line the sidewalks. Mom would have loved window shopping here. To her, envisioning the perfect occasion for a dress, or salivating over a menu, felt like a real afternoon out.

Kat leads me into Ben & Jerry's and treats me to a scoop of Cherry Garcia. Outside, we settle on the brick sidewalk, our backs to the building.

"So, why you? How did you wind up taking care of a woman old enough to be your grandmother?"

She licks the drips of her Chunky Monkey in a way that is not entirely unsexy. "Sophie and I are friends. When she and Curt decided she needed help, I volunteered."

"Yeah, but why? I mean, how did it start? Your family's in New York, right?"

"They're in New York *now*. My parents moved to Burlington when I was sixteen. Sophie's old house was in our backyard, and I think she liked having a girl around. We bonded. Back then, Curt basically saw me as a nuisance. Now I help with his mom."

"And your parents?"

"They get tired of cities pretty quickly. They left Burlington in the middle of my senior year."

"And you stayed here."

Kat nods. "I was accepted to the university, and finally—finally!—I knew I could be in the same place for more than a year. Sophie let me stay with her until school was out. Then I got a job and rented a room."

"And when did you start working for Sophie?"

She glares at me. "You ask a lot of questions."

"I'm trying to figure you out. I mean—I'm trying to get to know you."

Kat guffaws. "There's not much to know. I go to school a lot. I study a lot. I live with two people I hardly see. Working with Sophie pays the bills."

"Not your parents?"

Another laugh. "Definitely not them. Basically, they think I'm an unambitious mess. It's going to take me six years to finish school and they think I should take on a load of debt and push through in four."

"You're more patient than I am. I'm taking my AP credits to Tulane and hope to get out in three."

"I'm just enjoying the experience." Kat smacks her arm. "I hate these damned mosquitoes."

I assume mosquitoes are a regular fixture of Burlington summers. Kat doesn't appreciate my pointing that out.

"They're always awful, but this year they're especially bad."

We're sort of in the way of lots of people, but Kat acts like she owns the curb. Shoppers walk around us to get wherever they're going, and she just keeps talking. We tend to our ice cream, discussing loads of other things, most of which are trivial. I marvel at the fact that I've never eaten Ben & Jerry's in a cone. In Ohio (or, you know, Georgia), we just buy the pints.

Kat says, "I never really thought about that. I guess it's a luxury."

"Thanks for the scoop, by the way."

Kat's whole face changes when she smiles. When she's not focused intently on whatever it is she's always focused intently on, Kat is radiant.

"No problem," she says. "Thanks for the conversation. Most of my casual chitchat is with Sophie, so this is a nice change of pace."

The change of pace is welcome. I bite through my cone and consider how our respective lives have merged into this moment. "Kat, your job is really hard."

"Some days. But, you know? I don't mind. And I sort of owe her."

"How so?"

Kat stares at the brick facade across the street. "My parents are weird. I was this sort of, I dunno, commodity to them? They were always trying to craft this life that took them all over the place and when we moved here, my life slowed down. Sophie's house, the old house, was like a sanctuary to me. I mean, it wasn't peaceful. There were always a lot of people around, but it felt like a nest. Everything was always in the same place—furniture that had been there for ages, always comfort food in the cupboards, that kind of thing—and there was a routine. I really needed that. A sanctuary. Nevermind. It's hard to understand."

An inner tug-of-war erupts between my desperation to tell Kat I understand completely and my deeper desperation to keep my ugly childhood secret.

"I understand. Jill's house is like that for me. It's like breathing space. A homey place away from my family."

Something clouds Kat's expression.

Without divulging any of my family's secrets, I describe Jill's parents and brothers, and explain that I've always been like their fourth child. "I have breakfast there every Saturday. And, well, basically, whenever I can get away from my own house."

Kat nods. "Does Jill understand you?"

"God, yes. I mean, she gets why I need to leave my own house and we just—we connect on a really deep level."

Kat analyzes the asphalt. "That's nice."

"Sounds like we both are very lucky."

She shrugs. "I guess. At this point, Sophie just thinks she needs to save me from a life of abandonment."

"That sucks. Any time someone wants to save you, that sucks."

Kat stares at me, wide-eyed. "Yes! As if I need saving!"

When she stands, I stand, too. She chucks a sticky napkin in the trash and we wander toward the library.

I ask her about college.

"There's less bullshit than high school, you know?" Kat wants confirmation from me, but I'm not sure which bullshit she's referring to. "Okay, so we read Hardy senior year in English lit. I don't understand why Hardy can't just make his characters long for sex instead of talking about feeding a woman strawberries. It's bullshit. And poetry is worse."

I couldn't disagree with the poetry bit, but there's something about imagery that appeals to me. Surely Kat, who doesn't wear her heart on her sleeve by any means, understands that sometimes a message should be muted. Or veiled.

"Now I can study whatever I want. It's awesome."

"And you're studying microeconomics and American lit."

"Yeah. Nursing, eventually, but I have to get some core courses out of the way first."

"Why nursing?"

Kat definitely heard me, but pretends she didn't.

"Kat?"

"It's going to sound ridiculous."

"Tell me anyway."

She's quiet. "I feel like people don't see me, you know? One of the worst things we can do to people is not see them. Sophie thinks I need to be saved and Curt used to think I was a nuisance. People at school think I'm too busy for friendship or, worse, they see me as a threat to them, academically. No one really sees me."

That makes no sense.

Kat unlocks her bike. "I know I'm going to have a small life, and that's fine, but I want to really see people. I want people to know they matter to me, at least. I want them to feel seen and heard. Who gets to touch lives like that? Social workers, which would depress me to no end. Teachers, which would probably drive me mad. And nurses. Maybe a geriatric nurse."

I get it. "Hence your tolerance for Sophie."

"Hence my *enjoyment* of Sophie. She's really quite fascinating. She had a great life a long time ago, and she changed it completely to raise four boys almost single-handedly. And she did the bravest thing ever in divorcing Big Curt. When MS started taking over her body, she didn't run back to that marriage. This is a strong woman, and hardly anyone notices."

I certainly hadn't.

"So, in this world where she often is tethered to her house or, worse, her own bed, I'm still interested in her stories. I still want her opinion. I notice her. I value her."

Kat is proud of this. She also is proud of her T-shirts. Today's Sharpie art is a caricature of Gene Kelly, who I am told was Kat's very first crush. She lights up when she talks about him, even now.

And she loves her hair. Every girl I know covets someone else's locks, but not Kat. She calls it her best feature.

"Other than my feet," she says. "I have great feet."

I can't tell. Feet aren't really my thing.

At the bike rack, Kat's shorts don't cover a millimeter of leg when she straddles her bike. Her legs are great the way Gretchen's are great: lean and strong.

"I feel like taking the afternoon off from studying," Kat says. "Where should we go?"

I'm not lugging around all my crap today, so it's high time to go exploring. I have nothing to show for my eighteen days in Burlington. "Treat me like a tourist. Show me all your best stuff."

"You're on," she says, and we're racing again.

Hanging out with Kat is exactly like hanging out with Jill . . . except she's not Jill.

To the beach, around campus, to the south end of the bike path and then the north, we see it all. A seedling sprouts in my mind: I can do this. Kat and Curt could be my people—my real friends, not just temporary stand-ins for the ones I'm missing. We could hang out and eat at the deli and maybe the university would accept me and I could live here. And what is four more winters, really? Burlington has everything I need: pick-up soccer, a free-ish library, thousands of potential new friends.

Burlington also has a science center.

"Let's go on my next day off," Kat says.

"When's that?"

"Sunday?"

Sunday is definitely a day for friends. "Sounds like a plan."

Over burgers at a little cafe, I pepper Kat with questions about her classes and how she spends her free time.

"What free time?"

That's obviously rhetorical, so I veer us back to college-related conversation.

Two hours later, Kat leads me back to Curt's house.

"See you in the morning," she says.

After she speeds away, I change into my Chucks and go out for a jog. A few miles later, my legs start complaining about how I've treated them today, but I don't care. I can breathe again. I feel like I'm back.

Or maybe I'm me for the first time.

Thirty-two

Thanks to Curt's computer, I haven't been to The Byte for days. And thanks to Curt, I have a little extra money and a whole lunch break to catch up with news from Laurel Woods.

The Byte is just the same.

Jill's Instagram is bare, of course. In two days, it will be full of recaps from swim camp. I love debriefing her after camp. I've always secretly—or not so secretly—envied Jill's weeks at camp. It sounds like one huge party, with grueling practices sprinkled between. Being a counselor is probably even better: no practices required.

Internet news is slow today. Gretchen is away in New York until tomorrow. Tucker doesn't mention Jill at all, which is weird. He does share news about Grant, though: *Doctors expect Grant to recover fully. Now let's hope OSU coaches think he's been punished enough.*

Oh man. If Grant can't play next year, he'll be a wreck.

I need to head back to the deli in five minutes. Nothing from Gretchen, but a new one from Gary is staring me in the face: *I Forgive You.*

He forgives *me?* This I have to see. It won't change anything, but I have to know.

I once read about a spy who could read letters through sealed envelopes. I wish I could hold a candle behind the monitor and see what he wrote without seeing what he wrote.

Sitting on this side of fear—where I feel like he can't find me, and I know I have been smart about staying hidden—I just want him to disappear. Cease to exist.

I am so over this. There are some things in life you can't take back: things you say, the way you make people feel, your youth when you're sixty-five and can't get out of bed by yourself. Gary can't take back what he did to Mom. I can't take back abandoning Gretchen in Jill's kitchen.

But *he* forgives *me?* My fingertips brush the keyboard, flirting with the letters.

It's kind of disturbing that he's emailing me at all. Nothing will eclipse the fear I felt after he murdered Mom. Even an empty threat can't make things worse. If he can't track me through this email, there is no point in not opening it. Morbid curiosity lurks at my fingertips. I open the message.

A little pop-up box reads *This image has been downloaded in HTML,* but I can't find the image. Instead, Gary has written pages of bullshit justifying everything from slapping me to murdering Mom. His lengthy exposition blames everyone—his parents, his old bosses and colleagues, our neighbors, my mother, and me—for everything he's ever done. When I get to his forgiveness—for my horrid, irresponsible behavior, including scaring off Renee—I stop reading and log off.

The man is delusional. Then again, if he's forgiven me, maybe he's done with me.

Halfway to the deli, I realize I am a complete dumbass. If Gary could track email I send, I can track him, too.

One thirty-cent printed page later, I'm headed to Curt's with my best—only!—clue to Gary's whereabouts. At the convenience store, I borrow a Sharpie to blacken out my email address.

Curt takes the page and tools around on his iPhone for several minutes.

Not for the first time, I think Jill would love Curt. He's totally into this Gary stuff, which is just a game to him. Who cares that he doesn't know how dire the situation may be?

I can't help butting in. "What are you doing, exactly?"

He points to a row of numbers and periods. "I'm tracing that."

"Could you maybe explain like I'm five?"

"An IP address is kind of like a phone number. I got this number, and want to see who it belongs to. I did a reverse lookup, not helpful."

Curt goes through the motions and flashes his smartphone at me. "Hostname is a T-Mobile hotspot, so not like a company or residence or something. Dead end. So, we'll try Googling for geolocation based on the IP address. Could pinpoint his location."

Awesome. If Curt can find Gary, I can tell Jill on Friday, and be on my way home this weekend!

It could happen.

It probably won't, but it could.

Curt taps around on his phone again. "Yup!" He faces his phone toward me. "Spokes Coffee in Elyria, Ohio. Any idea where that is?"

Elyria, Ohio, obviously.

"There ya go," Curt beams." Now you know he's not here."

What a huge relief! Jill was right. Of course she was right. He's not coming after me at all. I can't wait to talk to her. Well, to apologize and talk to her.

"Can I borrow that a sec?"

I could call Dale, but I really want him to find Gary before I reveal my location. It has to be Jill. She isn't allowed to have her cell at camp, and she's probably locked it away somewhere so the little boys can't play with it. My call goes directly to voicemail.

"Hey, Jill, I found Gary. I mean, in theory. I didn't find him in person. I found him through an email he sent me. It's a long story. Tell your dad he's been using Spokes Coffee in Elyria. When they find him, use your Instagram time stamp thing and I'll call you. Hope camp was fun! Home soon! Infinite Summer! YAY!"

This is awesome. We know exactly where he is. Or where he was at 1:37 p.m. yesterday.

It's only a matter of time.

He's cornered.

Thirty-three

In 46.25 hours, Jill will be back from camp.

After a long day at the deli—when someone smeared shit on the walls of the girls' bathroom—Curt has coerced me into keeping an ear out for Sophie while he goes on yet another date. Kat stays to keep me company, but she's so immersed in her microeconomics notes that I can easily steal peeks at her still-radiant face. Every few pages, she pulls an Oreo from the long sleeve between us.

She offered me one, but eating Oreos with Kat feels like cheating on Jill.

Shortly before eight, Kat closes her book quietly, looks me straight in the eye, and says. "Done!" Two Oreos are her reward. She's a twist-and-licker, like any normal, self-respecting person.

Kat says, "So. Graham, we covered my stuff. What's your thing? What do you want to do with the rest of your life?"

Stay alive. Catch a killer.

I don't like being on the other end of questions. "Travel, I guess."

Kat throws her head back in a round laugh. "Been there, done that. It's overrated."

"You've lived in several places. I'm talking about going everywhere. I want to travel the whole world."

"I've seen some of that, too. I went to India with Habitat for Humanity when I was twelve."

Kat describes the house she helped build and how she made friends with children despite the language barrier. I want the whole story—how they got there, why they went, what they saw—all of it. Her eyes sparkle as she describes the family whose house she was building. She talks about the games the children played, and I realize she was wrong: she would be an excellent teacher. But nursing will do.

"Were there goats in the road in India?"

She stares at me like I'm a goat.

I raise my hands in defense. "I'm sorry, I've never been to India. But I read *National Geographic*, and there are always goats in the road in India."

"No, Mr. *National Geographic*, there were not. Not everything is as it looks in magazines."

"Hey, I wasn't trying to offend you. I'm just fascinated. And jealous of your travels."

"Why, where do you go?"

I could lie. I really could. I know enough—about the United States, at least—to cobble together a decent road trip itinerary. But I don't want to lie anymore. "Honestly? I've never been anywhere. I've lived in the same small town since I was born, and the same house since I was four. Before I came here, I never even left my home state, except for dinners just over the border."

"So what do you do with your time?"

After hearing about my soccer team and physics Olympics, Kat wants to know about all my friends, so I

ride tangents about friends and euchre and Sunday dinners out for wings. I confess that vacation to me is a day
at Cedar Point with Jill's family—only I call it "a huge
amusement park" because I think Cedar Point is a one-off.
I don't have a car or a passport or a real suitcase.

"But I want those things. I want to go everywhere, in
the US and abroad. I've seen every episode of *The Amazing
Race*! Surely that counts for something?"

"God, you are so average," Kat says. "I mean normal.
You're so normal."

Average is spot-on. If we are our experiences, then I
am an average, small-town guy. I'm not completely worthless, though; Tulane has seen something in me, enough that
they're paying to educate me, and clearly my closest friends
see something in me.

But everyone—even the most boring, vapid person—
has friends, right?

Compared to Kat, I am average. She's this interesting
and multidimensional creature, and she's just a year older. I
don't even know how to become interesting from here. I
can't even explain it to her.

Her stare is unnerving.

"What?"

"I can see the wheels spinning in there," Kat says.
"You're about to come up with something big."

I can't help smiling. "I just always thought I would
become this interesting and worldly person once my
life began."

"Life is—"

"I know, I know. I'm living my life, blah, blah, blah. I
hear what you're saying. What I mean is, thinking of this as

already my life, I'm not sure how to shift gears and make myself an interesting person."

"Oh, I think you're very interesting, Graham. You're empathetic. You're curious. You're kind of mysterious. Very interesting."

Curt's footsteps on the back porch are Kat's cue to slip her books into her bag.

"Also, just do things that you think are interesting."

Easier said than done.

"Also, always say yes."

"Say yes what?"

"Say yes to everything. You're invited to the Holocaust Museum? Say yes. Someone wants to spend a weekend fishing in a rowboat in the middle of Champlain, say yes. You hear there's one empty spot in a Japanese class or are offered chicken feet for dinner or are asked to volunteer, say yes. When faced with opportunity, say yes. That's how you become an interesting person—by doing interesting things."

Kat and Curt have their business discussion. Sophie would be embarrassed to hear them talk about her bowels, so I excuse myself.

Putting together my bed, which gets less particular every day, I try the yes on for size. Yes, I'll camp in the Adirondacks. Yes, I'll go hear Mastodon. Yes, I'll sit through a lecture about the evolution of the human brain.

I send a promise out into the void: I will become more interesting once life resumes. Or right now, at this point in my life.

I'll bet it's a lot easier to say yes when you aren't trying to suppress a childhood worth of secrets or hide how much your family is struggling. Those chapters of my life are closed. Even if my life is just resuming, and not starting from scratch, I think it's going to be a lot easier from here on out.

Especially if Gary is caught. I hope he's caught. Haven't I endured enough trauma and hard knocks? Can't I just catch a break?

Okay, I caught a break with the job. And the couch. Can't I catch another break? Just one? One big break.

Thirty-four

Just twenty-one hours until we heroically lead police to Gary, I need to go for a run to keep myself calm. After eight hours of dishes and toilets, running is like the new normal's lifeline to the old normal.

Kat pokes her head back into the house while I'm Mister Rogersing my shoes.

"Down and Dirty is playing at The Hub. Want to come?"

I don't even know what Down and Dirty is, but after last night's little life lesson, I can hardly say no. Kat knows this. "Come on. We'll walk. It's a nice night."

On the way, Kat enthuses about the band. "They're great. Mostly covers, but maybe three years ago they started writing their own stuff. It's good. Suits, you know, all the moods."

"All the moods?"

"Yeah, you know. The blues is about pain and love and loss and sometimes hope. They do it all."

Blues music has never seemed nuanced to me.

Kat has more to say. "The blues always get me a little, I don't know, frisky?"

That gets me a little frisky, no I-don't-know about it. "How does that work?"

"Like when I'm listening to B. B. King, or Keb'Mo, or ancient LPs of Buddy Guy alone in my parents' basement when I was sixteen. It just feels deep, like this very basic, very human rumble and sway. I want to be holding onto someone, grinding our hips into each other and running our hands all over each other's bodies. Or Ray Charles, which is technically R&B. It makes me want to take off my shirt. Is that weird?"

"No." It's freaking hot.

Imagining her taking off her shirt drives me wild. I'm not proud of this; I don't want to be one of those shallow guys who gets excited over any old topless girl. But Kat isn't any old topless girl. She's interesting and smart. And kind.

But she's not Gretchen.

Is thinking about another naked girl cheating? On my not-really-actual girlfriend? I don't know. But either way, I can't get the image of topless Kat out of my head. Maybe I'm cheating, but only in my head.

At eight thirty, the place is still pretty empty. An old red jukebox in the corner blurts out tinny blues while we wait. I have to shout to be heard. "So, when did you start listening to the blues?"

"In ninth grade, I had this friend who loved the blues. She spent all her time and money on sneaking into blues clubs and buying music online and reading about the blues. It was sort of thrust upon me."

That's just how Jill dumped heavy metal into my head, though I still hate it all these years later.

Kat launches into what I can only call a soliloquy, all about her friend Dawn, who was the best friend she ever had, and how life went downhill when she left Chicago. "I called her Dawg because, well, you know. Kat and Dawg? We were fourteen. Everything is silly when you're fourteen."

Kat has loads of stories about sneaking out of Dawn's house to go catch a show, or eating food that her parents forbid her to eat when she was at Dawn's. Eyes wide, she recalls little adventures they took around Chicago on a day when their school inexplicably lost power.

"And then, when my parents moved us to Austin, Dawn found a new best friend. We drifted apart. I hung onto the blues, though." Her voice is light, but a lot of pain lies just beneath it.

The lights dim and people keep talking—loudly— while these three guys on stage start plucking strings and adjusting microphones and all that. It doesn't seem very professional to me.

When they start singing, though, it's magic.

I have heard some blues before—background in the house or accidentally when someone's iPod was on shuffle or in a movie once in a while—but this is different.

First we're bouncing to an upbeat song, the singer smiling because we're in on the secret. His face contorts in anguish when he slows it down. There are maybe fifty people here, some gathered at the bar, others dancing right next to their tables. Every single person is moving, so the mood in the club ebbs and flows with the music.

Yeah, the blues are nuanced.

The blues are sexy. Pop singers have all these albums about making out or getting it on or getting someone to fall in love with you, but all they really need to do is turn on the blues. Maybe that's why there's no main-stream blues stuff. Everyone would be getting it on all the time.

"Thanks for bringing me," I whisper-shout near Kat's ear.

"Can you feel it?"

"I can." I don't have a wild urge to start dancing, but I am moved.

"Hear this? They're covering Ray Charles. 'Sentimental Journey.' Come here."

Kat drags me to the darkest corner of the joint. "Wrap your arms around me and close your eyes."

At my first middle-school dance, I tried to find girls' hips with my hands, and kept us arms-distance apart. You could have driven a school bus between me and Maddyson Sutch, with room to spare.

When my arms were wrapped around Gretchen in our mini-forest—ages ago now, really—my hands weren't so much wrapped around her as they were exploring her back and midsection and perfectly rounded butt.

Aiming for something between dancing with Maddyson and making out with Gretchen, I hug Kat loosely.

"Closer," she says, and I pull her toward me. "Now, hold onto me. Let go of yourself. Keep your eyes closed and feel the music."

How the hell do I let go of myself? I stand still and listen for a few minutes. *The night time is the right time / to be with the one you love.*

Kat digs her fingers into the spaces between my ribs. She shuffles one of her feet between both of mine, and then we sway slowly, forward and back instead of side to side.

It's impossible to separate my body from my brain, to sway, to let go and live in the moment. Kat bends her legs and our swaying deepens. And suddenly, letting go feels remarkably easy.

My other senses sharpen when my eyes are closed. Kat's torso feels warm through our clothes. She smells so strongly of patchouli that she must wash her hair with it. Maybe she smokes pot and uses patchouli to mask the scent. That's what potheads in Laurel do.

Laurel. Hundreds of miles away, Gretchen's body also is warm beneath her clothes. Kat's waist slopes smoothly toward her hips, which seem wider than Gretchen's. Gretchen has those tiny dimples above her perfect ass. And that hair I can run my fingers through ten million times.

"You're thinking again, Graham. Stop thinking and feel."

I feel like I want to be with Gretchen, who said that same thing to me exactly six weeks ago. And maybe I can't be with Gretchen, but I want to be. I want to lose myself in her kisses, in her hair, in her shirt. If I could go back to that girl who was mine for five seconds—if I could wrap my arms around her again—I would hold tight forever.

But I can't. For now, wrapping my arms around Kat is okay. For now.

Thirty-five

Kat's patchouli lingers on my clothes this morning. I'm mummified in sheets after a night trying desperately to keep warm. What the hell happened to summer? Burlington is freezing.

With my eyes closed, I imagine Kat's cheek pressed to mine. Mostly, when my eyes are closed, I still think of Gretchen. Pushing both girls out of my head, I get ready for work.

Curt and I walk to the deli through dense fog. I've never seen anything like it. People materialize from five feet in front of us and disappear five feet behind. I can't see across the street, or that there *is* an across the street.

"This is really weird."

"It happens," Curt says. "In August it happens a lot. It's weird for July, actually. It'll burn off this afternoon."

I hope he's right. Being so disconnected from my surroundings is unsettling.

Everything about today is unsettling. My guilt over Kat fuses with my longing for Gretchen to form a Xander-shaped ball of ambiguity. I need to connect with Gretchen.

Check her Instagram or email her, or somehow feel like she's still there, just beyond my visibility.

"Mind if we stop for a cappuccino?" Curt says.

"Can you get it at The Byte? I want to check in online."

Every few paces, someone new materializes from the still-dense fog, and Curt knows practically everyone. All the hellos and howdies are going to make us late for work.

Nearly to The Byte, Curt says, "I can't believe you used to pay for their Internet every day."

Me neither. "I needed my fix."

"Your social media fix. You are an odd duck, Graham."

"Guilty as quack."

Curt snickers and yanks open the door. "You said 'quack.'"

Curt imitates a genuine duck as we wait in line: "Quack, quack, quack."

Now flush with cash from the deli, I splurge on a peanut butter brownie and large cream puff from the plastic case.

When Curt strikes up a conversation with the cashier, I survey the customers preoccupied with caffeine and Wi-Fi. Yellow Backpack Girl types frantically on her laptop as a small group of tourists argue emphatically in Japanese. Some guy with a hoodie pulled over his face stares at the mug in his hands. He reminds me of me, two weeks ago. The sadness of holing up here day after day seeps back into my mind.

"Change?" the cashier says, and I pocket my coins.

Curt starts a conversation with the woman behind us in line. She's wearing leather boots in July. It's not that much of a cold snap.

The Byte seems almost lively, now that I'm in a better headspace. Yellow Backpack snaps her laptop closed to chat with the guy next to her. The Dice Guys arrive and commandeer the table next to Hoodie Guy, who rewraps his hands around his mug.

A flash of blue on his right hand. I whip back toward the counter. No other man past age twenty wears a gargantuan gold class ring with a sapphire birthstone.

Could it be?

No. I'm being paranoid again. Gary said he forgave me. Besides, he's in Elyria, Ohio. My trail is cold.

Still, I can't force myself to turn around and check. A tiny part of me thinks it's not a random stranger. Shuffling a little closer to Curt, I check out Hoodie Guy in the huge mirror behind the counter.

Curt makes a date with Boots while Hoodie Guy sips his coffee. The guy is definitely wearing a huge ring on his right—no, left—no, right ring finger. He shakes the hood a little further back on his head, and I recognize that nose. His short forehead and wide face. Covering my own face with my hands, I shield my reflection.

From Gary. At my café. In Burlington. Where my trail was cold.

I can't move.

I have to move. My life depends on it. *My* life. Right now. It all comes down to this moment. I can't lock myself in Jill's bedroom. I can't assume the fetal position and let Mom take one for the team again. I can't run away.

And, for the first time, I don't want to. I want to end this. Gary's destroyed my past, but I want to control my own future.

What does that even mean? My stomach flips over. I'm going to be sick.

Controlling my future requires getting out of range and calling the police. I tug Curt's sleeve and whisper, "We have to go."

"Two minutes," Curt says, accepting his cappuccino from the barista without missing a beat of his conversation with Boots.

I drop my pastries on the counter and frantically fish through my cargo pockets for the knife. Palming it, I pull up my own hood. It's ten paces to the exit.

A huge group of people floods through the door, blocking my way.

I can't get out. I need to know that he hasn't recognized me. I turn and find Gary's seat empty. Where—

He grabs my forearm and spins me to face him.

This is where it ends. Here, in an overpriced Internet café in a tourist town, seven hundred miles from where I'm supposed to be. After only seven hours and one awkward kitchen encounter with Gretchen. Here, four weeks before my life was supposed to begin.

"Stop running from me." Gary pulls off his hood. He looks like hell. Or like he's been through hell. He hasn't shaved in several days, and his face is ashen and gaunt. His other hand is empty. No gun, or knife, or anything.

He's going to use his bare hands on me, just like he did on Mom. I try to jerk away from him, but he holds tight.

This is my life; I'm holding onto it. "Get off!" I kick as high as I can and get him in the knees. Gary arches back, screaming in agony, but he holds tight to me. The café goes still.

"Graham?" Curt, my friend, is confused.

"Curt. Call 9-1-1. Tell them there's a fugitive here."

Frozen, I keep my eyes locked on Gary's. They're deep, dark brown like mine, but bloodshot and empty. I search for something in his cold stare, something to tell me what's going to happen, hoping that somewhere there's a shard of humanity left.

"Curt. Please."

Curt says, "Wait, you're serious? Is that—"

"9-1-1. Now."

Gary is so close that I could spit in his face. I whisper, "Dozens of witnesses. And my friend is buddies with the police. Fucking. Let. Go."

He won't. And even if he would, stunned bystanders are still lingering in the doorway. I'm cornered.

Gary grabs my other arm, and I'm eleven years old again, about to get thrown into the wall for losing the remote. Or I'm four years old, being tormented for crying over my broken arm. I understand why I peed my pants that time; right now, all my organs are threatening to unload.

Gary's voice is low. "You know what you did was wrong, and I can forgive you. But right now, I need your help." He loosens his grip very slightly. "You can set things right. You and I both know what happened to your mom: she provoked me, and I reacted."

I'm a soccer player. World football, not American football. I've never tackled anyone before. I jerk back-ward, releasing my arms from Gary's grasp. Every muscle engaged, I jam my right shoulder into Gary's gut, with the full force of my body behind it. Together, we tumble across the stretch between the counter and the storefront, shattering The Byte's front window and rolling onto the sidewalk. I land on top of my father, who's on his back, stunned from the impact of his head against the sidewalk and struggling to catch his breath.

Screams and shouts echo all around me as some people rush to get closer and others scramble to get away.

Springing to my feet, I pull out my knife. A bit of peanut butter lingers where the blade meets the handle. "Don't move. I'll use my knife. I swear to god."

Gary is still.

Curt is talking to the 9-1-1 dispatcher.

"Gary Fife!" I shout. "Tell them he's a fugitive. From Ohio. Who murdered his wife."

Gary tries to sit up. My knife threatens very near his chest. "I said don't *move*. You're done hurting me."

Gary watches me grip the knife tighter. He's out of breath. "I'm not here to hurt you, Alexander. This is you and me here. I'm the only family you have left. You know I'm not a murderer. I went there that day to talk to you. Your mom said you weren't there, but I know you were. So you *also* know that she provoked me. I didn't have a choice."

I could just carve out a space in his gut. Sink my knife deep into his body and let his guts seep out.

"I'm not here to hurt you," he says again.

"Bullshit. That's all you've ever done."

Curt stands inside the window frame, "Okay, man. Let's cool our heads." His feet sort of tap dance across broken glass as he steps through the window, hands in the air. "Put the knife down, man. The police are coming."

Gary flashes a grateful smile at Curt before refocusing on me. "Your mom and I were like oil and water. I kept trying to have a life and she kept making me jump through hoops and play house and all that crap. And then I'd try to have a life again, and she would never let me."

"Bullshit. You didn't like your life, you should have changed it instead of beating her into submission."

Gary squeezes his eyes shut. "I need you to be with me on this, buddy. We can get through this together."

Maniacal laughter bursts from my body. "*With* you? Are you kidding me?"

"Look." He tries to right himself, but I kick his supporting arm out from under him, widening my stance and moving the knife toward his throat. He whispers, "Do you know what it's like, Alexander, having a person keep you from who you were meant to be?"

His words hit me harder than his backhand ever did. Part of me—something bigger than me—fights to get out of my body and into the knife and thrust straight into Gary's gut. My brain keeps trumping the impulse, but the impulse keeps coming back. I flip the knife handle left and right. I could take care of this right now. I want to gouge him. Make him scream. I want him to pay. To beg for mercy. I want him to fear for his life, to be scared to sleep, to know how Mom felt, that last time, when he closed her windpipe so she couldn't even beg.

I want to kill him.

But Mom was right: if I kill Gary, I will become him, and that would be the greatest injustice to her memory and everything she did to keep me safe.

I need to keep it together. Deep breaths, slow words. "That is *exactly* what you did. *To me.*"

To keep from crying, I bite the inside of my cheek so hard that I taste blood. The pain shapes my resolve.

Everyone—or everyone who's left—is watching us. Watching me.

"Uh, Graham?" Curt says.

"Curt." I keep my eyes on Gary. *Deep breaths.* "This is Gary Fife. He killed my mother. He beat my mom for years before he killed her. He beat me up from the time I was just a kid—kicked me down a flight of stairs, used my head to knock holes in our drywall—and he always explained why it was my fault. For a long time—for years!—I believed him. And I was so ashamed. But I'm not ashamed anymore. It wasn't my fault, it was his fault. And I am not him. I'm me."

I am not him. The thought bursts the dam and I'm sobbing in the street.

"I get that you're angry," Gary says.

"You have no idea. I want you to *suffer.*"

"I just exploded—"

"You murdered my mother!"

I may not *be* my father, but I am my father's son. That thing inside of me wages war with my brain again. I desperately want to stab him—to kill him—to avenge my mother and my childhood and every single way he fucked up my life. But my brain keeps saying no. *Acting in anger will lead to a lifetime of regret.* Those were almost her last words, but not quite.

My brain—and my mom—is still winning when the police arrive—in three cruisers, no less. A minute more, and my rage may have overpowered me, but I'll never know.

Officer Amy nods at Curt while her colleagues take in the scene. Curt gently touches my arm. "It's gonna be okay, man."

I let an officer take the knife. I don't need it anymore.

The crowd disperses, Gary winds up in the police cruiser, and I have a genuine physical breakdown, vomiting in the street and crying uncontrollably. Seventeen years of garbage pour out of my body, as if I have been waiting my whole life to dispel them.

Curt stands by me, his hand on my shoulder, assuring me as I hurl.

With the vomit and tears, my nausea and fear and anger evacuate until I am just Xander. My life and my body are my own, and Gary owns no part of me. I am my mother's son. Exhausted and empty, I still feel stronger than I have ever been.

———

After another two-second trip in a Burlington cruiser, I'm back at the station. The interviews are shorter this time, mostly because Gary is here to tell them what he did.

Gary found me. And he didn't kill me. And he's going to prison.

And it's over.

The café owner, probably awestruck over the whole murderer thing, says not to worry about the window. The cops don't exactly see it that way, and I may face misdemeanors for battery and destruction of private property. That's fair. The police are fair.

Once I've provided the officers with Jill's address and assured them I have a safe way to get home, they let me go.

They will extradite Gary to Ohio as soon as possible.

I may never see him again. I certainly will never talk to him again. "Can I talk to him for just a minute?"

Officer Amy eyes me, confused. "You're kidding."

I assure her I have only one question. There's just one thing I need to know. She escorts me to an interrogation room and whispers with the guy who's holding Gary.

Curt is behind me, his hand on my shoulder, as I stare at Gary.

"I need to know how you found me."

Gary grins. "I'm a smart guy, Alexander."

"Tell me."

"I inserted a one-pixel transparent web bug—a tiny, invisible picture—into my messages. When you opened my email and that little picture loaded, the server log gave me your IP address. I tracked it to the café and have been waiting for you since."

My shock and confusion must register on my face. Gary smirks at me. "I know the Internet like the back of my hand. I can find you when I need you."

"Not from prison, jackass," Curt says from behind me. "Maybe you'll get on a ten-year-old computer to play Solitaire for twenty minutes twice a week, but they're never gonna give you Internet access in prison. My friend here is safe."

I'm safe. I'm alive. Content with that miracle, I head for the door.

"Alexander?" Gary shouts. "Alexander!"

I don't need anything from him. I never did.

"Let's get out of here, Curt."

On our way back to the deli, Curt doesn't quite know what to say. "So, uh. Alexander?"

"Xander, actually," I say. "I thought I saw his car. That day I was peeking through the blinds at the deli? I was terrified he was going to hunt me down and kill me."

"He said he didn't want to hurt you."

"Yeah, well, last I heard, he did."

"You have some heavy-duty shit in your life, man."

"Not anymore I don't."

It's really over. Gary is done. The levity is surreal, in the best possible way.

At the deli door, Curt says, "You should probably take the day off."

It's tempting. "Tell you what. I'll head back to Ohio tomorrow. Let me finish out my shift, finish what I've started."

"You sure?"

"I'm sure. Can I use your phone first?"

"Course, man." We share a look—of understanding, of grief, of relief—before Curt leaves me outside.

The hostel is only a few steps away, but I can't believe how far I've come. Curt's phone weighs heavy in my hand. This is my actual homecoming call, and I'm making it myself.

Jill won't be home from camp yet, but her parents should have picked her up already. I dial her dad.

"Dale Bernard."

"Chief? It's me. It's . . . Xander."

"Fucking hell. Hold on. I'm driving."

Janice gets on the phone. "Hello?"

"Hi, Janice."

"Are you okay, honey?"

There's a commotion—a happy one—and a second later Jill is on the phone.

"It's over." The story spills out of me. She repeats every line back to her parents, so it takes a while to get through it. I leave out the part with the knife because I will never tell her about the knife.

Plus, I'm not ready to process the murderous rage I felt with it in my hand.

When I'm done, Jill says, "Hold on. We're pulled over. Here's Dad."

Dale is incredulous. "How did he find you?"

"Online. He tracked my emails."

"No way."

"And he was waiting at the Internet café where I've been checking my mail."

"Well, that was stupid."

Dale is so right. This could have ended horribly.

"I just sort of thought Gary was blowing smoke up my ass with all his Internet tracking stuff. And then I got the brilliant idea to track him, and I thought I could be a hero because *I* knew where *he* was when he sent the email. He was in Elyria, by the way."

"I'll be damned," Dale says. "I thought you were safe up there."

That bounces around in my brain for a few seconds. "Up where?"

Gargantuan pause. "Uh. Up in Vermont?"

"You knew where I was?"

"Not immediately, no."

"How long have you known?"

"A few days. I talked to Mack Davies, the captain up there, after he picked you up for sleeping in the park. Convinced him to report back on you."

Well, shit.

"I'm glad you're safe, son. I hope to see you in Laurel as soon as you can get back."

"Thanks, Chief."

Jill's back on the phone. "He's wearing the cat that swallowed the canary face again. You're in Vermont?"

"I am in Vermont."

"What happened to New York? Have you been lying to me all this time?"

"No, Jill. I did go to New York. Now I'm in Vermont."

"You have some nerve."

"And soon, Jill, I will be back in Ohio."

She considers whether to stay pissed or get excited. "Oh my god. It's over! You're coming home!"

Excitement wins. I'm going home.

"When, Xander? When will you be back?"

"Well, it's not exactly a straight shot, but I can probably leave tonight or in the morning. The trip takes a whole day, though."

Home in a day. It's over.

Gary is going to prison. I am free of him, forever. Shaking this burden from my shoulders, I grow another two inches. Seventeen years of horror and abuse. Seventeen years of fear, gone. It's over. I get to live. And this time, my life is my own.

Mom really would be proud of me. Her absence leaves me raw, still. I find comfort in knowing I am her son, and I'm living as she would have wanted me to live. She would love to see me living without the despair I carried—despair she and I both carried—for so many years. That burden exhausted me. It debilitated her. It is gone. We both are free.

A sob escapes from Jill on the other end of the line. "I need you to come home. I need to see you to know that you're okay."

"I'll get right on it."

"You're sure you're okay?"

"I'm fine." I think I'm fine. I'm not really sure how I am.

There's a long silence. Well, not silence exactly, since we're both kind of crying. For very different reasons.

Jill gasps and shifts into fifth gear: "Xander, we can go to Quaker Steak on Sunday. I will invite everyone. EVERYONE! Oh my god. It's summer!"

Riding Jill's emotional roller coaster isn't remotely fun.

"Okay, Jill, I need to try to get a bus ticket and see when I can get home. Let me figure out everything and I'll call you back."

"Okay. My phone is dead. I'll charge it at home. Call Dad's cell if you need me before five."

"Or I can leave a message, like a normal person." I smile. A genuine smile, for the first time on this side of life.

Jill laughs. Oh, how I have missed that laugh. "Xander, I can't tell you how happy I am. Mom promised the three of us will do a road trip all together in August to take you to Tulane. I'm trying to convince her you and I can go alone. Oh, I can't wait for you to get home. You get to start over with a whole new life."

We hang up a minute later, and that phrase repeats in my head: *a whole new life.* Of course, this whole episode isn't something I can just leave behind. Kat is right: This is my life—every wretched, terrifying moment.

I'm free. Completely free. The ugliest parts of my life end with Gary's arrest, and now I can move forward.

I'm laughing like a maniac who has just been released from prison unexpectedly. Because I have.

Curt pokes his nose out the door. "You gonna be okay?"

It takes me a minute to get my laughing and crying under control. "I am. I think I'll be okay. I can go home tomorrow. Or today. Probably tomorrow."

"Good on you. Lemme know how I can help."

"A Reuben?"

Curt grins. "Extra special breakfast Reuben, with extra dressing and root beer. You got it."

Thirty-six

My last night at Curt's house is just like my first. He's in his date clothes in the kitchen. I swear, my time here might have been better served mining his brain for dating tips. Seriously.

"Tomorrow, let's leave at nine to get you to the station. Sure you feel alright?" he says.

I do. I feel alright. "Yeah. And Kat is here for company."

Curt whistles low and slow. He mouths, "Good luck with that."

Yeah, that's something else I have to get through.

"Thanks, Curt. For everything. Have a great date."

A sly smile. "Oh, I will."

The second he's out the door, Kat narrows her eyes at me. "You're leaving?"

Jill's iPod pings. Someone is sending messages at nine on a Friday night.

"Yeah! I mean, sorry you found out this way, but yeah. I'm going home tomorrow."

In the middle of the kitchen in her John Lennon shirt, she opens and closes her mouth several times before finding words. "Well, thanks for listening. While it lasted." She starts packing up her books.

Ping! Ping! Ping!

"While it lasted, Kat? Hey, why's it gotta be like that?"

Kat crosses her arms over John Lennon. "I just didn't expect this."

Ping!

I probably shouldn't pull out the iPod, but someone is trying really hard to reach me. A quick glance at the screen shows five messages from Gretchen. Gretchen with her long, tanned, muscular legs.

Kat says, "You're leaving tomorrow? In like twelve hours. Could you hold off with the texts for five seconds?"

Probably. I send a message to Gretchen—*Occupied at the moment. I'll be online later*—and tuck the iPod in my back pocket. "Sorry. Sorry. You were saying?"

"I said thanks for listening. Thanks for seeing me, you know?" She heads for the back door.

"That's it? Aren't you gonna stick around?"

Kat shrugs. "I have at least an hour of studying for my Saturday class."

"You were just needling me about texting. How about you do your studying, I'll catch up with my people. Then we can talk. I'm not leaving right this second."

We migrate to the living room, where Kat curls up on one end of the green velour couch and cracks open a textbook. She *is* lovely.

I ping Gretchen: *Here now.*

She isn't online anymore. Jill is, though, and she gives me the low-down on the last seven hours.

Every ten minutes or so, Kat shifts into a new position. And finally Gretchen is back.

Gretch: *I am SO EXCITED!!!!!*

Fraught with expectation and exclamation points. Five exclamation points. We're going to be just fine.

Me: *Me, too. I have so much to tell you. Are you coming to Quaker Steak Sunday?*

Gretch: *YES!!!!! Jill invited everyone.*

Me: *Yeah, I know.*

Gretch: *Maybe Monday I can have you all to myself? You working?*

Me: *Doubt it. Haven't been in touch with the cages since I left.*

Gretch: *Yeah, you sort of disappeared.*

Is that an accusation?

Me: *I hope you understand why.*

Kat says, "One more page and I'm done."

"Uh huh."

Jill pings in a separate conversation: *Gretchen is coming Sunday.*

Me: *Yeah, she told me.*

Jill: *Did she tell you she suggested you two could come alone in her car?*

Me: *Nope. Good! She wants me all to herself.*

Jill: *I love her, but she needs to get in line.*

Me: *Ha! Give me a sec, I'm talking to her.*

Jill: *Tuck wants my full attention anyway. Talk later.*

Me: *K bye.*

Gretchen has been pinging while I chatted with Jill.

Gretch: *So, Monday? The Italian Festival starts Monday.*

Gretch: *They have more rides than last year. We could get a pass.*

Gretch: *Their Napoleons are gorgeous. Gelato.*

Gretch: *Or Italian ice, if we want to go low-brow.*

Gretch: *We should just wander around and try everything.*

Gretch: *Except the Red Blood Cake, of course. Blech.*

Gretch: *Hello?*

Me: *Sorry. Definitely no on the Red Blood Cake*

Me: *But yes on everything else. I'd *Rome* anywhere with you.*

Gretch: *OMG. I have missed you so much.*

She has opened the door. Maybe I can push it open a little wider.

Me: *Really?*

Gretch: *So much!*

Gretch: *The puns. The snappy banter.*

Gretch: *The make-out sessions in the middle of nowhere.*

"That's a Cheshire grin," Kat says.

"What?" I glance at her quickly, then back to Gretchen on my screen. "Just getting ready to see my friends, you know? It's been awhile."

Me: *They have forests up here, you know.*

Gretch: *What have you been doing all these weeks, exactly?*

Oh shit.

Me: *Nothing! Promise!*

That's not exactly true. Gretchen probably would not consider pressing my body against Kat nothing. I wouldn't consider a date with Evan at the Mocha House nothing, either. But maybe Gretchen considered that nothing the way I considered the blues bar nothing.

Gosh, she is slow to reply.

Very slow.

Gretch: *Okay. Well, we have a lot of catching up to do.*

Gretch: *As previously discussed.*

Me: *Yes!*

I am super excited about making out with Gretchen, but I'm holding out hope for more than making out.

Her hair getting tangled around my fingers. Her legs, maybe tangled up with mine. The kissing thing is good. Her body is amazing.

My body is getting too excited just thinking about it.

Me: *Let's start catching up as soon as possible.*

"Okay, I'm done for the night." Kat scoots closer to me.

Gretch: *I was thinking maybe I could drive you home after QS on Sunday?*

Me: Cool.

I can't look at Kat. "Cool."

Kat is right next to me. "I just thought, you know, we could talk. What with it being your last night and all."

Gretch: *Great! I'll tell Jill.*

"Graham?"

Gretch: *She and Tucker have been inseparable for weeks.*

I hold up peace fingers to Kat. "Give me two seconds." Every few seconds, she bounces a little, like Jill does on our way to concerts.

Gretch: *So she shouldn't mind.*

Me: *I can't wait.*

Me: *Hey, I need to get offline now.*

Gretch: *No problem. Can't wait to see you!*

Me: *Chat or email later, okay?*

Gretch: *Yes! Both!*

Me: *DEF see you Sunday*

Me: *AND Monday!*

Gretch: *YAY!!!!!*

Gretch: *Night, Xander.*

Me: *Night.*

Giddy, I tuck the iPod into my back pocket and turn to Kat.

"I meant what I said," Kat says, scooting closer to me. "Thanks for seeing me. I mostly keep my head down and mostly don't notice other people not noticing me. But with you, I felt like I wasn't invisible, for the first time in a long time."

I appreciate her gratitude too much to call bullshit.

She scoots closer. "Ah, Graham." She wraps her arms around me and kisses me on the mouth.

"Whoa, whoa, whoa!"

She pulls back. "Sophie is out cold. I promise she won't hear a thing."

"It's not that, It's—"

"Is it Jill?"

"No, definitely not. But what are we doing here? I'm leaving tomorrow."

"We're celebrating," she says, and then John Lennon is over her head and lying on the floor. Kat is in front of me in shorts and an iridescent green bra.

Every time Victoria's Secret catalogues arrived in the mail, my mother launched into a litany about how real love and sex is very different from love and sex in the media. *Women only pose like in those magazines when they're joking or trying too hard.*

Boy, was Mom wrong. Kat is kneeling with her hands propped on her knees, which gives her cleavage. And she's sincere.

Two girls coming on to me within a few weeks? Unheard of.

I spent most of high school pining for Gretchen and going out on dates with girls who simply agreed to go out with me.

Kat puts one arm around my shoulders. "I really like you, Graham."

"I like you, too."

She shakes her head. "No, I mean I really like you. You get me. And you're just . . . open. Free. Totally honest. I love that."

Those words, *totally honest*, bounce around my brain while Kat kisses me. Kissing is one of those bicycle skills: once you learn, you don't forget.

Man, I love kissing. And I could use practice, so I quiet my mind and kiss back.

Kat kisses down my neck, which feels amazing.

"I know this isn't a lasting thing." *Kiss.* "But I want us to have this moment." *Kiss.* "One of the things we'll tuck into the pockets of our memories and pull out years from now." *Kiss.* "I'm working on college and working for Sophie and working to ensure my future." *Kiss.* "But I want to do this one thing right now. For me, right now."

I can't really fault her for that.

Kat untucks my shirt and moves her hand along my naked belly, her nails brushing the top of my shorts. We could both be naked in two minutes.

No one will ever find out about this. Whatever comes of Gretchen or my first girlfriend at Tulane, this first time will be behind me. I will have the experience with someone who is clearly wild about me.

Or wild about Graham. That trips me up. If we're going to do this, I want to walk into it honestly. I don't want to sully it with lies, even the tiniest ones.

"I have to tell you something first."

Kat's big brown eyes are expectant. I can't believe I'm about to blow the whole deal. The truth can wait for the morning. Hell, the truth can wait forever!

Kat leans away from me. "I can tell by your face that this is something big."

I nod.

She's getting a little hyper again. "Maybe it's something we should just leave unsaid. Maybe we can just understand that we're both feeling something big here. We can enjoy the moment and you can tell me in the morning."

It's my get-out-of-jail free card. I leave in the morning and she will never know.

But I will know.

"Kat, I'm not going to say what you think I'm going to say. Yes, it would keep for the morning, but I want to tell you while we still have time to discuss it."

She sits upright and leans against the couch arm. "I'm liking the sound of this less and less. I'm not asking for a relationship. Obviously I can't be tied down."

She might be as screwed up as I am. How can I put this gently? "Look, Kat, everything we've done together has been great. I feel—changed, because of you."

She covers the shiny bra with her arms. "Less and less."

"I'm trying to have a real conversation here."

"You're killing the mood, Graham."

"That's the thing." *Deep breath.* "My name's not Graham."

Kat's hands and arms dance around her torso, trying to cover all her bare skin simultaneously.

"Relax, I'm totally the guy you know. I promise. Here is the short version: almost six weeks ago, the day I was supposed to graduate, my father murdered my mother.

259

He was looking for me when he did it. I was ... terrified! So I took my fake ID—with the name Graham Bel from Wheaton, Georgia—and I took off. Two days later, I wound up in Burlington. And for a while, I hid out, panicked that my father would find me and kill me. I slept in the woods, I holed up at a hostel. I tried to get into the homeless shelter. That's another story.

"Eventually, Curt gave me his couch and a pseudo-job to keep me afloat. And things got better. And then I met you, and things got good. And today, my father *did* find me, and now he's going to prison.

"That's it. I'm really going to Tulane this fall. And my name. My name is Xander Fife."

I haven't said my full name for weeks.

"So you have lied to me about everything." Kat pulls the blanket over her bare chest.

"No. Well, about that one thing—two—yes. I'm actually from Ohio, not Georgia. But I swear to you: everything else is true. I run a lot. I love the blues and hate football. I love soccer and sunshine and ice cream and really, really love to read. I'm dying to travel."

"And Jill?" Kat's really weird about Jill.

"Jill is my very best friend, and has been since I was four years old. She helped me through all of this."

Kat snugs the blanket around her torso. "I want the whole story. The long version. Absolutely no lies."

She cries when I get to the part about Gary and the domestic violence shelter and she cringes when I tell her about that night with Jill on my parents' floor. I almost leave out the woods with Gretchen, but at this point I don't want to hold back.

I feel naked, but telling the story of my life is freeing. Everything is real again.

"And that is everything. Scout's honor." I follow quickly with, "I was never a scout. And, one more truth: that day, when I opened the door to find you standing there? I thought you were smokin' hot. I really had expected you to have green eyes like a cat, but that's not why I stood there with my mouth open. You make quite an impression."

Kat grins. "They're my favorite shorts. One day, my jeans were too short, so I cut them off at the knee, and every time they looked too shaggy, I cut off a little more."

"They're working for you."

She laughs. "Graham—Xander—Is it Alexander? Or Zander with a 'z'? Were your parents hipsters?"

"It's Alexander Fife. No middle name. Jill started calling me Xander, because Alexander was stuffy and Alex seemed square."

"I can get behind that." Kat laughs, and then she's crying hysterically.

What have I done to this poor girl?

"I just thought I had found something here," she says. "A real friend, in you. And now you're leaving, and you don't want to be something other than friends and . . ."

Her crying is almost loud enough to wake Sophie. Hugging helps calm her down.

She still smells like patchouli.

And she's half naked.

Focus.

I am being a good friend to Kat, and good something-more to Gretchen at the same time. I stroke Kat's back, in a friendly way.

"I feel like I'll never really connect with people." She gazes at me. "Or have a real boyfriend."

"Of course you will! But it's not me."

She sniffles. "I know. Gretchen is waiting."

"Maybe. But that doesn't matter right this second. I like you, Kat, a lot. You said that you wanted to have a moment to hold onto forever. How about a friend instead?"

She shrugs.

"No, I'm serious. My time in Burlington has been bizarre and askew, and I would have gone insane without my lifeline to Jill. And then I met you, and life got immeasurably better. So, while you're here and when you feel invisible, you'll have me."

"Long distance relationships fizzle."

"Are you kidding? I live on the Internet! And I am not Dawn. I'm not going to disappear. And don't discount what you have done for me here, either. You're *my* friend. I want to hang on to *you*!"

"I'd like that."

Kat scoots closer to me, gathering the blankets and pillows around her like a nest. Without a second thought, I put my arm around her. It feels genuinely friendly.

We're quiet. There's nothing more to say, really. I suspect she's lost in thoughts as deep and dark as my own. Where do we go from here? I mean, separately. Where do I go from here? Where does she?

We've been sitting like this, not talking, forever.

Kat stands and shakes off the comforter so she's just in her tiny shorts and shiny bra. "This was 100 percent not how I thought tonight was going to work out."

Me neither.

"I'm so glad we talked instead," she says.

"Me, too."

Kat shimmies into her John Lennon shirt. If I had held off for twelve freaking hours, we might be a tangled mess of nakedness on this couch.

But then there would be lies between us. And a huge mess between me and Gretchen. Instead, Kat and I know each other. Really. She knows everything, and she doesn't shun me. That's pretty amazing, actually.

"I love that John Lennon T-shirt."

"He's the one who said, 'Life is what happens when you're busy making other plans.'"

My life. I'm trying to change it, but until it changes, this is it. I'm living it.

Kat tucks in her shirt and brushes her hair out of her face. "Sorry for dumping on you this week. I never told anyone half of that stuff. Thanks for letting me talk."

"I loved hearing it." I wrap her in another warm hug.

"I think I fell in love with you a little tonight, Xander."

I want to hang on to her. I want to clutch this moment with my entire being. "I think I love you, too."

The lovely Kat says, "I need to head home. I'm mentally exhausted. Like we just did a triathlon, you know?"

"I do."

Our hug is like reverse tug-of-war: both of us waiting for the other to disengage. I refuse to let go first.

Kat whispers, "Oh. This is it. This is the moment I'll take with me out into the world."

When we finally let go, Kat delivers a chaste kiss on my cheek. "Good night, Xander."

"Good night, Kat."

If I ever see Kat again, it won't be for a very long time. With the couch to myself, I rest my head inside Kat's little pillow nest, my conscience clear. I was true to myself, and true to her, and true to Gretchen. And what else is there, really?

Thirty-seven

Running back to something takes a lot longer than running away from it.

I can't wait to get off this bus. After this small step backward into Laurel Woods, I can catapult myself into the future, one in which I can embrace my own name and my past.

Forget the catapult: I can start doing that today. Right now, I am an orphan. It is a very strange and disquieting feeling. I am homeless, in a completely different way, and this time it's permanent.

I have other labels now, too: the guy whose mom was murdered and whose father is going to prison. But now, I own it. And in two short weeks, I will turn eighteen. I'm already a different person than I was on the last day of school, or in the mini-woods with Gretchen. I have tasted life—my own, interesting life—and I want more.

My Greyhound shudders and lurches, and I hear *more, more, more.* More music. More books. More people. More understanding. More discussions about everything and nothing and what makes everyone else tick. More travel.

I have been missing Laurel for weeks, but now I want one more Reuben from Curt's. Or one more hour at the Free Library. One more walk to Ben & Jerry's. One more biking tour.

Hugging Sophie good-bye this morning opened my Mom wound a little more. I hope Sophie improves. I'm glad she has Curt and Kat. I'll take a bit of Sophie with me. Curt and Kat, too. And probably Bingham from the hostel, which already seems like ages ago. Of course, he still knows me as Graham.

Being Graham Bel taught me a lot about being Xander Fife. For maybe the first time in my life, I belong to myself. And I am just fine. And interesting. And good.

Part of my heart is buried with my mother, and a huge part of it lives with Jill. But I love Kat, too, so part of my heart will travel with her. And a little piece of my heart stays in Burlington, where I made it on my own. And next month, when I finally—finally—make my way to college, other pieces of my heart won't go with me.

Maybe that's what life is: a series of tearing your heart into tiny pieces and giving them to other people. Maybe as soon as you detach yourself from someone you love, you can never be whole again.

Okay. So what part of my heart is mine?

THIRTY-EIGHT

One second I'm standing in the Youngstown Greyhound station working the buckle on my backpack and the next I'm nearly thrown to the ground by one hundred pounds of squealing Jill.

Tucker's not far behind, hands in his pockets. "Hey."

I wrap my arms around him just as tightly as I had Jill. "Congratulations, buddy." I cock my head toward Jill.

Tuck stands up a little straighter. "It's not like that, Xander."

"I already told him everything," Jill says. "Don't be weird."

"There is such a thing as private relationship business, Jilly."

Their focus is off me as we walk to Neapolitan. Tucker calls shotgun while I'm stuffing my bags into the trunk.

"Nuh uh, I have been gone twenty-three days. The least you can do is let me sit in front."

Tuck folds the seat forward. "Rules are rules."

I climb in the back, and we're off.

Jill says, "Mom emptied Ryan's room after you called, and my brothers have been bunking together. She says you might need privacy."

"Which is more than she's doing for me, by the way," Tucker says. "Janice watches me like a hawk. Lights on when I'm over. A genuine curfew, even on the weekends. Janice framed a photo of us, and I'm not even allowed up to Jill's room to see how it looks on the wall."

"Your reputation precedes you, Tuck. What's the photo, Jill?"

"The three of us at Quaker Steak. She paid Gretchen to snap it in May. Mom framed it as a graduation present, one for each of us."

"Sweet."

Jill has more and more and more. "Nine Inch Nails is playing at Blossom on Thursday, and I'm sure we can get another lawn ticket for you. Tucker refuses because of *the noise*, of course."

Tuck says, "That's hardly fair," and they quibble all the way home; I can't get a word in edgewise. It's good to be back.

The weight of the air changes when we reach the town limits. We pass the Dairy Queen, and I wish I'd eaten more Ben & Jerry's in Burlington. Ben & Jerry's is light years ahead of DQ when it comes to flavor.

Still, DQ is home.

Jill parks in her driveway and I glance at my own house, two doors away. A brown and yellow real estate sign hangs from a post next to the driveway.

Jill follows my gaze. "It went up last week. I didn't want to tell you on the phone."

"It's okay. I never need to step foot in there again."

Janice is yelling at the little boys. We duck into the backyard to find Ryan running around, completely naked.

Janice says, "He is covered in baby oil. I have been try-ing to catch him for twenty minutes."

Same old, same old. Last time it was Vaseline.

Janice wraps her arms around me. "Welcome home."

"Thanks."

"Now, I would like nothing better than for you to live with us this summer. What do you say?"

"Sounds great."

Janice beams. "That is exactly what Jill said you would say."

My best friend knows everything there is to know about me. Rather, she knows everything I knew about myself when I left Laurel. I desperately need to fill her in on everything else. I want her to know about Curt and Kat and Burlington. They're important parts of me now, and things still don't feel real until I tell Jill.

All this time, I thought life in Laurel was going on without me. In reality, my life was temporarily not here; I took it with me and made it my own.

I turn to see Jill and Tucker holding hands, something Jill has not done with anyone since the fifth grade. Life is different now, and it's rolling forward.

———

I'm sifting through all my crap in Jill's unfinished base-ment because I can't stand my Burlington clothes for one more second.

Janice comes down to load up her washer. "Sorry it's such a mess. We had to move everything very quickly."

"Hey, I appreciate you got anything at all." I'm hoping she got some decent clothes, although I guess everyone has already seen me at my worst. I want tonight to seem like more of a date than just a night to hang out.

Janice points to one dented box. "That one's your mom's. Most of her stuff I donated, but I kept some things I thought you might like to have someday."

Memories of Mom flood my mind. She only exists in memories now, which is both nauseating and freeing. If I can let go of the negative and abusive memories, her life can be all happiness and love. Maybe that box is full of things that made her happy. Her Beatles bookends, maybe. Or her favorite books. Or the scarf she knitted me, complete with seven holes.

I need to see what is left of her life.

I unfold the flaps and find her pillowcases on top. Then a sweater and other clothes. I turn my back to Janice and bring a handful of T-shirts to my nose. I fight back the tears, but they win. Mom's voice has been in my head a lot, but it's harder to imagine a scent. And here she is. Ivory soap and cardboard boxes and—*big inhale*—Mom. It's heaven and holidays and home. I breathe in the fistful of cloth again.

Love you, Mom.

I don't need anything else from this box. I especially don't need the file folder from the day before Mom died, but I'll bet it's in here. What a mess. I made a mess of her life.

Janice touches my shoulder lightly. "You okay, Xander?"

"I can't help but think if it weren't for me, she would still be alive."

"Actually, I'd argue she would have died a long time ago if it weren't for you."

"If it weren't for me, she never would have stayed with Gary. I'm sure you've worked out that they got married because she was pregnant with me."

Janice purses her lips.

"It's okay, Janice. I've done the math."

She puts her hands on her hips, drops them, and looks at the ceiling. "This is a conversation you should have had with your mom."

No kidding.

Her voice is quiet. "You got the math right, but the story wrong. Your mom got pregnant with you because she thought Gary would marry her."

I don't believe it. "No way."

"A year or two ago, we had probably too much wine and got to talking about high school. She told me how head-over-heels she had been for Gary. For over a year, they were crazy about each other. He took her to Cleveland and Pittsburgh and Columbus and they dreamed of traveling the country together. Gary had a bit of a wandering eye, though, and your mom was desperate to keep him. When she found out she was pregnant with you, she hoped he would settle down with the two of you. That's how she justified it: Gary would stop ogling other women once they were married."

I don't know about this. In some sense—if it's true, which I'm not willing to concede—Mom choosing Gary makes things better. In another sense, what happened to that guy? An adventurous father would have been awesome. We could have been a real family. Then again, maybe family is like life: it's always the real thing, though not always the version you want.

No one would have wanted this life, but it's mine. That family was mine, too, and I'm done lying about it.

"Janice, I'm sorry we lied to you about him. I was living a lie for a long time."

"You weren't living a lie, Xander. You were ashamed of your parents. You kept secret the things that were happening in your life. You didn't keep yourself from people. The Gary stuff, your mom? It's tragic, it's awful, but those are things that happened to you, not who you are."

I actually appreciate the after-school-special sentiment. I remember how light—how free!—I felt when I confided in Kat. I want all of life to be that light. And maybe when I get to college I don't need to tell everyone my life story, but when the topic arises, I won't be embarrassed.

Not everyone needs to know everything, but some people deserve to. I check my watch. Gretchen is probably already waiting.

THIRTY-NINE

Quaker Steak is in three hours, but I needed to see Gretchen first. Alone. She said she'd meet me, but she's not here.

The fields are full of soccer matches. I choose a bench that faces the pee wee games, where four-year-olds chase the ball for an hour without keeping score.

Eyeing the thin line of trees that separates the park from Gretchen's neighborhood, I wish I had searched harder for my old phone. Maybe I wasn't clear about where we should meet.

No Gretchen. Ten minutes. Fifteen. Just when I decide she has changed her mind about the whole thing, Gretchen steps from between two trees. She brushes her hair away from her face as she searches the fields. When her eyes find me, she smiles, and I congratulate myself for sitting so far away.

For a minute, I'm just a guy waiting for his smart and beautiful girlfriend to walk across the world's largest field. It's one of those moments that will become a forever memory. A happy one.

Okay, she's running now, but that's maybe because I was staring too hard. She kisses me like it's the most natural thing in the world. I will replay this over and over in my head.

We share the longest hug in the history of the universe. This isn't how I expected our first date to happen. It's exactly six weeks late, for one thing. "I'm so glad you agreed to meet me here."

Gretchen laces her fingers through mine and starts walking. "I would have met you anywhere."

Walking together feels like the most normal, natural thing. Like nothing ever happened. Gretchen stops and kisses me lightly, then not so lightly. I wrap my arms around her back.

A little boy—or girl, it's hard to tell—squeals, "Ew, ewwwwwwww," and we erupt in laughter. We kiss again, picking up where we left off, as though these last weeks didn't happen.

But they did.

I pull away from Gretchen and grab both of her hands. "Gretchen, I want to be here with you, doing this. Right now. But we need to talk first."

"I thought we agreed that we've been talking for years and needed to catch up on . . . other things." Her cheeks are the softest shade of pink I've ever seen.

I run my fingers through her hair. It's still heaven. "We'll get to that, I promise. But this can't wait. That's why we're in public right now. We have the rest of the night and all of summer for the other things. All the other things, I promise. But hear me out: there are things about me that you don't know."

Gretchen admits that she does know, now. She recaps for me what she's seen on the news since my mother died. She knows Mom was abused. And I was abused.

I stop her. "But there is more that I was afraid to tell you. There is so much more that you don't know."

She can't look me in the eye. "You don't have to tell me. I understand."

She leans in to kiss me, and again I pull back. What is it with my brain? "No, Gretchen. I need to tell you. So that you really know me before we . . . get into the other stuff. Which I promise I cannot wait to get into with you."

Bewildered, her gaze shifts endlessly from one of my eyes to the other. "Alright."

Sitting in the sunned grass, legs crossed, holding Gretchen's hands, I share the whole story.

She listens intently, and my life feels real. This life, right here. Right now.

Acknowledgments

Now that I've earned my author badge, I want to acknowledge several things:

First, that I cannot write with my captivating daughters underfoot. Megan Thornton, Brooke Monroe, Rachel Noveroske, Sierra van Burkleo, Tessa Boutwell, and the Napping Gods ensured I had the space and time necessary to write and edit this book.

Second, that writing novels is a team sport. Sarah Quigley, Anique Drouin, and Amanda Blau provided invaluable insight. The Thomas Ford Library Teen Book Club contributed honest and heartfelt feedback. My editor, Nicole Frail, and her intern, Alexandra Ehlers, transformed crucial aspects of Xander's story.

Third, that Heather Booth's keen editing eye improves any book immeasurably. She sharpens my focus and precludes my embarrassment. She also is the 2015 Illinois YA librarian of the year!

Fourth, that even my uncanny sense of direction cannot navigate the publishing world. My agent, Andrea Somberg, is my compass.

Fifth, that my high school English teacher, Maxine W. Houck, is always right. (She also is the person who said, "It is not the answers authors give, but the questions they raise that make them interesting.")

Finally, that without Charles Bacon's unwavering support, I never would have found the confidence required to become an author. Seventeen bonus points for you!